The Soul Trek
A Story of Love, Faith and Destiny

Volume II

Djana Fahryeva

www.thesoultrek.com

2010

No part of this book may be reproduced, stored in a retrieval system or transmitted in any form or by any means without the prior written permission of the author, except by a reviewer who may quote brief passages in a review to be printed in a newspaper, magazine or journal.

This book is a true story of backpacking South America, Central America, South-East Asia, India, Nepal, China, Mongolia and Russia. The places, routes and travel information might not be up to date and cannot be used as a travel guide in third dimension.

Edited by Spica Aldebaran.

ISBN: 1452800820
ISBN-13: 9781452800820

For soul trekkers worldwide.

Contents

Volume II
A Story of Faith

Time and space are interconnected.
Changing the volume of space
you are changing the speed of flow of time in it.
In a limited space, the flow of time slows down.
If space is expanding, then time,
correspondingly, must accelerate<<<<<<<<

I am in Pokhara, Nepal. It is almost 10 PM. I just finished up a two week trek to the Mt. Everest Base Camp where I joined a group which was made up of 4 Americans and 1 Australian. Meeting people from other countries while traveling is as big as any part of traveling and it was a nice dose of home as we had no communication issues and shared a very sarcastic sense of humour.

The major component was John from Cairnes, Australia. He works as a consultant on an oil rig, most recently in the North Sea. He gets one month on and one month off. He is the definition of work hard, play hard. He could drink and party and almost got us killed our last night in Kathmandu. He headbutted a kid after playing pool. Apparently, the kid was mouthing off to him. As they got into each others personal space for a handshake, John just dropped his head on this mofo. The kid fell like a sack of potatoes. It seemed like it was from a movie. We got escorted to the other side of the bar and greased the bartenders a bit. After some more drinks, meeting a few ladies, and getting our lives threatened, we left.

We walked right into about 6 kids who jumped John. We fought them off and I am told they shook our hands afterwards b/c we put up a good fight. We walked away virtually unscathed. This is ironic b/c minutes later John kicks some local Nepali persons car and gets blindsided by the owner and has a beautiful black eye to show for it.

Tourist season has just ended so the place isn't too busy and I can get accommodation cheap. There are many Israelis here who have just finished their mandatory stints and they are only 21 or 22. All cool cats.

In a week I will be joining a 7 day course of meditation at a Buddhist monastery. I have been awaiting this opportunity for a while. I will live and eat there. I am excited and nervous. After our night time meditation it is silence. This will be time to read and catch up on journal entries and keep me away from bars and hashish. Dude, if you just take a normal stroll in Nepal you pass marijuana plants.

I am not sure my purpose for writing this as it doesn't have much of a story, also it is hard to write b/c I just covered a few characters and few moments in time, but it's all the things that happen in between and the things I am forgetting right now that make all this a life-changing adventure.

I keep saying it, and I will continue to ask people to join me. Even if just for a short period of time. Sorry, for any misspellings. I will try to edit next time. Prob. after the monastery stay.

Love

James

I. Panama City.

Panama City Voyagers Hostel. 3/5/2008.
The reminiscence. The memory. The scent of the flowers. It was parsley. My perfume. *What are you wearing?* Stop watching me like this. I can't bear you knowing my every thought and emotion. Am I closing down? As I feel my heart breaking into tiny little pieces. I feel a grudge. I reminisced in tears how it opened one life I was happy in. One life. One man. One
Taking a break. *Somehow you are the only real truth. So profound and beyond anything else I have come across in my exhausting path. Is it the pain that binds us? Is it an illusion? I can't understand. I can't tell whether you were real or I dreamed you into my life. A little glimpse. Your essence. All my writing is always about you and how you made me feel. How amazing everything around me became.*
I don't want you to torture me anymore.

So why do I keep me in you.

In the prison of the memory of you.

I need to let go, lovingly.
I almost forgot while traveling across the Atlantic how important you had been. But I want to go back.

Panama Canal at Miraflores Locks. 3/4/2008.
The emotional code is running its perpetuating patterns.

The Bridge of the Americas joins two continents at Balboa. Panama City. Pan-American Highway starts at Monterrey, Mexico and ends at Valparaiso, Chile.

Walking around Panama City is a lot like walking downtown Kathmandu. That said, crazy drivers, honking, tonking, beeping, running one over and driving further. We took the chicken bus for a change. THAT was interesting. No chickens. Just old American school buses.

It is funny when you don't know where you are going. Not speaking Spanish making things harder. I guess there will be no other way I will have to learn the language. You ask the driver, he keeps nodding his head, si, si. Whoever is trying to help you with directions really has no idea where Casa el Carmen is - apparently a must-stay hostal. We were so tired when we eventually made it to the said location...we just continued walking back to our hostel.
Finding an ATM that works is another story. "Cerrado" says on the door.

- Signomi, kirie!..- as I see the puzzled look on the securidads guys face, Greek being the language I picked up in bits and start speaking when people don't understand English. - La puerta...es cerrada...
- Tarjeta!

I see. You need insert your card to unlock. Who would have thought. WHAT!? I am blonde. I am allowed.

Mi cama en el hostal. 3/15/08.
I woke up to the sound of a plastic bag muffled around by a girl on the neighboring bed. So annoying. Only a girl can make this sound. No guy would be fiddling with plastic bags at 6 in the morning.

Breakfast consists of local made coffee with a powder creamer and toast of local bread with green mold bits and spiderweb around the edges. Put butter on top, jam, and spoon. Goat cheese. Bearable for 12 bucks a night.

Still no Spanish whatsoever. Easter week soon.

Tocumen Int'l Airport. Loving someone.
Boquete to Costa-Rican border.
Hearing their voice to starting to smile.
Valleys around the Baru volcano.

Their smile makes your heart quiver and weak in the knees.
Quetzal park. Caldera springs.
A look into their eyes sending shiver through your body and ascension of energy.

Soaring of emotion.

Electric pulse. Connection of grids.

Bocas del Toro. "Mouths of the bull" *en Espanol.*
Spring breakers sweating, drinking, jumping off trampolines and salt mud water all over my blue jeans.

I walk along the shoreline for an hour and a half to get through the jungle and deserted surfer beaches. I feel so lonely. I feel you are always going to bring me to tears and no matter what I do you will always torture me with your ways. You stay with me.
I hardly stand it. It's a bit too much. A parallel lifetime. A parallel reality. I want out of this stupid game. Out of the physical grid.

....it turns out I am still here. Switched computers as the connection blows. I still wonder where you are. What you do. I could connect to you using our cords that always work. But...can I feel you, because I love you?
I can't. All I feel is pain. I feel pain.
It is tough and hard to bear. Maybe I should get away from the water. Storm brings wet, humid, yucky smelling stuff ashore.
I live in a nice yellow Caribbean style beach house. I wish we were here together.
I painted this morning, laying in a hammock. Fuscia for the first time. Your blues is not for me anymore. You came out of the blue and always come through to me when I think of you, in my painting.

I have to say I am not as good a blogger like you are. It is hard to upload pictures. Almost impossible. Okay, no, I will not look at your picture and have my heart break again. It is thoughts of you. ...but continuing to go on with you would only be further bonding and my knowing it is not the same anymore. I am so scared. I am so scared.

There is a path of fear, and a path of love. What would you pick?

I just finished off the most incredible 5 day trek of my life.
I am in Tibet.
I arrived in Lhasa after five days by jeep from the Nepali border. I teamed up with two other travelers and we decided to ride our 25-day Chinese visas which they REALLY don't want you traveling w/o a tour group, but the politics I will save for another time.

After a tour of Lhasa and seeing the Potala Palace, where the Dalai Lama would reside had he not been exiled, we decided to trek from Ganden to Samye Monastery. This was no well-trodden trail as there pretty much wasn't a trail 75% of the time. There are no teahouses or guesthouses to sleep and eat at like if you trek to Everest or do the Annapurna Circuit in Nepal.

We spent a full day getting supplies. 5 days worth of breakfast, lunch and dinner as well energy snacks. Porridge for breakfast, breads with peanut butter and jelly for lunch, and baked raman for dinner. Snacks, fresh onion, ginger to put in our noodles. We rented stove, kerosene, tent, etc.

This was an 80 km trek from start to end going through passes of 5,228 and 5,256 meters - something like 18,000 feet, about the same height as the Everest base camp. Here the oxygen levels are half of what they are at sea level. The team was Lynn from the Yukon Territory, Canada and Brian from Texas. I could never ask for better trekking partners as they never complained, were fun, open-minded, adventurous and experienced. Especially Lynn whom I personally consider from the North Pole. She has been exposed to camping and cold weather her entire life and she taught us how to use the GPS since China so conveniently decided that topographical maps weren't necessary to sell to the public.

Day 1.

Wake up at 5:30. The sunrise was amazing, so on went my headphones and out went the bus-ride. An hour later we arrive at Ganden Monastery. Very legendary and historic, though not much of the original remains b/c of the cultural revolution like all monasteries in Tibet.

The juxtaposition between old and new monastery buildings was fascinating. Everywhere you turn there is something else to steal your attention. The monastery is surrounded by mountains, rivers and blue sky with white clouds that I have never seen the likes of before. Everyday these clouds get me. They are stunning white floating ships.

We begin the kora walk (clockwise walk around temple complex where there can be many Buddhist religious items such as stupas, mani stones, prayer flags, prayer wheels, and many monks) out of the temple complex and then pulled off and embarked on our trek.

A few hours in after trekking under blue skies and amazing landscape we are invited into a yak herders home. This is a burlap tent that they use in the summers while they let the yak graze (yak can only live at high altitudes by the way - or they die). It was a father, mother, and daughter. They have the most incredible scenery. Surrounded by mountains, a river, green grass for yak. Simple and beautiful.

They tried to give us yak butter tea. This is enough to make anyone throw up. Just melt some butter in the microwave, maybe add some hot water and try drinking it. Tibetans supposedly can drink up to 40 cups a day of this shit. We opted for the boiled water which is a normal drink. The mother was relentless in filling out glasses.

I should note that yak dung is used for many things. One big thing is that they burn dried yak dung for heat and cooking. There was quite a lot of it inside the tent all piled up. You don't smell it and you don't think much about it. Then again, I did have an epiphany the other day. If I have been in Asia too long b/c when presented with a Western toilet or a squat toilet I seriously debate which I'd rather use.

Lynn teaches Brian and I how to use GPS while we trek and we finally get to camp ground. We setup camp and started to boil our sweet potato raman with soy and hot sauce. I brought my i-pod so we listened to a little Jack Johnson before bed. PERFECT!!!!!!

Day 2.

Witness and feel the effects of mother nature like you wouldn't believe. We are in a green valley surrounded by mountains as far as the eye can see. I watch the clouds wrap around a mountain to my right like a ghost. It then turns right onto our path. First rain. Within a couple of seconds we are engulfed in clouds and being pelted with hail. We switch to rain and protective gear. The temperature drops so fast that by the end of the storm I can't feel my fingers. I started out the storm in a t-shirt, hoping I could stay that way.

This ends and it gets hot again. I actually have to take everything off down to my t-shirt again. However, it is not long until the hail strikes again. It would happen a third time as well.

This is all happening as we are pushing onwards to our highest pass at Shugala of 5,256 meters. It was an uphill battle - both exhausting and oxygen deprived.

We camped this night at 4,900 meters. Setting up camp, food, and keeping warm were our priorities. We are always near a river. So we filter our water immediately. It is all about teamwork and we were a great team. Never a problem and we had a 3 man tent where our body heat kept each other warm.

It was cold but weather had subsided a bit. I decided to wash dishes alone in the river and I just stayed there for an hour. Taking it in. The mornings are cold and you need your fleece as you watch the sun slowly ascend and then surpass the mountain peaks at which point it is warm and you strip down to one or two at most layers of clothing.

We've all heard it before. DON'T FUCK WITH MOTHER NATURE!!!

(I would also like to point out that I slipped at some point. Difficult to balance with heavy bag in a storm. Didn't feel anything, but my wrist kept on swelling up as the days passed. I bring this up for one reason. My friend and I went snowboarding in 8th grade. First time. I fell and landed on my wrists and my left one hurt quite a bit. I waited for my friend and the other assholes we were with to come down. You stopped so thanks for that. I tell him about my wrist and his response is, "Put it in the snow". I'll repeat. "Put in the snow" was his response. He then continues down the hill. It ended up being broken. This memory brings to memory the time we were walking so cool past my car on an ice day when I came to pick him up for school. As he looked over he slipped and landed right on his back. Ha. It's stills so funny in my mind. That's karma for you bitch!!!!Love ya man).

Day 3.

We head to our second and last pass of the trek of 5,228 meters called Chit lu. At the top of this pass you are greeted by the clearest and highest elevated lakes. It is photo shoot time, time to chat with yak herders, and just about lunch time b/c you wouldn't choose anywhere else to eat and we just topped another pass.

Looking back at the pass from the lakes it looks incredible b/c the pass looks like a sheer vertical wall of rock.
Looks impenetrable.

Day 4.

Just wanted to quickly mention the 'moonrise' we saw over the mountains this night. This thing peaked it's curious head over the mountain and then quickly surpassed it. It then became more than just a nightlight. Brightest fucken moon I have ever seen. I mean we stared at this thing for a while. I could see our camp and the neighboring farmland and village with complete clarity. Our shadows were long and prominent. The moon kept an aura over the mountains as long as I could stay up for. Using the mountains as reference points we were able to watch the globe turn. Bright stars would appear and then simply rotate behind a mountain and disappear as the moon kept rising. Simply amazing
- Baxter ate the whole wheel of cheese!!!

Day 5.

Walk 10.5 km in about 2 1/2 hours on a rock dirt road. Quite different than the beautiful valleys we were in with no sign of human life around. We are in sort of civilization and we don't like it too much.

We arrive at our destination of Samye Monastery. This monastery is in the shape of a mandala - the Buddhist Universe. I climbed 400 m to the top of a mountain for an aerial view. Very cool.

I surveyed, took pics, and then went quickly to the monastery. They had a religious ceremony happening: people dancing around in masks, offerings, instruments. People crowded tightly around to watch. Many people on roof tops.
I just did a circumambulation while turning prayer wheels letting my thoughts go with them and took pictures of the four tall different-colored stupas.

We 3 met back at 4 PM and had to figure out how we were getting to Lhasa. This involved getting transportation to a ferry crossing, taking the ferry across the river, and then the bus to Lhasa. Not so easy.

This was made even harder b/c though we had visas and a permit for Tibet but you need different permits for other places. Samye is one of these places, but the Chinese won't even issue a permit unless you are with a guided tour. So you just have to chance it. If you get caught without a permit you just have to act dumb (easy for me).

We thought we'd be fucked b/c we were the only Westerners there. In fact the most beautiful thing was that we saw not a soul for five days except for Tibetan nomads - yak herders.

It is also interesting to note that we think that we are looking around surveying different parts of the world, but we were being more closely observed than anyone. Tibetan people are fascinated with Westerners. They literally come right into your personal space and stare at you. Imagine the awkwardness. They touch your arm hair b/c they have none and are so surprised by it. You lift your shirt and show chest hair if you really want to shock them. There are quite obviously many other cultural differences. So we learn from each other. I especially love when old women stick there tongue out at you as far as it can stretch. It is a sign of respect.

Anyway, we hopped on a tractor with a bunch of Tibetans and headed to the ferry. We got about 300 meters and the tractor breaks. Terrain has already changed to desert. Apparently, the bolt holding the trailer and the tractor together had popped out. You expect these things to happen in 3rd world, and they do all the time. We just sit and wait to see what the next move might be.

Canada and Texas think that New Jersey should be able to fix a car. Fucking stereotypes. You know me, I'm a true auto-mechanic.

Nonetheless, I try my luck. After surveying the situation and watching 6 people fail at fixing this I decided to stick my hand in there. The bolt was stripped, therefore not able to be screwed and had to be stuck through four holes perfectly lined up. I pulled some oil from the engine and lathered up the bolt and my hand till it was black as night. Then we lined up the two parts of the vehicle, and I eventually got that fucker in there. Had to push down and then hammer it using a wrench. Hammering was the only thing the wrench was good for in this situation. There was no nut so the chances of it staying in seemed slim on a bumpy road.

Anyway, the tractor is fixed and my hands are now not allowed near anything.

We arrive at ferry around 6:30. The ferry is a large wooden canoe with a motor engine exactly the same as the tractor had used. Comforting for a change.

Again, we are the only 3 white people. Most are Tibetans. They are on the boat with their eternally tanned and leathered skin. Their trademark sun- and wind-burnt cheeks.

Little one with an LA Dodger hat on where the top zips off to form a visor. A very old woman next to him trying to make him drink Chang - rice fermented alcohol of choice of Tibetans.
Old Tibetan women party man. They can drink and make sure you do too.

A women to my right dressed in traditional Tibetan garb drinking Chinese Pepsi. When she is done she tosses the can into river.

Brian and I are in the back of the boat by the engine frying like bacon. Lynn secured a seat up front and was given an umbrella to block the sun by a nice Tibetan woman.

I can see the cutest little kid in front of Lynn in his mothers lap. Head shaved except for a wide pony tail in the back. Lynn tells us after the ferry ride that this cutey just bent down right in front of her on the ferry and just took a shit. The mother was eating some bread. She was attempting to clean the shit with something while simultaneously eating.

There was also the really really old and really really cute old woman with spectacles bigger than magnifying glasses. She had her turquoise and gold scarf wrapped around her head and was always smiling.

With the help of some 'exfoliating' sand from the river I am able to get most of the oil off though I still look like an auto-mechanic who hasn't showered for days or shaved for weeks - all of which was completely true (except for a surprisingly fresh rub down with some almond soap in the river we camped near on the 3rd day). I, of course, did this nude. There's only yak and my fellow trekkers around. God knows I don't wear clothes if I don't have to.

Lhasa was a shock when we returned. It seems we had forgotten how much construction goes on by the Chinese, just exploiting the shit out of Tibet's natural resources. All that's left is "Little Tibet" as I call it. Barkhor Square and this is where we went and ate our first real meal in 6 days.

BRILLIANT!!!!

Either of the two. When you love, you don't fear.

If the phone rings in a second and snaps me out of this trance I am in, I will forever remember you never came. You never came back to say I am sorry.
But no matter how bad it hurts to be without you...
I will live.
..with
or without you.

And if you leave it all up to me I'll make it right.
Whatever we face I will always stick it out for us
because I am, again,
your heaven sent,
loving you unconditionally,
truly, madly, deeply,
I know you wanna hold me when you read this,
I know you feel the same.

Many people that have been on my mind that I wanted to know I have been thinking about a lot. We find ourselves in either place all of our lives. It's a good thing. It feels good to be found. It is also good to be lost for those are the times when you need to find something about yourself. When you find that 'thing' it means that you are a little more knowledgeable, perhaps wise, perhaps more complete, and more importantly you are found.
So we must embrace all the things, good and bad that happen during our life. Perhaps we should not even categorize them as good or bad. They are just things that happen.

We have a tiny bit of control as we make decisions. Obviously with a clear head and wisdom we can make better decisions. But this is very hard when you are in the middle of something. Especially something brand new. You really want to do the right thing, but you find yourself smack in the middle of a situation that you have never encountered before. You don't want to hurt anyone, you don't want to act selfishly, and you want to make the right choice.

Seems Impossible.

We always go on blaming other people or the situation. If it wasn't for so and so or if that didn't happen. But the harsh reality is that these things seem to happen b/c of ourselves. We are ultimately responsible for ourselves. Other people may see it much more differently. They may also have different circumstances around them making them feel differently or might have more or less access to knowledge than you do.

I personally encountered a situation that I am admittedly clueless on how to handle. It is a tender one. I see it as a positive thing though it feels so negative now. I want to do what is virtuous.

To me it means to decrease whatever pain there may be in the future or to make it pleasurable. Not to act on the short term though it could hurt so much more in the short term. I will try to believe that truth will prevail in the end no matter what. I am also with time becoming much less clueless.

You have to be in tune with yourself. Be in perfect harmony with yourself. Know yourself. Then you don't need to worry about finding the right person or direction in your life. She/He will be there. Opportunities will be ever present. It will be more or less obvious.

In respect to a love, that person could be there right now, but without a clear sense of reality you may not know it. You need time but that time may not be there. Scary. That's where faith comes in.

Well, I am getting into something a bit deeper here. Good for a late night chat.

But I do want to talk about my last experience which relates to having a clear mind and thus does relate to being lost and found. It was in Cambodia. I am still in Cambodia. Taking a 3 day beach break before I go into a 10-day intensive meditation course called Vipassana.

Before I came to the beach called Sihanoukville, I had the special and unique opportunity to live with monks for a week. I befriended a 26-year-old one named San-Tey. I met him at a practice meditation class he held where we talked briefly about

Buddhism and meditation and he invited me to come to his *wat*. After finishing up the 3 days I had left on my Angkor Wat (kick ass) pass I showed up as I said I would.

They realized that I am quite easy to please and very simple (the best compliment you can get from a monk!!! - unfortunately my mind is not so simple as some of you that may be reading this may be laughing at now). I met the Abbot - the Master, as San-Tey introduced me one day.

I have met just a few men with eyes that seem beyond this realm we live in. Asia is a much more spiritual land than the West and I had the fortunate experience of being blessed by a few of these people. You look into their eyes and you know that they know a hell of lot more than the average human. It's incredible. The few that I have met are imprinted in my memory. Wow. Especially One right now.

Anyway, the Abbot's eyes and his calm nature made him stick out of the crowd. Perhaps the fact that he was sitting above everyone on a lawn chair helped too. He spoke Khmer and San-Tey translated. He liked me and told them to take me in and give me a bed. I had slept on a tile floor in San-Tey's room the first night. He tried to offer me his bed, but I refused. He said that he thought that all Americans were used to luxury. This is a constant battle out here. Everyone thinks that you have all the money in the world. I explained about bums on the street in NYC. Then I slept on the tile floor.

Woke up at 4 AM and sat in back of the 400 year old temple while they chanted for 45 minutes straight in Pali (the Buddha's language). The temple looks and feels its age. Only candles lit and at least 30 orange robed monks sitting on ground and chanting. From young novices to older monks. It's beautiful. It is early in the morning so no disturbances and you feel the spirit envelop you. The temple is alive.

I sat in the back with a white robed nun who chanted with them every morning at 4 AM and every evening at 7 PM. Her hair always wet, her robe perfectly white, always seemingly clean in this dirty environment. I am not.

And so begins the simple life of the monk at Wat Bo. It is very dirty here. It is Cambodia. I must have had 500 bed bug bites by the time I left. But you stop thinking about these things as you travel out in Asia. You see snakes and bugs the size of your hand. It's normal. Just look around. Don't need to ask any questions. Children naked. Children with ripped clothes. Children selling books and other things till midnight. Taxi drivers never leaving you alone. And after saying no to the taxi for the fifth time they try to sell you weed, coke, speed, ecstasy or heroin. They will do whatever they can for a buck. Or less.

They can be so annoying, but they have nothing. What would you do if you were in their shoes??

Have a hard time with the beggar dilemma. Promoting it is a bad idea. The children just give the cash to parents. Best to give children food. They will eat right then and there.

So back to the monks. We would eat at 7 AM. They would collect their alms in their buckets by walking around the streets and people on their knees will give food to the monks. The monks are poor but are provided for.

They eat. When they were done I would eat. They saved food for me. I was not to eat with the monks. This was a little weird but outside of that we hung as if we were all brothers. I watched movies. I played chess. I sat outside and talked to San-Tey about meditation and Dhamma (Buddha's teachings).

I am used to so much stimuli and live for adventure. It was hard to sit and just chill all day. But this is part of the secret. They eliminate external stimuli. They meditate and chill. They are not always serious. They are normal people. They laugh and joke and smile more than we do. Just lead less complicated lives on purpose.

Minimalism is their middle name. Happiness comes from within. It's not an ice cream cone. Sure it brings temporary pleasure and that's cool, but it ends real quick. What we search for is eternal happiness. We must eliminate negative emotions the best we can. Has anyone seen anger get anyone anywhere?

Their beds are wood planks. Their rooms quite unhygienic. Where I slept I would watch large crickets jumping around on my mosquito net. Large cockroaches. The monks barely notice them at this point.

They were all so eager to learn. I loved it. At night I would have 7 or 8 monks sitting down in a room and I would teach them English. Much on pronunciation, vowels. I would read to them. It was good practice for my teaching skills too. I felt more confident and I was teaching more effectively everyday.

One day some random dude asked if I would teach an English class for him. I said sure. I had nothing to do. The Wat was also within a village so there were monks mixed in with Khmer.

Next thing I knew I am in front of 30 Khmer/monk students staring at me. No-one even tells me what the hell I am supposed to teach.

I take one of the students books and ask what they did last time. Fruits and vegetables. Okay. I can do this. Just get over the anxiety.

Many people have told me I have a blockage in my throat chakra. Well, lets get that fucker out!!!!

So at first a little annoyed and nervous. But that quickly turned into a feeling of happiness. I was able to get the whole class to listen and to get them involved. By being animated and having them come to the board and answer questions. They loved it and thanked me so much after class. I met some of the Khmer teachers. Their English was bad so it must have been a treat to have a real English teacher.

Well that was over.

Wait. Nope.

Next one hour class. Teacher decides I would be a great thing in the classroom. Okay.....so I did it again. Was really tired. However, next thing I knew I was teaching another hour of English to the monks in their private rooms. 3rd session in a row. All good though.

San-Tey has built great respect for me (I must have really fooled him:) and takes very good care of me. They insisted on me having a bed with a semi-cushion on it. They gave me free food everyday and everyday San-Tey helped me with sitting and walking meditation. Teaching me to be mindful.

I think I could have stayed there a while and really cleared my mind. But the taste was great and now I move on.

Not to mention how sweet they were. Man. Making sure I was fed. Giving me gifts. Making sure I have water, my mosquito net is up correctly. Everything. Bringing me to tea time. Talking about Dhamma or American wrestling. Brilliant really.

Life is short and it takes on real meaning when something significant happens in your life. So don't pass it off as a cliche.
My feeling is that we must learn to glide and go with it. No need to force or push. I am not saying I have mastered this at all. I haven't. I have hopefully learned much. I am attempting to apply much to my life and I am happy to share my experiences, whether, deep or shallow, funny or sad, good or bad.

Yes, remember life is short. Remember as my father says that we must enjoy the passage of time.

Remember as the monks say that there is no past or future. Only now. We are not permanent creatures. Look at now.

Remember we are all the same. We all have blood. We all have a heart. We have the same body make-up.

When I see someone on the street I try to remember that they are no different. Yes, different upbringings and circumstances in their lives. But in the end they think and they feel and they want to be loved and to love too.

It's nice to always smile even if they don't smile back. Start a conversation with someone if you feel compelled to. Sometimes it's hard in NYC or New Jersey. Who gives a fuck? You are the weird one if you try and talk to someone. They may think that you could have an ulterior motive. Whatever. You might make a great friend too.

I am just babbling. Oh well.

You guys know how to reach me. Anytime boys and girls.

Also, when I get back I want **all** my alcohol. One night. No holds barred. It's on. Leave the weak at home, um I mean bring them. We are all the same :)

II. Grids of Mexico, Peru and Brazil.

<Sandboarding in Ica, Peru. Miles of sand-dunes with one single oasis. On to a 35-hour bus to Cusco.
Llamas, alpacas and Quechua peoples dressed in traditional garb. Train on to Aguas Calientes to start the Inca Trail.
High on endorphines trekking through the jungle to Machu Picchu.

<<*Ormeno* bus to Puno on the Bolivian border, overlapping Lake Titicaca on to Nuestra Senora de la Paz - world's highest de facto capital city at an elevation of 3,500 meters above sea level. Loki hostel - great people, great space, made out with a hot guy who turned out to be a Mormon (can't have sex before marriage).
On to Koala Hostel at Potosi silver mines watching the miners chew coco leaf full of alkaloids to moisten their throats and prevent them from suffocating.

<<<From Lagoa and Leblon to Jardim Botanicou. Gigantic lilies - but they say these are nothing compared to *Victoria Regia* we will see in the Amazon. Unsuccessfully looking for malaria pills. I was staying in *Girl from Ipanema* hostel when Gustavo picked me up as we listened to Ivete Sangalo on the way to his place. I met his brother, Ricardo, and their empregada, Sonia. Corona beers to celebrate good times in Miami. Ate at Garcia e Rodrigues in Leblon, came back as I lay on his bed and seduced him, our lips locked, hands everywhere, the lights were out, as we made passionate love. In the morning we went at it again and then had banana shakes for breakfast. I visit Christ the Redeemer

on Corcovado mountain and look out at the *favelas* and the beaches. *Teleferico* to Pao de Acucar - the "Sugar Loaf" rising out of the waters of the Guanabara Bay of Rio-De-Janeiro.

<<<<On the procession of the Cirio of Nazare, Brazil's largest and greatest event, having planned to go have an ultrasonografia and having done a pregnancy test, my period started. We found out that we can get malaria "shots" in a free clinic and boarded the long-week boat to Manaus in the middle of the Amazon river. 5 nights going upsteam is always unpredictable, rainy, stormy, hot, humid, sticky and never comfortable. *Forro* music of the North-East of Brazil sounds like American country folk. Non-stop. I got sick. I had no problem until after 3 nights and the stopover in Santarem, halfway between Belem and Manaus, where I went to Altar do Chao to snorkel, watch pink dolphins, kayak and all that good stuff. It seemed time was faster when I kayaked all the way in the bay, by myself, alone....*dispersed words echo in my mind...waiting for you, is like waiting for rain...disappointing and unnecessary.* Earliest morning I crossed the border as the immigration official stamps me into Peru for 90 days.

<<<<<The Amazon basin is comprised of seven million square kilometers with 60 percent in Brazil, 13 percent in Peru and the rest split between Colombia, Venezuela, Ecuador and Bolivia. It comprises the largest and most species-rich rainforest but I did not see anaconda.
Tres Fronteras border crossing in the jungle between Colombia, Peru and Brazil. Board the 6 a.m. twelve-hour speedboat to Iquitos: gateway to Peruvian Amazon.
Stayed at Mad Mike's who also publishes *Iquitos Times*.

Went on a jungle tour and swam with pink dolphins, fed bananas to monkeys, got ill with diarrhea, eaten by mosquitos, scared by alligators with flickering eyes in the dark and stayed overnight in an Amazonian jungle lodge. Iquitos could only be reached by plane or boat so Cristina and I hopped on a plane on to Lima.

<<<<<<The screen of my laptop is cracked as I left earphones in between the keyboard and the screen and closed it...
Information is in the hard drive.
Tulum, formerly known in Mayan as "City of Dawn".
Stayed at Lobo Inn off Main Highway.
Mix shredded tomatoes, jalapeno peppers, cilantro and sweet onion in lime juice: get salsa. Mash ripe avocados, shredded jalapenos, onions and cilantro in lime juice: get guacamole.
An egg starts to fall down the fallopian tubes into the uterus: get my period.
Swim in a sacred cenote, or "Well of Sacrifice".
Had to head to Distrito Federal to extract the hard-disc from my *Acer* and sell the skeleton on *Mercado Negro*.

<<<<<<<The Sun enters Serpentarius and Via Combusta. *Go to* Chichen-Itza. Obsidian blade for self-sacrifice. Bloodletting.
Cancun, MX. Hostel Quetzal on to Merida and Uxmal.
Jaguar, Mayan symbol of power, divinity and domination.
Thirteen crystal skulls. 2012. Odd one out.
12 around 1. Judas of Iscariot.

<<<<<<<<Temple of Inscriptions at Palenque - the largest Mesoamerican stepped pyramid structure. Built as a tomb. Hieroglyphic text on the Inscription Tablets.

<<<<<<<<<San Cristobal de las Casas.
Highlands of Chiapas state: mountains, flags, icons of Santa Domingo Church trigger the memory. *I in my soul*, I look into his eyes: from my visual memory. My head span in the subtle connections I felt when I remember connecting with his Self - his Soul. My Soul. Our Soul. A bouquet of yellow daisies.

<<<<<<<<<<A Mayan shaman performs a cleansing with prayers, flowers and copal incense. *Yo tengo dolor de corazyn. No quiero pensar de il no mas.*

I loudly cry into the pillow until he leaves me to sleep in my cold hostel bed. I head to the Church of San Juan in the village of Chamula.

On to Distrito Federal to get new fillings.

The entire 1 year + has been illuminating in many ways. I am currently in McLeod Ganj, Dharamsala, India. It is an extraordinary place and home of the Dalai Lama and the biggest Tibetan Refugee community in the world, located in the Mountains of Northern India. For these main reasons it has quite a different vibe than many other parts of India and the air is cleaner.

This time is amazing as well, though quite different. This could be for many reasons. One reason is that the Dalai Lama is giving public teachings and it has drawn in quite a crowd from around the world. Dharamsala is always a big destination on the tourist map in India.

The type of people it has brought together is what has proven to be most extraordinary. I have never felt so comfortable with total strangers in my entire life. All walls are down and there is no differentiation of who you are or where you are from. Because of uncountable causes and conditions we are all here together now and that's all that matters. RIGHT NOW. And we all know it!!!

From day one you could see there was a special vibe. This was evident when just a few days before the teachings we were plotting down our seats with cardboard, tape, and markers. There were about 7 of us who didn't know each other from countries ranging from Latvia, to Poland, Australia, Britain and so on. There are separate sections for other countries that don't speak English and within minutes of picking our seats (which basically proved to be useless b/c so many people pack in there) we were all joking around and exchanging hugs and pictures. So easy and felt so good and so real.

Anyway, after speaking to my parents for two hours I went to pay. However, I couldn't. My money belt was missing.
It contained everything: cash, credit cards, and passport.

I did not panic as these things I can accept and there is no reason not to have hope. Little did I know I had more than hope on my side. So I walked for 15 minutes back in the dark and avoided the howling dogs who like to hassle me and got back to my freezing room. Woke up late as I was exhausted, but got on the move as I had a lot to do. I ended up missing the Dalai Lama speak that day as well as the next.

However, instead of teachings I got direct experience with the power of kindness and compassion (which is what the Dalai Lama constantly conveys) as well as many other lessons. I hope that they are just not experiences, but things that I internalize and can use in everyday life. I first went back to the area and place where I thought I lost it all. Not there.

Next to police station to file a report. This was a test in patience. They looked at me like they had never seen a white person. At least not one as dirty as me. They start speaking in Hindi and going thru a very disorganized pile of papers. Eventually they find one that is an example of a report of stolen items. They had me copy this example and then they rewrite it themselves. After a lot more paperwork that seemed so senseless I left with a stamped police report which would have proved necessary. And my whole point was to get the word out there that my belongings were missing. So next I made a flyer with all the pertinent information: bought tape and started putting up posters everywhere I could. I had already been blown away from the people I had met (which I have good stories about), but this is when I began to be knocked off my feet.

I ran into a middle aged gentleman from Canada named Chris that I had met in Bodhgaya, India. He told me of all the people that have had this problem and gave some good advice and then offered me 1,000 rupees (39 rupee to the US dollar) or ~$25. I declined. I had about $100 in traveler checks that I had been holding onto in case of emergency. I decided to remake the flyers with my photo so I had passport photos made. The Indian man owning the shop, knowing what my issue was, gave me the photos for free.

I then made several copies of the new flyer in Western Union. The Western Union is where I cashed my traveler checks earlier. They almost did not let me but I remembered my passport number and I guess the gods were on my side this day as they have been recently. In Western Union an Australian girl gave me some advice for the flyers which I deemed very useful. She told me to write "reward offered" at the bottom. This would prove helpful especially if it was stolen as passports can be sold for good money on the black market.

She and her friend took some flyers and said they would post them for me. The afternoon teachings were ending at this point so I knew a flood of people would be surging out of the temple complex. I found some of my friends including Margy from the US, Jeremy from Britain, and Raymond from Latvia who took flyers and offered me money and help. I was and probably should have gone straight to the Internet café to cancel credit cards which I knew would be hell at about 4 PM, but I didn't. I just wasn't worried. I went to a special gathering up at the

Tushita center and was so glad that I did. Was there with good friends. Got served tea and food.

Up at Tushita I saw my great friend Roger. A man in his 50's with a white beard down to his belly. He is a jolly man with a heart of gold. True compassion and a great sense of humour among other things. We befriended each other in Nepal and have become very close since then. He automatically offered me money. I, of course, said no. On my way out he gave me 1,500 rupees and would not take 'no' for an answer.

Afterwards, I went to the internet and canceled my cards. The owner of the Internet shop stayed open late for me even though he lived 6 km away and his wife was calling him. He would not take money from me and offered me 50 rupees for a rickshaw back to where I live as he said the walk was dangerous. I refused but the continuous flow of people's genuine kindness was really starting to infiltrate me.

There was an Indian man who spoke perfect English in the Internet shop that saw my flyers and heard my phone calls. With absolute and complete heart he offered me his prayers. It came straight from his heart and he gave me his advice. Like he had known me for along time and could feel any pain I felt. I also forgot to mention a man named Todd. He is originally from the US, but now resides in Dharamsala. I don't know him well but I had his contact info. I called him from the police station and he told me to use his address to have anything sent that I might need. After finally leaving the Internet shop around 11 PM I ran into my Italian friend named Claudio. He asked wuts up. I told him. He brought me over to a group of six people that instantly reacted as if my problem was just as much their own. I never met any of them before.

Each of them took many flyers to post around town. One guy from Israel named Mordechai reached into his pockets to give me money faster than I could say hello. Then one little sweet girl came up to me and looked at me and just said, "Keep thinking positive and it will come." Anyone could say this and you could be like "whatever." But she meant it and I believed her.

This was the icing on the cake. Are people really this nice? What is going on here? You'd think this would have a been a long and bad day. Perhaps hell for some. I was never to upset. Just figured I had some work to do. However, the extraordinary thing is that I felt better at the end of that long day than on most days. It was people's mindblowing kindness and it didn't stop there.

People cared and wanted to help. It made me feel truly good and made them feel good to help. To me it is proof that genuine happiness comes from being good to others. Not desiring things for ourselves but the desire to do what is good and virtuous for everyone. Our lives are constantly being affected by the people around us, and it just makes sense to help them as much as you can. It comes back to you too.

Just think how good it feels when someone does something good for you for no apparent reason. It feels fucken great. Imagine if we always did this for each other all of the time. It seems that once we find some peace in our turbulent lives and create some space in our minds we can then help others.

So off to bed. Woke up and missed the teachings a 2nd day. However, I really did receive teachings on this day just like the first. These two days put together were enlightening and taught me so much. After dealing with credit card company's for a little while I went into town. While I was in the Internet café another total stranger heard me on the phone and offered me money. Never ever saw him in my life.

Once into town I ran into Raymond. He said that he was going somewhere but felt it more important to help me. He said that he would help me make better flyers on the computer with my image scanned in. Just outside of his hotel I ran into the girl from Western Union and the little girl who told me to keep positive. Both had the same message for me. The little girl came up to me and told me that she saw a sign at the main temple about a yellow moneybelt with an American Passport in it.

On my way to the temple I saw Roger, my great Australian friend. He handed me 600 rupees which came from two amazing women named Nancy and Margy. Raymond waited as I made my way thru 1,000's of monks, nuns, and lay people from the teachings completely filling up the street. Finally I made it to the temple. I made it to reception and they told me the office was closed. But I told the main security guard, Tibetan man named Karma, the situation and he walked with me to the office and had it opened for me.

There it was. My yellow money belt with my passport. I gave them verifying information and went on my way. They said a Tibetan nun found it and turned it in. Whomever had it, must have taken the cash and tossed it on the street. Cash gone and credit cards now canceled, left me still with no money. But I had my passport which contains my India Visa. Saved me a trip to Delhi to the US consulate which could have taken weeks or a month. I can stay in Dharamsala and do what I intended to do.

I ate with Claudio, the Western Union girl, the little girl, and a few others I had met and had a nice meal and conversation in which we dedicated at the end. I was walking back to my place when I ran into Hanz from Austria. I shared a sleeper with Hanz on the 14-hour bus from Delhi to Dharamsala. They sell two tickets for a spot big enough for one of me. So you share this uncomfortable space with a total stranger. This is not at all weird after being here for while. In fact it is totally normal. Personal space does not exist in India. Hanz knew I had lost money. After speaking for a moment he took 500 rupees and stuffed it in my shirt. I tried to give it back to him and he was already far away and just waved. He waved and I lost it for a moment. On the road all alone I found tears rolling down my eyes. They were of both joy and sorrow.

Joy b/c of the faith it gave that people are good and deep down I know that everyone wants to do good and not to suffer and would do anything to be shown the kindness that I received.

Sorrow b/c the solution is so simple. We can be happy by simply helping others, but this is so rarely the case even with people close to us. It was disbelief in the power of humanity and the power of kindness in action. It was disbelief that I was staring at the solution to so many problems in which we face.

Many of us get so busy and consumed every day that we leave no space for others. I find myself guilty of this all of the time. We find ourselves upset and always needing to do one more thing and then we'll be satisfied. Always desiring the next thing. It's no-one's fault. We are products of our environment.

I saw the positive energy that consumes this place come to me when I needed it. I try to do my best for other people and it came back to me when I needed it.

I ACCEPTED the situation. This is so important. I was ready to have to ditch my plans and spend time in Delhi and possibly have to go home. So acceptance of ourselves and our situations is integral to our happiness and health. Fighting makes things worse. I know this from repeatedly making the mistake over and over.

It seems acceptance of the unpredictability and ever-changing nature of all things is one of the main channels to achieve serenity. It seems we need to Let Go. Because in reality we have so little control. All the planning in the world does not mean that things will turn out how you planned. There are ways to many conditions each affecting one another. We are actually lucky if things turn out as planned.

Getting my things back involved patience as well. We all know how important and difficult patience is. When I mentioned the people that helped along the way, I mentioned their nationalities for one reason and one reason only. To show that it does not matter where people are from. Many of us have very different lives, beliefs and circumstances. Especially, between a Westerner such as myself and the Indian shopkeepers who were endlessly kind to me.

I know that our lives are not even remotely similar in how we survive. However, we are all exactly the same when it comes down to helping one another and wanting to find happiness. There is just no difference. So the world came together and helped me in Dharamsala, India.

I was passionate about what I was doing b/c they were my important belongings. But it is this passion that shows that you can accomplish many things if you really care about it. It is all about your intent and motivation.

And even if you 'fail', you really haven't. You have made a difference even if you don't know it by being an example to everyone and to have strength and fight for what you believe.

So many lessons learned or to be learned. It was as if this was a test for me. To put all that I have learned through out the year into practice or at least to see if I can actually begin to see the ultimate reality things. I think I pulled some of the lessons from it. The real goal is to internalize these lessons.

I tell this story not b/c I lost/had stolen my things. I wouldn't write to tell people that. I would just get shit from you :)

It has been long since I wrote and I have so much to share. I can't upload photos b/c of camera card issues but at some point I will try to accomplish this if can find the right facilities.

I was in SE Asia for a while before coming back to India.

III. Back< INdia.

<<<<<<<<<<Randall gives me his hand as I make my last step before Wayna Picchu. "You can't sit on the rocks," - says one of the guards, "they are falling down as thousands of people trek up here every day. Did you know that it was named One of the New Seven Wonders of the World last year? Yes. Along with Taj Mahal, Chichen Itza, Christ the Redeemer, Colosseum, Great Wall of China and Petra??"
I stand up as the clouds reveal the Lost City of the Incas.

<<<<<<<<<Salar de Uyuni in the South-West of Bolivia on the border with Chile. Incahuasi island of giant cacti adorn my camera along with Andean flamingos and pyramid-like heaps of rock salt. The salt flats formed as a result of transformation of prehistoric lakes. The flamingos are pink because of feeding on pink algae. Salt blocks were used to build the Salt Hotel where we spend the night.
Our tour guide says that when covered with water, the Salar becomes the largest mirror on Earth, five times better for satellite calibration than the surface of the ocean.
The tour ends at San Pedro and we cross the border - a small house in the midst of the Atacama desert.

<<<<<<<<Frida Kahlo and Diego Riviera lived in Casa Azul, in Coyoacan district of Mexico City.
It is now called Museo Frida Kahlo and houses numerous catrinas (literally, "elegant") - skeleton dolls from ancient tradition to symbolize Dia de Muertos or All Souls Day.

Sugar calaveritas and pan de muerto. Agua horchata!!
The museum is two blocks away from Leo Trotsky's home,
Russian revolutionary and Marxist theorist.
At 18 Frida was in an accident which crippled her.
She started to paint.
Second turn of Lilith.

<<<<<<<At the top of Templo de la Luna of Teotihuacan.
I cover my shoulders with a white shawl. Gaze out.
The Sun enters Via Illuminata.
On through the Avenue of the Dead.
I receive the reconnection throughout the electromagnetic grid of
the past, present and future. Detachment. She left him.
On to the pyramid of the Sun.

<<<<<<Bariloche of Argentina or Little Switzerland.
Skiing and snowboarding, hot chocolate and cheese fondue.
Watch Nahuel Huapi Lake from Cerro Campanario.
Catch a cablecar and hike the glacial valleys of Cerro Catedral.

Chilean border is nearby but Consulate is closed.
Continue on The World's Most Dangerous Road as described by
Che Guevara in his Motorcycle Diaries.
All the way.
On to Uspallata, nearby Mendoza, one of the Great Capitals of
Wine, which also served as location for filming *Seven Years in
Tibet*. Mountain-biking for four hours. Milk tea in *Tibet Cafe*.

<<<<<To cross overland into Brazil from Argentina.
Go through customs at Foz do Iguacu.

National Park of gushing waterfalls.
The largest cataract is Devil's Throat at 82 meters.
Park includes rides, a lagoon to swim and butterflies to watch.
Drink some yerba mate, a traditional infused beverage.
Mate gourds and typical bombillas (straws) for sale.
Along with bows, arrows and other mics of the *gauchos*.

<<<<Capoeira, olodum.
Martial arts, music, dance and african drums. Sao Salvador.
Bay of All Saints.
North-East of Brazil calls up the best Carnaval.
Agua de coco is coconut water sold for 2 reals.
Samba to
"chorando se foi que um dia so me fez chorar..."
Lambada by Kaoma.
"...crying was the one who one day made me cry"
Lacerda elevator from the Pelo to Model market.
Ferry on to Ilha da Itaparica and Morro de Sau Paulo.
"Suerte!" - yells a young boy, - "You are beautiful!"

<<<Pisco sour. A cocktail of rum, lime juice, egg whites, syrup and bitters at Barranco's Backpacker's Inn which holds title of the *Best Hostel* voted by hostelworld.com. Owned by Chris, a British expat, located next to a surfers' beach of the romantic and bohemian "ravine" neighborhood of Lima, also one of the most popular within the worldwide surfing community for its beaches and yacht-club.

<<"Paulista?"
Florianopolis, Santa Catarina.

48

Brazil's South holds the German yearly beer festival.
A wet-suit to surf the waters as private lessons are only 35 reals in Lagoa da Conceicao.
Rain and storm hurt.
Idan from Jerusalem shows me an overland route from Cancun into Monterrey, MX.

<San Blas = 365 islands for each day of the year.
Andi and I take a boat from Carti - to a Cat island on Monday, Dog island on Tuesday and Cow island on Wednesday.
The indigenous Kuna Yala inhabit the islands - originally refugees from Columbia who came to Panama...

Ushuaia @ Tierra del Fuego. World's End.

Tibetans to Carrot Cake

Not a clue where to start. Just inspired.

Decisions. Not easy. But when you just follow your heart, where your feet take you without even thinking, no mind involved you end up doing the right thing even if it is extremely hard.

I wake up feeling my sinuses once again rocking my world. But it's something I have learned to live with and I know it will pass as it always does.

The Dalai Lama is back in town. Unbelievable. You hear his unforgettable laugh as he has a pretty wicked sense of humour. Today I did not see him, but spent about 3 hours with Tibetan refugees. Two hours with one who is an ex-political prisoner. His story is one to sober the most insensitive and his attitude (one of some level of contentness) enough to make you wonder how we ever get upset.

He deals with kidney and stomach pain from the beatings in prison. That's the physical part. He mentions not forgetting the face of his 26 year old monk friend who was killed in jail by Chinese police right before his eyes. That's the mental part.

But we do a good job jumping back and forth from his 25-day trek/escape over the freezing Himalayas to Nepal and about his prison days to how the hell Tibetans drink that nasty butter tea.

And so I am brought back to what seems like yesterday but is close to a year ago now. I am back on a trek thru Tibet where I met nomadic yak herders. Tonight a man told me his family is from a village near Ganden Monastery. This is the place where I began my trek and in the same day met my first nomadic yak herder which he says his father was. I wonder if I met his father.

Blissful were those days. I am now in Dharamsala again where the Tibetans end up after they flee their ravaged country.

How lucky I am to have gotten to see Tibet. Getting in now is near impossible. So I have a bit of a reference point. Everything is hidden from us.

Time spent in candle light vigils, and having conversation classes with Tibetans. Time spent at the Dalai Lama Temple. Time spent reading and catching up with old friends. Time spent making new friends. And way too much time eating the Tibetan special from this bakery that has the best baked goods and may kill me soon. So irresistible. Such a test everyday. Most days I lose.

This reminds me of the month I spent at the monastery in Nepal in January. I lived in a freezer box. Had five fleece blankets on me and candles burning to keep me warm.

Was one of the best months of the trip.
Went there with the intention to try a private retreat as I came from a month spent in Bodhgaya, Bihar, India. I succeeded to an extent. Read a lot. Got introduced to Thicht Naht Hahn among other great writers and books. He was a great friend of Martin Luther King and one of the most notable peace activists of our time. He resides in France now as he is in exile from Vietnam.

It most reminds me of the monastery though b/c of the people. One of the most interesting people on this trip and One I met in Nepal that was most influential to me.

And so I had a million thoughts in my head and can't find them now. So much for single pointed concentration. When you haven't written in a long time and you are feeling it there is just too much to say it seems.

Ah, perhaps it was the 3 days I just spent in a village outside of Dharamsala. When in this town, part of the state of Himachal Pradesh, it's hard to realize that you are actually in the Himalayas and amongst serene beauty. It is around you but there are many distractions.

It begins with meeting a guy who calls himself Yogi (real name Tasneem from Kashmir). Skinny as hell, talks with an English accent, studied English Literature in Mumbai and seems to always have a Western girl. He communicates with Westerners and knows how they think to the point where it is scary. What is more scary is that he can turn on his Hindi accent like the flip of a switch. You would never know that he knows a lot about you without knowing you.

I wanted to go to Karmapa's Monastery as he makes appearances on Saturdays. Yogi heads to another house in the village as the sun begins to set. I head to the bus stand to wait for the local bus. I am in pure debate about what to do. Go back to town or spend the night in the village and have a nice village experience.

I then see Sarika and two of her friends. Sarika is part of the same NGO as Yogi that I somehow found myself working for the past two days. She is more than this though. Though she, Yogi, and her father Ajay head up this Himachal Children &

Development Organization (HCDO) project she has become one of the foremost leading people in AIDS awareness in the world. She is only 25 and she has two titles. One is the secretary of HCDO and the other is the Deputy Chair and/or Regional Youth Caucus Rep. of India for the Commonwealth Youth Program. Anyway, I see her and I know Yogi went to her family's humble abode in the middle of the forest which I wasn't about to find as the sun was setting.

She is about to leave and I ask if I can come with her. She says okay and so there was my decision. I was staying the night in the village of Garoh. We walk and I hear about what made her the prominent person she is today.

We pass the nutjob Yogi on the never-say-die Enfield. Sarika and her friends (one who is her cousin and apparently a huge folk singing star in India) tell me to pick up rocks (sharp ones) and throw them at him as he shouldn't leave me at the bus stop unattended (though it was my decision). I have no argument as I would love give this complicated enigma a nice jolt :)

Back at the humble abode I have another glass of chai. You get in with some Indian families and you are doomed to drink chai all day. No problem. It's awesome and with super fresh milk in the villages as it comes from the cows you see. And it ain't butter tea.

I watch yogi and Mata Ji (mother) argue and argue in Hindi. It's hilarious. Sarika tells me they always argue.

I then watch a documentary made on Sarika and her work. Well it starts with an episode on a Bollywood star. Than a real star - Sarika - someone really helping the world. Then last episode they meet.

Under the night sky Yogi mounts the Royal Enfield. Behind him is young Sau. Perhaps 8 years old. Behind him is me. So 3 on a bike is totally normal. Helmets - NEVER. Feel the wind in my face on a night of perfect weather underneath the stars. We get back home and I am shown my bed. It's like 9 PM and I think I'd like to go to bed. I also know that we haven't eaten yet. Mother is not in sight. Kids in bed. We are in a room next to them. Papa Ji comes in with some King Fisher Strongs. I haven't drank in ages. Two glasses and I'm tipsy.

I'm asked if I like chicken. I haven't eaten meat in a long time but I know I eventually want some. It's close to 11 PM. Then the placemats come out. So does the rice, dahl and chicken. FUCK YEAH!!!! I eat that shit up like a dog hits up humans leftovers. Chapatis too!!!!

Mr. Pathania asks about my sinuses. He is sincere and I am told he is a man that if he sees someone walking down the street that looks in need of some help he asks what's wrong and takes them in. He gives me a program. I am sure it's one that we have all been on. I'll explain briefly. First 7 days - eat a leaf from the Neem tree each day. It must be fresh and sit in the sunlight and be from a branch with an even number of leaves.

Day 7-14 - same procedure but with mint leaf.

Day 15-21 - same but with Tulsi tree leaf.

Day 21 - find special root and pull it out of ground and wear around my neck for a day.

Day 22 - 28 - Neem leaf again.

I am told that this opens up all blockages in the system.

Fuck it. I'll try it.

Next day. We pull Neem tree leaves off plant and eat together. But it ends there as I don't have these plants at my disposal and I am leaving the village at around noon this day and little do I know with all the perfect timing. But back to waking up on this day. I wake up as if I am hungover. We have chai. I notice when I wake up there was 'new' Indian man sleeping on another bed in the room. Once outside drinking the chai I see a Western girl standing in front of me and Yogi. WTF is going on. I should not be surprised by anything anymore but it is quite amusing.

I never meet any East Coasters in India but right before me is some girl who goes to Brown University and arrived at 1 AM on a bus-ride that left her head bruised and her mind traumatized as the bus somehow arrived 2 hours EARLY. This bus had to drive thru the mountains. YOU have to be on an Indian bus to really understand this. It's chaos even when they are not flying. Traffic in India can be compared to nothing at all. It is truly unique and can give you a heart attack, but it works. Just like the rest of India it works. The honking, the weaving, the speeding, the motorbikes, the pollution. And it works. Put a Westerner to drive here with no prep and they would be dead soon. Put an Indian in the West with no preparation and they too would be dead.

The Indian Man who I saw when I awoke was named Ajay and is the backbone of HCDO. Great heart on this guy. Around 11 AM we get rice, dahl and curd and somehow an Indian man who on this day at least did not move on Indian time. Ajay knows I want to get to the Karmapa and gets me, Lizzie (East Coast girl) and himself in a taxi to the Dharamsala bus station which he pays for.

We arrive around 1 PM and the bus I need is there and ready to go. Ajay mentions that when you do something with your heart it all works out. I get on bus still unsure as the ride is perhaps 20 minutes and I think the Karmapa will appear at 1:30. The bus is not leaving and I am contemplating getting out.

I see a Tibetan woman and a Westerner. The only reason they would be on this bus is to see the Karmapa (somewhat equivalent to the Dalai Lama - sorry for not mentioning earlier). I ask and they yes and he will appear at 2 PM. I get there and on time and I get to see him. It all does work out. No worries man.

Ran into a girl I met from a few days back and we went to the nearby Norbulingka Institute - art institute for Tibetans. The grounds were dreamy and the artisans were amazing and so sweet and happy to talk and let you take pictures. Thangka painters, wood carvers, metal sculptors and more. I have made plans to make an excursion to Sherab Ling this coming Sunday. I will parcel books, clothes, music, movies and more. See the Dalai Lama one last time this round and see some other people. I will also attend a closed door (maybe 10 of us going) sitar player concert in the Cafe Delicacies. It promises to be special.

I also desperately want to write about BBQ spiders, frogs, and ducks for sale as food at bus stops in Cambodia. Or bats and other dead mammals for sale at some of the markets in Cambodia. Or a car ride in a trunk to a waterfall as it gets dark and the car gets stuck and we walk to a waterfall in which we end up swinging from vines in to the water fall like we literally are Tarzan.

But I cannot forget the electric nights on the Mekong River at 4,000 islands in Laos.

A hammock, a candle, a joint, great company, the Mekong roaring beneath the stilts of a $1 a night bungalow as the sky lights up in pink colors due to electric storms consistently but never raining on our special little island of Don Det. And thank you to the Australian baker who decided to make it his home for the last 3 years and made sick ass doughnuts and carrot cake that every visitor craved.

Thoughts pouring in like the monsoon.

Oh the moments.
Oh the people.

Just to be alive when they are happening.
To be aware. So important.

Well, that's a weird ass all over the place journal entry for your asses. I'm out. Literally. I'm getting kicked out of here. And I can't stop eating sweets. This place will be the death of me.

I love people and I love life.
In the morning I may feel differently but I know that that will pass too and I will come back to what I know matters most.

You, me and everyone else.

Spread love and it will come back to you.

Kay. Scatterbrain is out.

IV. Malaysia.

LAX check-in. Four seats in a row. *If You Could See Me Now*.
20 minutes before landing into Kuala Lumpur of 100 degrees, humid and smelly.
Golden Triangle at Pujangga Homestay. The KL Tower.
Batu Caves. National Mosque - Masjid Negara.
Crimson table-runner for my mother. Nasi lemak (white rice with coconut milk) for breakfast and nasi ayam (rice and chicken) for dinner.
Reason to go to Malaysia: see Petronas Twin Towers - 88 floors of reinforced concrete with steel and glass facade - motifs from Islamic architecture.
The reality of a hollow object is in the void, not the walls that define it. The power of the void of the towers is increased by the pedestrian bridge. The supporting structure creates a portal to the sky - a door to the infinite.

Forbidden Love in a Monastery. *Go to Thailand*. Bus to Butterworth. Ferry to Penang. J is in front of me. J is inside my soul vision. J is within. J is here, too. Love Lane Hostel. Love Lane. Running shoes. Hopelessly try escape hysteria. Must be a reason. Pain within. Creator. Wizard. *Believe in me*.
Faith is energy. Uplifting. Inspiring. Run, run and run...Return to the hostel and go online.

What am I doing? Just because I felt lonely for a minute I am going to give in to the urge to write to him after all this time and all the e-mails he had already ignored and left unanswered????
I can hold on to my integrity no matter how bad the pain gets. I go to a Gompa across the street as a nun welcomes me and blesses my mind. She speaks English and gives me study materials as I weep. She says she sees I love him but my mind

put an end to our communication now that my heart is trying to break out of the prison my mind had put it in.

Manjushri Mantras.

I leave a generous donation for the CDs, go back to the hostel, log onto facebook and add James into my friends.

On to Thailand. Joy of being on the road. Getting off one bus, getting on another one, stopping for a cigarette, getting coffee at a 7-11. *The feeling double-sided.* Something that felt so beautiful turned out to be such a mess. The story channeled. The energy bubbling. Run to him. Be with him. Again. After all this time

...after all this pain on the bus to Krabi. Mind needs to find out what this means. Check in. Bored, angry, tired, starved, frustrated. Using US dollars, exchanging little by little into Thai Baht. Break into tears. *Tell him. Explain everything.* Without residue, without holding back.

But our story...part I, II, IV and X keeps me from writing. Closest Internet cafe. Our connection. Innermost truth within. The pull I feel. The children I see. This is so *strong* again.

This is *not* a sign.

Subject: A New Page
"Dear James,

How have you been? I have been very different and I needed a VERY long time to get over our connection and what it was doing to me. Recently have I read your blog to hear you mention going back to the monastery in January...I was so relieved as I knew why I was having visions of you again, in Jan 2008. I saw you there. On the stairs. I wrote to you every day, but every-time I finished an email I shoved it, as my logic kept saying that this can't be real again. I didn't trust my heart. Afterwards I moved to Miami and embarked on a what I like to call "Search for everything" in which I have been to Peru, Bolivia, Argentina, Brazil, Mexico, Honduras, Belize, Guatemala and Panama. It is the last leg these next few months and I just entered Thailand. I love overland travel so much, and by the time I come to Moscow, I would have crossed thousands of kilometers by train, bus, boat, and I would have been to Siberia - very mystical, like Tibet.

I have visited NJ at some point while I was in America, and it felt very romantic. I loved Hoboken, if not the winds. So I was on the bus today, as ever. The image of you kept coming up in front of me. I denied it again. I started crying. I felt so much aggravation and pain over the fact that I have been through so much before, with, and after you, but I still haven't learnt to let you go. And thats when I knew I had to face the simple truth. I still have feelings for you. It never really goes away.

And then I thought, but what was I to do with it, after all this time, all this pain. One thing I knew: I wont be in this alone.
If you wont let me.

I understood a very big problem for me was the fact that I was alone in it for too long. I needed you to help me through this. To speak to me. Our dialogue is so important. So no more jumping to conclusions, no more obsessions and compulsions. I have grown over and passed that. and this is why I am writing to you today. Because I realized. I am unhappy. I am suffering because I am not talking to you. Because your spirit, your essence, your memory, haunts me when I enter a Buddhist temple or smell incense burning. I cried on a nun's shoulder yesterday and she told me to go to Chiang Mai to do a puja with a monk.

And at this minute I wanted you to be part of this. I want you to know what I'm going through. What I HAVE been going through all this time: living in our connection.

I have accumulated enough strength and will-power to clear the fear and doubts I have in regards to you, me, us.

I want to find out if this means anything to you, or not. If you want to get back in touch, whatever it would mean, or not. If our connection is just my connection, or it really is OURs.

I hope you like it. I hope you respond.

Tell me about your experiences.
Much love to you,
:)"

Phew. Catch a boat to the infamous Railay Beach. Gorgeous scenery makes me feel the same as when my heart connected to his and our channel of energy was open. Find a lodge to sleep for 400 Baht: the cheapest bungalow. Challenge myself into rock-climbing to the presence of a tall guy in a bandana with blue eyes, wide shoulders and dark curly hair. Makes me feel good. Next second it hurts like hell. Pray James replies. Pray he replies saying anything. Just about anything.

I have recently learnt that Alex Garland was really writing about the Philippines in his book, *The Beach*. By making it seem as it was in Thailand, he kept the Philippines safe from backpackers. Ferry station close-by Surat Thani. Familiarity. A girl. A reflection. I pull out a chair and excuse myself into her private world. She is Dutch, humble and fascinating. Four hours on the ferry as we arrive to Ko Pha Ngan and catch a ride to the Full Moon Party Beach. I forgot the name of it but you will know once you are there: it is full of backpackers.

J's is energy imprinting...hologramming....overwriting....in my reality. Ivonne and I walk into a restaurant as I notice a hot guy with the corner of my eye as I swing past him picking out a table, walk back to the table we started from and sit down. Ivonne tells me about her week of diving in the Similan Islands off the coastal border and leeches in the jungles of Northern Borneo around a village called Kuching.

We order Pad Thai and beers as I light a cigarette. The hot guy indecently makes his way into our conversation and tells us about a Canadian dude who owns a tourist agency down the road. The indecent hottie is from Northern California.

He just flew in from Kathmandu.

He was there for New Year's.

He just did the 16-day Everest Trek.

By himself. Alone. No guide. "What's the big deal!?"

Anyone can trek to the Everest in December all alone: the trail is marked. There was no shower for a week. But today he is clean, shaven and hot: wide shoulders, dark hair and blue eyes. Into himself, sad and angry about something.

What kinda guy would trek alone to the Everest for New Years????? The kinda guy who would strike my immense interest and break my heart.[1]

I have to run for the hills as the attraction between us is so strong. Ivonne and I walk out of the restaurant as I burst out in saliva as to how much I was attracted to the guy and I realize I don't even know his name. We get beers, go back to the bungalows and I confess "I am on this journey to forget him: get rid of the pain that binds me to him. When fear took over when I first bungy jumped in Phuket...standing on the tip hearing: 3, 2, 1, Bungy! I said his name to heavens and then I jumped."

- Wow, he is really in your heart.[2]

She sets me off on a ferry to my pre-booked five-star hotel in Ko Samui. How easy is the program. Just see if it works, do it for a day or two, and if it doesn't, forget it, move on, and on, and on...my high school friend Nomin is doing ESL training and we meet at the Three Monkeys bar in Chaweng Beach. This time around Thailand is overdue...I should have been here a long time before...in a life that was maybe easier. Perhaps it is just coinciding with my memories of traveling to Spain and Italy with my family when I was a child. Something long ago...you know?

---

[1] Is every guy I am gonna be attracted to going to come from the Everest Trek or Buddhist connection?

[2] said Ivonne.

Wat Suan Mokk, a Thai Buddhist monastery in a tiny town called Chaiya. My room is full of flies, mosquitos and filthy sheets. The nun who checked me in doesn't understand what I mean when I say I need a puja. I hand-wash my clothes and hang them to dry. I try to fall asleep but the bugs bug me as in a haze I see J's spirit floating atop my mosquito net in a cross-legged position. Next morning I buy my ticket for the third class train to Bangkok at 19:07, grab my bags, head to the train station as I am one hour early. I logon on to book a hostel. Two facebook notifications: James has accepted your friend request and James has edited details on how you know each other. I confirm that we *traveled to Nepal in the spring of 2007*. I click on his updates. He had just posted photos from Israel. He still looks as hot and sweet as I remember him. He had just returned from travels. Still searching, he went to motherland: ancestry land. The meditation retreats were not enough and there is more for him to experience. Log off with a sugary taste of reconnecting.

Never shut my eyes on the train after 8 hours of contemplating on how independent and self-driven both of us are and how we find our missions regardless - as we are independent individuals as we connect in our goals. It is amazing how I can still feel him.

In Bangkok: Myanmar Consulate at 8.30 a.m. Apply for visa. Indicate "therapist" as profession. Official asks "what kind of therapist?" Answer "massage therapist". Looks at my passport photo, tells me *krasivaya*.[3] Issues me a single-entry one-month visa. Catch boat to the backpacker ghetto of Khao San Rd. Buy ticket to Yangoon, capital of Myanmar. Visit the biggest Wat Pho in Thailand with a giant reclining Golden Buddha and Wat Phra Kaew.

---

[3] *Beautiful* in Russian.

V. Myanmar.

The annual solar eclipse in the XII house of ancient teachings, religion, secrets, mysteries, foreign countries, jail and limitation.
Thai visa runs out January 25th.
Obama's inaguration on satellite TV.
Witnessing history traveling the world.
I board the plane to Yangoon, sending out a powerful message to meet someone to travel with. *Regain faith, believe in love again.*

Stamped into Myanmar and look for the guy holding the sign with my name who is supposed to be picking me up: cute, wearing a long checkered Burmese skirt. Another foreigner getting picked-up is Lars from Sweden of 37 years old, working in China teaching English. We get on the minibus to the hotel and plan our day as everyone around us probably wonders why we stay in different rooms as we make such a perfect couple. He has blue eyes but he is old, fat and reminds me of my ex-boss, Sasha. The way he smiles, the way he laughs and makes dirty jokes. He calls me "honey" as we circle the main stupa in Yangoon square. Being here with him may cause a *connection*.

My awareness blocks it. We continue exploring the city looking to find a shop to buy local currency. The city of Yangoon suffers from decades of neglect as the buildings are crumbling and the paintwork is chipped. But within it...lies the charm. The European architecture remains from the times of the British colonization. There are no banks or ATM machines, so whatever amount of money you came with, that's all you have. Locals approach us, greeting with *minglaba* = hello, offering to take us to a "shop" to exchange our dollars into Burmese kyats. The rate is 1 US Dollar to 1,000 kyats.

We go to the only place that has an official currency exchange joint - the Strand Hotel - also one of the city's most famous landmarks. Apparently they can give you a "cash advance" - a charge made as a purchase on your credit card if you need to take money out of your account while in Myanmar. They would charge 15% for it.

The name of our hotel is Ocean Pearl Inn and service is fast, staff is attentive and sweet, breakfast the next morning is filling and yummy. I meet an American couple and we take a bus to Chinatown for celebration of the Chinese New Year. The ticket salesman waves a 400 kyat note. I debate as to "why?" usually the bus costs 200 kyats. A young local guy explains that this is a better quality bus so it is normal to pay more than for the normal bus. He speaks perfect English. We giggle about it, get off the bus in Chinatown and eat dinner. Lars tells me about his earlier travels in SE Asia and that the most impressive sight for him was Angkor Wat in Siem Reap, Cambodia. He says that I should go to Luang Prabang in Laos: a cute town of smiling people...temples...the strongest impression comes from the very first sight you see, and for Lars, it was Angkor.
For me...it was Swayambhunath. But my soul is too tired to experience something like this again.

The Burmese guy, Soewin, or John, as he calls himself, brings me a jar of thanakha - compressed yellow powder/paste - made from ground bark for women to decorate their faces. Him and his girlfriend Thet Thet from Shan state pick us up from the hotel to go to Bago - a small town two hours East of Yangoon. As we walk through fruit and vegetable markets, I notice how many people's teeth are red. John says it is from chewing betel nut leafs, an old tradition in Myanmar, which strengthens the teeth. He also says that in Burma you cannot tell someone's gender or marital status from their name. There are only seven names - one for each day of the week.

Bago's most famous sight is the 55 meter Reclining Buddha - Shwethalyaung Buddha. It is said to depict the Gautama Buddha on the event of his attaining nirvana, holding his head with his arm means attainment of the 'point of final liberation from cyclic existence'.

On to the Bogyoke Market which literally means "General's Market" - in reference to Bogyoke Aung San - the father of Burmese independence movement, national hero and most famous martyr. John tells me that Aung San is to Burma what Mahatma Gandhi is to India - except for the fact that Aung San was a soldier and founder of the Burmese Army. He was murdered along with five ministers and had left a widow with three children. His daughter, Suu Kyi, was only two years old when it happened. She stepped into her father's activist shoes 41 years later - and was awarded a Nobel Peace Prize for "one of the most extraordinary examples of civil courage in Asia in recent decades". In contrast to her father, Suu Kyi is committed to Gandhi's philosophy of non-violent protest.

John, Lars and I visit the Shwedagon Paya - the pagoda to which British writer Somerset Maugham referred to as "a sudden hope in the dark night of the soul". It is the quintessence of not only Yangoon, but all of Burma: covered with 8,000 tons of pure gold, it is over one hundred meters high, its spire is crowned with a golden ball decorated with 5,448 diamonds and other precious stones. The courtyard is stone-tiled, polished by millions of bare feet of pilgrims. Each Burman must at least once in his life come here, to touch the wonder, sit down and in the quiet, see the Boddhi tree, offer flowers and incense to the Buddha.

The legend surrounding the pagoda's construction is of two Burman merchants who traveled to India and met the Buddha under the sacred boddhi tree. They offered him cakes and honey. As a measure of his appreciation Buddha gave them eight sacred hairs, plucked from his head. On their way home, four hairs were given to kings en-route, and the other four were presented to the King of Burma who enshrined them on the holy Singuttara Hill - which the pagoda stands on. The story goes that when the golden casket containing the sacred relics was excavated at the site it contained all the eight hairs.

John tells me that each Buddha statue sitting around the main pagoda - is symbolic for each day of the week for a birthdate. I was born on a Friday and according to Burmese astrology I am ruled by the Venus and my sign is a Guinea Pig, which means naturally artistic and creative with tons of fabulous ideas. But have a hard time seeing them through to completion. This may be because I am going in so many different directions at once. But I hesitate to pick one thing because I bore easily and get tired of the same thing. Loving, kind and very sympathetic. Very sensitive to others, make a wonderful friend. So far...so true. John leads me to a Buddha statue and instructs me to make an offering by pouring water: one cup for each year of my life and o   n   e   e   x   t   r   a   o   n   e   . 1,2,3,4,5,6,7,8,9,10,11,12,13,14,15,16,17,18,19,20,21,22,23,24. *Good luck.*

Bus to Bagan after a lunch of fried chicken, rice and okra - and my favorite "topati" - avocado milkshake. Lars shares oreos and his ipod as we meet another foreigner - a French man named Sam. Again, mad bus, bumping on the road, stopping in the middle of the night for immigration formalities....???....hopping back on and hopelessly trying to get rid of the dizzyness.

Nyaung U at 5 a.m. is dark as a horse-carriage takes us to May Kha Lar Guesthouse with a beautiful smiling lady speaking perfect English. Straight to shower and sleep. Wake up and go jogging in a cute town with a nice crafts market. On to visit the temples of Bagan by bicycles.

Gaze out into the endless field of this ancient town of stupas and Buddha statues inside. The ones you can walk into are called *pahtos*.

Myanmar has the most stupas than any other country in the world.
In Buddhism the best way to make merit is to build a stupa - and those who built Bagan in the XI century were obsessed with it. Namely, King Anawrahta, who brought the three "baskets" of Buddhist texts - Tripitaka over and made Theravada Buddhism the state religion.

Theravada means "Teaching of the Elders" and it is the most conservative school of Buddhism and thus, as considered by man, closest to Shakyamuni's Teaching. The aim of Theravada is reaching the spiritual condition and freeing the spirit from turmoil...and delusions.

Monks in Burma are highly respected and according to the rules a monk cannot have contact with a woman, touch them, possess money or other assets - anything, except for hygienic items, an umbrella and a bowl for offering (rice etc). They eat only until noon, and the second part of the day they have water or juice. They sleep four hours a day, whereas the rest of the daytime is for prayer and religious rites.

Vipassana meditation is directed to control the mind by ways of observing the inner processes, breath and sense organs. During Vipassana 10-day retreats one cannot speak, look into the eyes or eat after noon. The state of deep enlightenment, which is reached in the process of meditation, clears the mind and opens its abilities, makes the spirit of the person free from material needs and karmic forces.

The Burmese aren't only deeply religious, but also deeply superstitious. Signs, lucky and unlucky numbers, as well as predictions are very significant to them, as along with Buddhism the Burmese believe in the spirits of nature.

Earthquakes and floods have destroyed many temples, few remaining stand out, and each one is unique in this site of 42 square kilometers, originally having had 5,000 temples.

A favorite of Burmese architecture were bricks covered in stucco, on which various complicated designs were engraved, the wall decorated with terracotta stelae. The biggest Ananda Temple, literally meaning "Temple of Bliss" houses the four Golden Buddhas, which receive daily offerings from the faithful. Thatbyinnyu Temple, literally "Temple of Universal Science" houses paintings of the Buddhas on teak wood walls.

Breakfast with the Frenchman and political borders.
Sam works on an oil rig in Angola and goes back to France every other month. I eat too much as I feel I will be digesting everything until another week. Do not eat in magical or spiritual

places as you don't need food to have energy. It is powerful already and you are attuning and absorbing. Also, you need blood in your head and your heart, not your stomach.

John and I say goodbyes as we leave the restaurant and Samuel and I explore sand paintings for sale. A unique technique....only done in Burma at the banks of the Ayeyarwadday river. Especially One with three laughing monks. *Life is not as serious as I see it.* As the painter's essence is embedded in the painting of Fuk, Luk and Sau, the Taoist Trinity of health, wealth and happiness. Samuel tells me about his visit to one of the most important pilgrimage sites in Burma - the Kyaiktiyo. It is a granite boulder covered with gold leafs pasted on by devotees which, despite all the rules of physics, does not fall into the abyss - and so it looks like it is on the verge of rolling down the hill. Legend has it that the Golden Rock is precariously perched on a strand of Buddha's hair.

Lars and I catch the 11-hour boat to Mandalay, the second capital of Myanmar. Superstitious Burmese kings often changed capitals. It was considered that each city has its measure of happiness, and sooner or later, the time comes, when destiny stops favoring the chosen place. Thus it is best to leave the city, having built another one - a fortunate one. Each new ruler was assured that the old city keeps memory of thoughts and actions of old rulers, not always attractive and worthy of memorials of descendants.

Holy Cow![4] Ayeyarwadday river is over 1,700 of navigable waters out of 2,000 starting in neighboring Chinese province of Yunnan, flowing into the Bengal bay. As we approach Mandalay

---

[4] An Indian Adventure by Sarah Macdonald.

72

Hill, which, according to a legend, once Buddha himself stepped on the mountain with his student Ananda, he predicted a good fortune to a great city, center of Buddhist faith, which will be built after two thousand four hundred years after his visit.

The sun is going down and we check-in to E.T. Hotel Soewin recommended. Lars has to eat and he is not going to wait for me to change so we can have dinner together. Grudge of agreeing to what he wants to do and neglecting my needs...on to to Lashio Lay: a Chinese buffet recommended by the owner of the hotel. Rice, chicken, broccoli, carrots and water. Lars gets an orange juice. Lars asks me what is wrong. Lars says I seem down. I just want to eat and do I need his permission to eat calmly in the quiet as he laughs saying "of course".

I look for fares for Chiang Mai but the flight had been stopped. The only way to get back to Thailand is to go back to Yangoon and fly to Bangkok. I walk by the moats of the Mandalay Palace - former king's home and nowadays headquarters of the Burmese Army. On to Mahamuni Paya, which means "The Great Sage Pagoda" - two gigantic lion statues - symbols of power and royalty greet me. Conquer the endless steps. Cautious about local astrologers and palm-readers. The *paya* is home to a rare sight - a Buddha statue which the faithful polish with their hands as they apply thin precious gold leaf to the statue. As I walk back down to the streets I wander to the Kuthodaw Pagoda which contains the world's largest book, at the foot of the Hill. In the grounds of the pagoda are 729 stone-inscription caves, each containing a marble slab inscribed on both sides with a page of text from the Tripitaka Sutra - the entire Pali Canon of Theravada Buddhism.

A rickshaw back to town costs 1,000 kyats as my mind is bubbling and I can't focus on my decisions. I am in the eclipse of time and consciousness. Start a meditation course in a monastery. Children. Mothers. Orphans. Volunteering or charity....and six months from now: results of the eclipse occur.

All travelers in Myanmar know not to buy services from the Ministry of Tourism, but rather use them as an information source. The ladies working at the MOT office tell me my option is to cross the border overland in Tachilek and go into Mae-Sai in Northern Thailand. There are no roads to the border and the area is closed from tourists (=opium fields). I would have to take a flight to the border, be picked up by a representative, pay him for declaring me, get stamped out of Myanmar and walk the bridge to Thailand. The permit to cross over-land costs 50 dollars which I negotiate, resultlessly. Moreover, it will take 5 working days...as I cry that I have no money left to stay here....I decide to go to Kalaw and trek to Inle Lake for 3 days. They say they will put me on a flight if a permit is issued for me...so I can fly out of Mandalay to Tachilek and cross the border. Adventure!

I go to Chinatown for avocado shake: *topati pju-ei nuan-nu-ne*. I book a bus to Kalaw, from where I will join a group the same morning. Yay. *Suddenly* my gums hurt. Genetic memory. Ancestral information.
Leave the dysfunctional situation.
I had slept for so very long even though it had only been 5 hours at Winner Hotel. I meet our trekking guide, Thet from Tauggyi and two other trekkers: Harriett and Tom from the West Midlands. I want to work for human rights. We walk to our first stop-over for some dahl bread and avocados. The hut of a restaurant is called the Himalayan Lodge. *How do the fillings affect my soul...my life...my energy....do I have more metal inside me now that I got amalgam fillings...*

Energies imbalanced...ate too much...was not hungry...but ate...and now am unable to sleep....demons in my mind...driving me...I run outside as vomit starts running up my throat and I puke outside the trekkers lodge.

Another 50 kilometers and sleep in a monastery. The head monk offers us to write something in his diary and leave a donation for the blessings we are about to receive. We cannot pay as we are skint backpackers and he does not give us the blessings. Thet explains to us that monks in Burma wear orange - like they would in Theravada Buddhism. Some wear a resemblance of crimson, like Tibetan monks. I ask Thet what is the difference between Mahayana, Theravada and Zen. He says the purpose of all schools of Buddhism is to attain enlightenment and free oneself from the wheel of samsara thus attainining liberation.

Lake Inle is the region's richest resource. The main town of the lake is Yangshwe and Thet says that the inhabitants of Inle Lake call themselves "Intha" which means "Sons of the Lake", their primary occupation: fishing and farming. Farmers cut land into pieces of two meters deep and the strips are transported to the farmers by water. The floating islands are worked on while the workers are still in their boat. Tomatoes, beans, cauliflowers are few of the many crops grown. Flowers like daisies and astras. "The Inthas are able to transform land and water to produce gold."

They built their own "Venice" in which everything is floating: shops, markets, even temples. The fisherman casts out his bamboo bow-net for a unique fishing technique: to catch the fish which hides in the algae of the shallow waters. They hold the net vertically at the bottom of the lake, the net spreads out and closes, catching eel, carp and catfish.

Thet gives me a ride on to Heho from where I catch another bus back to Winner hotel, wait for the night bus in a nearby cafe as I order *topati pju-ei nuan-nu-ne*, they bring me sliced avocado with powder milk on top.

I browse a local market and see cheroots - the flavored cigar Thet told me about. They are made from sweet-smelling herbs, tobacco and molasses, rolled together in a large corn.
Burmese women smoke, and make sure you do too.

When I was 15 my first spiritual teacher taught me a Mantra to rid myself from the attachment, guilt and emotional pain over someone who had not reciprocated. She taught me to pray for him to forgive me for the selfishness in our relationship in a past life in China when he was a painter and I was his wife with fourteen children.

Just like on the bus to Thamel I prayed for a chance/I got it/now I pray for closure....

I pray for release

I wake up as the bus makes a stop for dinner. I run around looking for a foreigner to understand how much the food costs. I am saving every single dollar. The woman at the canteen shakes her head in "no, no". Food is free.

Look at love
how it tangles
with the one fallen in love

look at spirit
how it fuses with earth
giving it new life

why are you so busy
with this or that or good or bad
pay attention to how things blend

why talk about all
the known and the unknown
see how the unknown merges into the known

   - Rumi

early morning, monks pass by to get alms: money, clothes and food for good luck.

Back in Mandalay. I have another day to prepare for my flight to the border and I need to go to the MTT and cry so they give me my permit. Push the envelope. I have learnt that another way to leave Burma overland would be on to China via a crossing named Ruili, notorious for the trade relations between the two countries, primarily for jade and pearl. The woman at the office feels my situation, takes pity on me and takes me out for lunch. I tell her I can't eat noodles because I am allergic to wheat as she pushes a bowl of Shan noodles down my throat. We walk back to the office from the street restaurant and my permit is ready. I kiss the woman's hands in gratitude and run back to the hotel to meet a cute young Dutch man named Mart. Just like Mart = March in Russian. I give him tamarind sweets as a goodbye present and leave in a taxi to the airport. Myanmar had been of French, Dutch and German people. I met a guy from Luxembourg who told me his first language is Luxembourg and I asked him what is Luxembourg and he asked me what is French or what is German?..

Upon landing in Tachilek, a rep picks me up and takes me to the border. It is nothing like I imagined...I thought it would be a dodgy crossing point in the midst of dense jungle but it is a normal border town not unlike any other I have seen. With a *paya*.

The rep takes my passport to the MTT Office. I pay 15 dollars and he hands me back my passport stamped: "Feb.08/2009/Left for Mae-Sai." I thank him and walk across the bridge into Thailand following the beckoning of the Thai flag - the three pillars of society: nation (red), religion (white) and monarchy (blue).

I am stamped in for 30 days by the Thai immigration officer. Mae-Sai is famous for jade, pearl, cashews and visa-runs to Myanmar. But I am now in a country with ATM machines and 7-11's. I am excited about doing Thailand during February. I want to be here to re-live the future in the last month in my cycle...and the hardest month of any person's year is the month of their birthday. The longest and most challenging. Enter...Mart...March.

I buy a bagful of cashews after unsuccessfully bargaining for jade which I know both my mom and sister would love. It seems unreal if one day my passion and hyperactivity can be stopped and subsided. I feel I will live forever. It seems that life is going super-fast. I live faster than I did. Time moves faster.

VI. Thailand.

I catch a bus to Chiang Rai: definitely out of the backpacker trail but I want to visit as many towns as possible in order to tick them off my *Cities I Visited* map. I wonder if J thinks of me. I wonder if he wonders whether I am well or ill, whether I am happy or sad, in health or in sickness...I wonder why he had not written back after all this time. A part of me is screaming at me for making the throw of subtle connection to him again...a cord remains until he writes back and I receive the energy back from him...now it has happened again like in the past and the cord is hanging strong but is weakening as the anger and obsession comes over me and takes me in like a wave.

I check into Pintamorn Guesthouse but find no-one to talk to. I must be strong. I want to leave. I feel energy stagnating in my guts. *If you are playing out a purpose, you are always doing it unconsciously.* True. Happening already. I just don't want to embrace it. That is the general idea.

I remember J and how Angels sparked around us when we saw each other. When we met. When we held hands. When we talked. We believed. I only wish it is not just once. I wish it happens again.

I get a Thai massage for a bargain price of 50 Baht: as the tiny Thai lady stretches me up and down, and around, I deeply sign and groan. I also exchange books in one of the numerous bookstores but am unable to connect with either book. Then why did I even come here??????????

I decide to go far out into the woods and explore the wild on my bicycle. Pedal for three hours. Buddha statues engraved in rock. *Go around the world having interesting conversations with strangers.*

Today the conversation is all in my head as I feel completely disconnected. Somehow it feels wrong to have accelerated my trip in Myanmar having another two weeks left on my visa...I feel the mathematical equation is out of balance. What would have been different had I stayed in Myanmar day-to-day of my visa?..The energy would be forming differently. I would be expecting to end something. Meeting other people. Shifting my grid.

I escape a traffic accident. Was going in the wrong lane. Was so close to hitting me. Turned away in the last moment. *Thank you, Angels.*

I leave for Chiang Mai on a three-hour bus through jungle. It is a unique city with four moats and four brick city walls respectively. The driver drops me off right before the West Moat: the Tha Phae Gate and explains that I should just WALK. On to Daret's House - according to the LP Guide, notoriously known for its cheap, tiny rooms and a cafe. I check into a tiny room with no windows. You cannot sit on the toilet straight - only side-saddle. Unfortunate as my stomach had been stagnant the past few days since I returned from Myanmar. I forced the energy of returning to Thailand and now my body is coping. *Leave for a few days so it comes back to normal.* I walk around town, find a travel agency and book a 3-day trek for 1,500 Baht. I make sure with the travel agent that there will be young people on the trek, not old farts, as happens to be my pattern. I walk the tiny streets inside the moat and on to a Sunday market of massage parlors, yummy Thai food, souvenirs and muay thai shorts; watch a show of singing and dancing adjacent to the Flower Festival.

A pickup truck with two benches - called the *songthaew* in Thai, picks me up me and we visit a Butterfly and Orchid Farm. One thing I learn is that vanilla essence is made of vanilla orchids, but those abundant in Mexico. When my father would leave on a business trip he would always bring my mother orchids. We would all get excited but he would say that in Thailand, they grow like weed-plants. We stop at a Tourist Police Office and a man with an American accent says our names out loud and takes copies of our passports. In case anything happens. We are going on a trek, hey. He gives us a number to call, if anything happens. Just that second we realize...neither of us has a *cell phone*.

The three-day hill-tribe trek outside of Chiang Mai includes the whole package: lunches, dinners, elephant riding, elephant trekking, an elephant show, bamboo rafting and white-water rafting. Long-neck Karen village. Burmese women who were forced out of their country came to Northern Thailand and are looked at as a major tourist attraction. Their necks can be up to 30 cm long as the metal spirals are a symbol of beauty. A single ring is placed around a girl's neck when she is five years old. Additional rings are added every three years and by the time they reach adulthood they are carrying ten kilos of rings. It is impossible to remove the rings as their neck muscles have atrophied to an extent where without the ring support, the women wouldn't be able to hold their necks upright and would suffocate. Our guide, Eddy, tells us that they are paid 1,000 Baht per month to pose for photographs. There are many myths as to why they have all that brass on their necks in the first place.

Some say, for beauty. Others, so that they are not taken for prostitution.

The elephant show in the camp is an every-day amusement show. Elephants carry so much weight on their backs - they take up to 4 people at one time PLUS the weight of the saddle - can cause them miscarriages and severe spine problems where they become disabled and helpless...and need to be cared for. First the tour agents amuse us with a show...and then they are selling us a tour to the elephant refuge camp. Elephants end up there anyway.

I watch one of them washed in the river. The ride on an elephant's back is anything but a fun experience. It is scarier than doing the bungy...but everyone else seems to be having fun. Bamboo rafting: we are placed on a raft made of bamboo sticks. I am given a bamboo stick to row the raft.

At night a Lisanne asks me if I need a tampon as I just got my period. I don't use tampons. She asks me why. I am afraid of them...and I find it unnatural. She asks me if I need help putting it in. I say no. She tells me she had done this before many times because she works as a nurse in a clinic for mentally challenged patients, so she had to help other girls take care of their feminine needs. We have a little party by the fire with music, chants and dancing. I throw off my shirt and make funny silly moves for everyone's amusement.

The last activity for the trek is white water rafting. The water splashes in our faces as we stream down a mountain river. The water is freezing. My hands are cold. My body is cold. I made no friends.

The past. I am still in Thailand. When *J's body was in Thailand, his mind was in Lala land*. I read an article about fractals of time. I wonder if it is fractals that I had been painting: repeating of patterns in time. As cycles repeat: the next one is more powerful than the one before. It carriers more meaning. Just like the equation of life. I was 12 and had an unreciprocated love/soul connection with a homeboy. It repeats itself 7 years later. *Con un americano.*

But whenever I talk about this connection...nobody understands.

I return from my trek to Daret's House to find there are no available rooms. I walk out of the lobby through the restaurant downstairs. My eyes meet the eyes of a man. We smile at each other. Mutual recognition. I pass by him as he sits down at a table.

- Why are you smiling at me?

- This is the land of smiles!

- Can I sit down with you?

- Please. Would you like to drink something?

- Yes. I love the papaya and banana shake.

- Where are you from?

- Moscow. I live in Miami. You?

- Austria. My name is Claus.

- Nice to meet you. I am Djana.

-   What do you do in Miami?

-   I am a holistic therapist.

-   Like a counselor?

-   It is more about astrology, spirituality and energy work.

We agree to hopefully see each other again as I need to check into another hotel and then I will go to the night market. I check-in to Moon Muang hotel, shower and get dressed.

The night market is a tourist mecca within the tourist mecca of Chiang Mai. Thanon Chang Klan - a road outside of the ancient city's walls: expensive hotels, food stalls with spicy Thai soup, market stands of handcrafts, handwoven scarfs in pastel colors, wooden and jade elephants, artwork of the Thai landscapes and *wats* - a Thai word for temple or pagoda - whereas neither describes the meaning of *wat*, and the funniest thing...that only really annoys tourists - a wooden frog with horns on its back and a stick in its mouth. The indigenous tribes living around the Golden Triangle - between Laos, Myanmar and Thailand, come here to sell them - they walk around and at times they try sticking it in your face - as if you cannot already hear it all over the place - rolling the stick over the horns of the back of the frog - making a "quack, quack!" sound.

I see Claus with his friends and run up to him to say hi. He kisses me on the cheek. His birthday is March 7th. We connect so very well. We go for a drink as we can't get enough of each other. He touches my hand and we leave the bar. He walks me back to my hotel, slowly puts the hair away from my face and kisses me on the cheek.

Jungle zipline, or Gibbon's Flight for the day. Also want to train *muay thai* - kickboxing and the national sport of Thailand. Found a camp called Lanna Muay Thai in the LP Guide and they have a trial class Sunday afternoon. I should get a scooter to go there because there aren't any buses or songthaews. I am thinking my further travel plans would be to *maybe* go to Laos by boat and then cross into Cambodia from the North and into Stung Treng - which people seldom do - but I am always the one doing it off the beaten path.

As the instructor finishes tying my legs together he tells me to hop into the elevator which will take us both to the height of 50 meters...from which I will jump.

...3........Bungy![5]

I ride my motorbike back to town and relax with a papaya +banana shake at my favorite Daret's House. I have the motorbike for the day so I go straight to the camp. Train today: return the bike tomorrow morning. If I decide to train for a week or so - I will just rent a bicycle. Hot sexy man boxing: Andy, a Canadian native. The star of the camp is Lucy, also a Canadian. She is petite, she came to this country to fight b/c people were *supposed* to be smaller here. A Thai man who speaks no English trains me to hit him hard in the protective pad covering his arm which he puts up to his neck. I lift my leg up high. Break, fight! I sweat. I drink water. I wear protective gear on my hands and legs. I want Andy. He reminds me of Vadim Kazachenko - the man of my dreams from my childhood and 80s superstar in the pop scene of Russia. I salivated/was infatuated with him when I

---

5 http://www.youtube.com/watch?v=YpSjd4S0hd0

was 9. After Vadim there was Sasha Tulisov - my father's business partner with whom I recall once going to an anniversary dinner in a fancy Chinese restaurant in Moscow.

I get up at 6 a.m. to ride my bike to the camp at Kiat Busaba. The sun starts coming up on the horizon. I change into my shorts and Andy, a Swedish man and I ride to a lake 20 minutes from camp in Andy's pick-up truck with his dogs. He is playing mellow rock music in his car. It is early and misty. It is romantic and pure. I think the man I will marry will not be American: he will be Canadian. He is a Native English speaker, and he is purer than the Americans I have met so far. He will have a truck and a house on the lake. Yes...I really do love *The Lake House*.

Long before any of this existed, my twin soul and I were united in love and devotion. Then I had to incarnate in Earth. My lessons and karma to work out with others involved walking a painful path separated from my twin soul. I had many lessons and passions with other souls to work through. I had many relationships to put closure on. I could not reunite with him. The desire to do so would keep driving me to search for that connection in men I meet in real life. They never reciprocate. Because there already **is** a man in my life. In Kathmandu my heart opened - my psychicness unfolded. I became aware of my own truth - regardless of J - that involves me walking alone. Because the one, the only, has given up physical form to be with me, protect me and guide me through this lifetime.

The Swedish man and I hop back into Andy's car, drive to camp and train for two hours. Muay Thai moves include kicking, punching, elbows and knee-strikes. From my instructor's sign-language I understand he is telling me that because with every move I am rotating my hip - the focus on core muscles of the abdomen are going to make my tummy fat melt away in a month.

As I kick my leg high up in the air and onto a gear piece by his ear - he laughs in my face. His laughter makes me mad and I punch him in the stomach and I kick him in the stomach and he falls onto the elastic bands holding the boxing ring together. It's for real. I kicked him!

And...break!

I grab two crab meat and egg rottees, take my scooter to the renter's place and lay down in bed.... feeling high...every muscle in my body relaxed with the injection of endorphins from the kick-boxing.

Once my Reiki teacher told me, No man will appear as long as your heart is busy with another.

She said there was a man standing on my left. Which is why I don't have to protect myself with a bag as I do on my right. Once, during an initiation, I heard clear instructions on my left - saw a pillar of light - joined him in the divine channel. I held his hand. It was one of the most profound moments of my life.

....I wake up from an afternoon nap and eat a gigantic papaya. As I had given the scooter back I will rent a bicycle from downstairs - it is safer and cheaper than the motorbikes. I ask the woman who runs the hotel for a bicycle - and I need to hurry up - as it is already half to three. She says she will give me a deal if I rent a scooter from her. I agree.
I drive to camp as I follow the traffic nice and smooth on the perimeter of the NE moat.
A truck pulls in my drive-way.

I hit the brakes.

Help me. Please help me.

I am in the middle of a three-way traffic road.

...help me

You're bleeding!

I did not want to drive today. Why did I drive.
What the heck is going on?

as darkness fills my eyes...
....Emergency room. Doctor says I need a stitch. *Why aren't you here with me...why can't you protect me from this...or talk for me instead of me*...I have to do it all by myself. If my twin soul had been incarnated with me in this timeline - I would not have done many things. The doctor says the wound is clean, gives me a shot of anesthesia and in a second, it is over: I am prescribed antibiotics and I come to the hospital every day for 7 days to have a fresh new dressing. I go back to my hotel and meet a Muzzy from Lake Tahoe. He takes great pity on me and stands up for my right before the woman who rented me the motorbike and gives me good painkillers.
A physical change calls for a program change. It is just the system's way of adjusting. Hitting zero point will make me revive and be re-born...just like a phoenix rises from its own ashes...but before it does...it has to die.
...I call my mother and Amina in tears of what had happened. Mom says they miss me so much. I tell them I feel so lonely and alone. I can't bear doing this no more. But I have to finish something here. I let everyone on facebook know that I've just *survived a motorbike accident on the way to muay thai.*

I stay in bed as my body needs energy to recover. I sleep a lot and slowly *crawl* outside the hotel in one of the *sois* to get rotisserie chicken, papaya, mangos, egg+crabmeat rottees. I buy a drawing pad and crayons and go to the Tourist Police office. I can't walk straight and it scares the shit out of me. *I will deal with any emotional pain, but please make me physically healthy.* I tell the officers how it all happened, they write a report and give it to me. The next morning I take it to the insurance company and get indemnified for the costs for the medical care...

I turn 24 in a week. I think party, I think celebration. First thing, I need to find a hostel. LP Guide has a Spicy Thai Backpackers. I meet the owners that same night: Noom and Pong - two real cool guys. I book myself in for a week and a half. We go to Sukontaa - a buffet restaurant with music and entertainment for only 139 Baht. There's a hot pot in the middle of the table in which you fry meats and greens and boil a stew of meats and greens around the center of the pot. A guy who looks like a Richard Gere or a Patrick Swayze makes smart comments about me getting my third plate of strawberries. Whereas he is getting his forth. The group goes to bowling and I join them.

The Richard Gere/Patrick Swayze lookalike is actually Luke from Australia. An unspoken interest. He says he thinks I look like Anna Kournikova. He had been traveling in the last year...he had left home around April and will be returning April of current year. It seems my soul mates are triggered to find similar things as me? Perhaps it is just the timing. When you find sparks from your soul family, you will love them. You will not be able to help yourself and this love will take any form appropriate. At a point in time we are all drawn to find one another...in our soul family. We feel the tug inside of us and follow the calling...of other facets of our being.

Luke and I have too much fun bowling and he encourages me to throw the ball when I can't throw for shit. I still have so many miles to cross in my travels...my journey just about beginning...and recovering from the physical intervention of surgery only means faster attraction of somebody truly important...who will help me make the transition.

I used to strongly believe that I am responsible for everything in my life...there is a higher meaning in every single relationship and event I encounter. I then faced things I did not foresee happening. A prophecy...a suggestion infested in my mind's eye did not take place in physical reality. So I do not believe it any longer.

My Spirit guide kept the Love within me alive. He would manifest himself in different forms...something that lingered of him in another man...when I was a child, it was Thomas Anders of Modern Talking whom everyone worshipped in Russia and Germany back in the 80s. His voice, his lyrics, his long black hair and pink lipgloss (!) were THE thing I needed to help me connect with the voice within.
Keep...love...alive
...as I feel the powerful pull. Spirit have ability to open up human's perception of them by seeing, sensing, hearing. Our emotional bodies always in resonance with those on a similar frequency. Many times men have for no apparent reason left or withdrawn. I knew the truth of it that my Higher Self had been creating the best conditions for my growth...and it is always with somebody moving out of your way.

I get up early to catch a songthaew to camp as we trek through the woods of the former Lanna Kingdom. Andy, Lucy, the Swedish man who really likes jumping jacks and I are united on this adventure. We pass by a waterfall and a poisonous green snake. I like everything about Andy but he does not speak to me. He is older....by a lot. Perhaps in his late 40s. I love his smile, his face, his hair, his posture, his power, the way he hits the body-bag and instructs others to hit. I fantasize how he could be my teacher. It would be so hot as he would instruct me in all kinds of ways.

Back at the camp he comes up to me as he catches me hitting the body-bag wrong...and shows me how to hit. He tells me I should hit air because if I keep aiming at the bag, my body will remember the limits. There are *no limits*. As I look into his eyes he is trying to understand what I am about. He thinks I am in boxing because a man broke up with me. Rofl.

Chang, chang!
Luke. *Hi, Djana*. Dozed off for a sec. I tell him about my bungy jumping career and he tells me about his skydiving career as he did Accelerated Free Fall which is a tandem jump of up to 14,500 feet with an instructor on your back, and also Static Line - where you jump alone, but the free fall is only four seconds. He likes to say *there isn't anything I haven't done*. I like to ask, *you kissed a man?*

"Wooohoo...yeah yeah yeah....when I get up all in ya, we can hear the angels callling us, we can see the sunrise before us..."
Mrs. Officer by Lil Wayne.
"...and when I'm in that thang, I'll make that body sang..."
Spicy Thai Backpackers is a single family house with 5 big rooms, 3 bathrooms, a big open kitchen with a pool table, a dining room and a big TV/DVD/Entertainment room. This is *the* place. It is amazing how just as once I set my intention to meet fun people, those who will make the transition with me around my birthday in a cute fun hostel like this...it comes true immediately. I just went and found it. Before that intention and

clear knowing, I did not even see the listing of this hostel...whereas it was in the LP Guide all along.

Energy. It is all about energy.

Luke approaches me but quickly realizes I am in my own zone of bliss listening to R'n'B tunes and leaves me alone....I decide to take a bath instead of packing up and marching to camp. I run the water and make bubbles in the tub and stick my leg out so that no water goes into my wound.

Ever since I discovered the allergies and food aversions, not to mention the fact that I only eat when I am stressed or bored or not smoking, I watch what I eat. Thai food is good and healthy, when it is free of the powdery white substance...monosodium glutamate, a.k.a. MSG. Spicy tom yam with bean sprouts, fish balls or shredded chicken, special Thai herbs that make it have the distinct flavor and of course, glass noodles. However recently I discovered it is not enough...that's when I reach for rotees - thin crepes, freshly baked rolls filled with banana slices, sweet milk or chocolate sauce. Breakfast in the hostel consists of coffee and toast with butter and jam. During the day I nourish myself with papaya... fruit of the day...every day...

Fried rice with vegetables and chicken is another favorite. At night, stalls open up to sell dinner. They are so good...cheap...and addictive. MSG is, anyway.

I explore Chiang Mai wats within the city walls as I wander off to the biggest one - Wat Chedi Luang. It is decorated with big rock elephants and white Buddha statues in orange robes. Apparently the rules of visiting a *wat* are that one must not touch, climb or even take pictures with the Buddha statues. Thai temples are white-washed buildings with distinct orange roofs and gold deco "dragon-like" *cho fa* - and *naga* tail-points. The

Gold Buddha sits in lotus-position with his right hand resting on the right knee with the tips of his fingers "touching ground" thus calling the Earth goddess Dharani to witness his enlightenment and victory over Mara...the king of demons.

In the afternoon the gang goes for a Sunday Roast. Luke and I have the best time at a pool atop one of the hotels. I notice he is wearing one of the rune symbols on his neck. He says it is an Aztec symbol for luck on the journey. His ex-girlfriend gave it to him when they broke up. Runes are powerful protectors as they are ancient symbols carved in either wood or rock: a symbol embedded in a medium merges energies to complete a power-guard.

Luke tells me to take care of the kids and kisses me on the cheek as him and the gang leave on a trek. I hang out with a new person every day...as we mostly enjoy going to the pool for 80 Baht. One day with a tall, chubby Mike from Canada. We hang out with a British couple as he goes on and on about how much he enjoys traveling alone and hates to feel tied up and attached. Ha. Next thing he "kind of offers" me to go with him to Cambodia with a detour through Laos. Thanks. But "I have other dreams."

I miss being here with Luke. We had fun as we ate papayas and bananas I prepared before leaving. *I officially love you.* Is what he said. Many months later he would thank me for being a part of his re-invention on his journey.

I buy a CD by Michael Bolton and can't wait to stretch to *Can I Touch You...There?* I buy two papayas and feel Mike really wants me to go to Laos with him. He says even if I don't go with him for my birthday he will still congratulate me on facebook. We go to the post office so I can send a parcel home. I chose slow mail which costs me 50 dollars for 3.5 kilos. The Thai man who happens to be a really manly woman yells at me for negotiating the price of the cardboard box which I filled with table runners, cute wooden elephant figurines, Thai-style bags, candles, postcards, scarves, other gorgeous typical Thai souvenirs and my Angel drawings from the accident-recovery//Frida-Kahlo period. She yells that people like me always cause trouble. I yell back at her for talking to me like that I will go to another post office shop. She yells at me to get out of her shop. I tell her I will call the police. She calls the police and I cry on the phone telling them I don't understand why she was so mean to me. Mike tries to bum in when he doesn't realize...it is a freak show. I arrange my parcel and we leave. I just made him like me less. So he wont wain on me. We return to the hostel and I slowly grind to Usher's *My Way* on Mike's *nano*.

Abby has an amazing smile and I can not get enough of her positive energy. She is allegedly having hot sex with the orange-haired Brit who is currently on the trek. As we hang by the pool, she goes on and on about how open and communicative she is with her partners during intercourse. She likes sex and she is confident with her men. Although she has a pretty face and a cute smile, she is not physically attractive: she is overweight, she does not shave her armpits and she does not pluck her eyebrows.
Mike left for Laos earlier the same morning.
On to the boat 3-day boat to Luang Prabang.
Abby and I walk back to the hostel as she keeps guessing whether she should jump on the orange-haired Brit when she sees him or should she hold her emotions.
My guess is they are not even back yet anyway.

As we stroll into the front yard of the hostel we see the orange-hair man as Abby gets nervous. She sits next to him and looks at him like a cat looks at a fish in an aquarium. It's kind of sweet that she has this affection for him.

I see clearly his interest in her is simpler: carnal.

We agree to go for dinner in a Western burger restaurant. I walk through the living room area and see Luke hanging out by the TV. He is wearing the same shorts as he does every day. I wonder if he ever changes clothes? As he is checking out my pastel blue dress, he says the trek was wonderful and I would have loved it. Also he makes me the center of his world every time we hang out. He asks me who do I like in Hollywood. Does he mean whose character do I like?...whose looks do I like...personality...?

    - I just mean, who would you shag!

    - George Clooney. Keanu Reeves. Angelina Jolie.

    - I love you, this little bit more!

It so happens that the orange-hair man's birthday is one day before mine. Noom says he will make a party weekend for everybody, buy me a cake and make a barbecue in the front yard.

Luke is listening to music on the computer. He says he never carries an i-pod or a music player, whenever he wants to listen to music he goes online. He refuses to go out and drink as he is being cheap...again. He tells me about his plans to go to Laos by boat and then cross into Cambodia in the North. I love recognizing similar thinking patterns. I always thought my soul mates would be doing the same route. Luke has been to Bhutan, officially the closest country in the world, recently opened to tourists, where Vajrayana Buddhism is the state religion. I tell him about my recent trip to Myanmar.

    - You've been to Myanmar? Wow it is nice to know there are people out there doing similar things as me.

Perhaps he should not go to Cambodia via Laos as there is a lot of red tape. In the jungle of SE Asia...poppy fields man...

Speaking of tape. I have three empty pages left in my passport. I call the Russian Consulate in Bangkok and ask them if they can stick a few additional pages in my passport until I get to Russia. They say no, they cannot. I call the Foreign Affairs Office in Moscow and they say the same thing. Luke puts on *Cidade de Deus*, a beautiful film about the settling of Rio de Janeiro, followed by *Forgetting Sarah Marshall*. We laugh and make fun of people and relationships as I go on about how men play women and Luke says it is a bit of both playing one another. I run to the kitchen and surprise him with strawberries covered in chocolate sauce as he exclaims that he loves me as everyone in the room salivates over the strawberries and our relationship.

The next morning everyone hops in the hostel's pick-up to go to the lake. Luke is giving me so much attention: watching and appreciating. He offered to buy me a glass of wine for all the fruit that we have eaten together. He tells me I spoil him. He takes pictures of Kelly, a girl from San Diego and I in bathing suits. His fantasies must drive him.

Is this a true soulmate?

He never hurt me, make me mad, depreciate me or undervalue me. He gives me time, love, attention, appreciation, praise and inspiration.

However himself and the gang are about to embark on a 3-day motorbike ride to Pai - a village in the jungle of Northern Thailand - and a chill place to be after the bustling mecca of Chiang Mai. I wont go. Still scared of being on the road. Luke wont push me but he encourages me to be brave and come with them...but it is also my birthday Sunday - which is when they plan to leave - and I feel I am about to become attached with a member in my group...and everyone else here...and I can't let that happen...so I stay in the hostel.

After swimming I jump into my little shorts and run down the road going around the lake. Luke calls me a real athlete. Kelly swims to the other shore - and back. She is one cute sexy lifeguard.

I fold out my Brazilian flag. *I love Brazil.*

I left someone there.

- You're a heartbreaker, I knew it! - exclaims Luke. He acts so much like Barney from *How I Met Your Mother*.
- That's not true! And it's not fair!
- You just said it.
- That's not fair! I still send him postcards! It is not my fault he only wanted to have his job in Rio and stay there and I had other dreams and wanted to travel the world!

Gemma, an English girl, steps into the conversation.

- Wow! Postcards!
- What do you mean?! I wish the one I loved sent me postcards as signs of attention!

The gang of thirty people stares at me as I lecture. Noom starts packing up and I put a dust mask on my face as we hop into the hostel's songthaew. The mask protects me from dust as I have had problems breathing before.

Sunday morning. Monks come out at 6 a.m. to collect their alms from people who want prosperity and good fortune in their lives.

We hop into the pick-up and I mention to Noom that I lived in a monastery in Nepal and haven't been in love since...I point out that our love had been spiritual...and more than any other love in the world. I tell him about bungy jumping. I tell them this year...I

need to do all the things I had put on my list before my trip to Tibet when I had touched the void and truth of life. In Lhasa.
I also need to hit the ATM machine as my card expires and I should withdraw the entire balance of the dollars in it and so I will carry them with me and constantly stress about carrying cash...and then little by little, exchange them into local currency.

As we get to Wat Doi Suthep and climb 309 steps on to white elephant statues, I have my mind blessed by a monk. I make offerings to the golden Buddha statues sitting, standing and lying down - all representative of the different states of Shakyamuni. *Do a puja.* I am so much more trusting to ceremonies and Buddhist rituals...perhaps now more than ever before.
I buy flowers, incense sticks and candles. *Heal.*
I make an offering to the Buddha statues. A monk ties a white thread on my right hand as a symbol of protection after blessing my mind. *Heal.*
Tell Me How Am I Supposed to Live Without You
by Michael Bolton and remember mini-golf the other night. Kelly and I got drunk up, swung our hips and dry humped golf sticks making everyone miss their holes. I love how uninhibited she is and that someone so pretty can be so sweet. She got distracted from our love-game to fornicate with a Glenn. They connected...during their stay at Doi Suthep. When he returned from it, I asked him how was it and how was Kelly, he said he thinks she is okay, but he doesn't really know...because you can't speak to anyone during the stay. Lol. Dah!

20th round in the neighborhood. Motorbike roar.
    -    Happy Birthday!! Happy Birthday sweety!!
Luke hugs me.
You look so sexy when you sweat.

Kelly and the gang wish me a happy birthday and hop on their bikes ready to leave. I wave them goodbye. He gives me a big fat hug and a wet kiss on my cheek while I am trying to put nail varnish on my toes. Luke holds the record as he had said HB five times. He tells me assertively that we should meet again on this trip. He will be traveling the area for another two months and we should cross paths in...Cambodia, for example.

As the gang leaves...and my trip clear and knowing that I will return to Bangkok I book myself on the Khao San Rd. Bus for 336 Baht (cheapest in town!) at the Daret's House Tour Desk.

I give Noom a pineapple as a goodbye and thank you gift.

I leave a pack of chocolate wafers for Luke when he returns.

Finally CM is over for me. Many stories, many choices, many things. And now, goodbye.

The cramped tourist bus drops passengers off by a 7-11 in Banglamphu at 5 a.m. on a Tuesday morning. I did not book accommodation in advance as I guess I was taking a chance. Everyone does when they travel.

I walk back and forth all hotels possible and without any luck hop on the first boat on the Bangkok river to go to Sukhumvit to *Soi 1 Hostel* as Abby recommended. Easy to find, very well air-conditioned, bathrooms in the hallway. I shower, change and fall asleep. As I wake up I eat everything I can find. Bad news as I get bloated. Angry and frustrated as I am thinking, why the hell did I get so scared and leave the gang?

So here I am......alone. Going jogging to one of the city parks and realizing that CM was paradise compared to the burning hell of BK. I have March 7th as the last day on my entry stamp. Last time in Thailand I waited for the last day so this time I decide to go to Siem Reap on March 5th. As I walk to the hostel past the skyscrapers of Sukhumvit, a young man with a British accent and a countryside attitude approaches me to find out whether I know how to get to the Brazilian Capoeira School. I don't. He wonders if I know Internet here somewhere. I do. I walk him to the hostel's computer. He says he thought I was walking him into my room. He checks his e-mail, thanks me and disappears out the door.

Talked out of visiting the floating gardens by the Australian owner of the hostel, I visit Ayuthaya, one of the former capitals of the Siam Kingdom. It is a city of gigantic Buddha statues - and I glare at the magnificent view of it...and realize how small I am. Siamese cats are actually related to the Siam Kingdom as said to have been sacred temple cats...

I book the bus to Siem Reap for 900 Baht (big mistake...huge!).
Go running in one of Bangkok's parks again....as hot and unbearable as it is...I still need my muscle-happy-hormones active. As I get on the train to get back to the hostel:
a sign pointing to Cambodia Embassy.

Catch a river taxi outside the hostel which is supposed to take me to Khao San Rd. to eat everything I possibly can. Tom yam, chicken fried rice, rotee, another rotee, and if I can still breathe, another rotee with bananas, sweet milk and chocolate.
I receive a wall post from Luke: he loves me and thanks me for the wafers I left for him and says they were delicious.
It is nice to have reciprocity, gratitude, attention and love.

VII. Cambodia.

...as we approach the border I realize we are about to be ripped off in visa fees. I should have taken advantage of the time I had in BK instead of eating and being confused.

I was scared to let anyone know...if I let the secret out what it would mean if it would put him in jeopardy...I could not allow that. I followed my instinct and kept the secret safe from everyone...including myself. Imagine...had I been conscious of the fact that I will never meet my twin soul in flesh in this lifetime and timeline when I was 12. When I was 15. 19. I knew it when I was 22. It's a catch. Catch 22.

It seems your own journey is the most important. At times you meet people who make you happy and you feel a bliss of union. Then they leave. *But can this be the lesson I am refusing to learn? At times you will come through to me.* I can float to your reality and timeline at *times...*like in my **dream**.

The Thai immigration officer stamps me out of Thailand and I walk across the border. The name of the town is Dodgy Casino Town. Not really. Poipet.

I sometimes question something I cannot memorize. If I let my mind focus on it. I let Spirit *whisper the message.* Let it talk through to me. I can speak it. Like my own words. Same goes to when I paint.

The officials tell us we need to pay 45 dollars in visa and service fees. One Canadian dude argues the price (stupid). He then tries to bargain it down to 20 dollars (what it costs at a consulate). However now that we have little choice - and the officials arrange them in half an hour while we have lunch - it is double the price. A visa fee is a visa fee.

We are stamped into Cambodia and still ill from the little sleep and air conditioning in the hostel AND expecting my period any day now, I am boiling hot. Our guide tells us we are booked on a bus, it will take off in 3 hours and arrive to Siem Reap around 8. The roads are very bad, he says. It never leaves on time, he says. It always arrives late, he says.

So he offers us to hire a cab for a whopping 10 dollars per person which will get to Siem Reap in 3 hours flat.

The change to Cambodia is apparent, sudden and beautiful. The people look and speak Khmer. I feel a connection to that world and culture. if only I was conscious of what past lives I had lived here and what I had carried over.

But sometimes conscious is not the point. Sometimes it keeps you...from playing out your part. If I knew my twin soul did not exist in this timeline...would I have given in to that strong feeling of meeting him in the Buddhist and Tibetan world...?

Actually...yes. That is exactly what I did.

Destiny can be such trickster.

Something...put into your mind...to play out a scenario.

Our cab drops us off just outside town. A rickshaw picks us up free of charge and takes us to Siem Reap Backpackers Hostel which both the Canadian chap and I booked ahead. Talk about soul-mates doing the same thing you are doing. In the same timeline.

Sometimes it is just overlapping of program. Or a glitch. It was not planned. Was it?

I did pick to go on this date. But the Universe...well...the Thai immigration officer gave me March 7th. as my day to leave the country.

Interesting how it forms. I would have never started boxing had I only had 15 days on my stamp for Thailand. I would have never gotten into the accident. I would have never found out about

103

Spicy Thai. I would not have met Luke. Luke...I miss him so much already. Never bond with anyone in any way. It breaks your heart.

But how the fuck do you love someone without bonding with them? I do not believe in this.

If you say you can love someone without becoming attached to them...you are full of shit.

Or you're in it for the sex.

The rickshaw driver is trying to sell his business to have us hire him to show us around Angkor Wat, as it is a huge complex and it can be anywhere from one day to a week to explore. Temples of Angkor are the heart and soul of the Kingdom of Cambodia and the main reason for over a thousand visitors everyday. It is a source of inspiration and national pride to all Khmers and today it is a point of pilgrimage to all Cambodians.

Receive answers.

Just like atop Machu Picchu a Spirit of the Ancients has told me to bring forth my spiritual work.

Tell fellow travelers about my true profession....have I done it?

...as I feel a total and complete disconnection.

At times....if you're not ready...*the knowledge will be kept from you.*

for your own good and protection.

Our hostel is big and surprisingly expensive for what it is. I jump into the indoor pool and start doing laps. I fall in love fast. If I enjoy something, I stick with it. I devote to it.

True teachers....have kept it all to themselves...they never made themselves known....they quietly did their job.

Famous psychics are such bogus. They are the control measure to keep the masses from the truth. distract peoples' eye from the real thing.
I shower and
....wipe my body dry as I get my period.

Opening of the crown chakra. Spirit activity. Connecting to the Other Side. *I wish everything I learnt in my travels and spiritual work would have a creative outcome.* All this is recorded in the Akashic records of the Soul's journey and DNA.
Painting DNA strands. Graphic works of doodles into beads forming a string...
The Canadian chap never finds me so I go to walk around alone. I have fried rice with chicken and Khmer beer, return to the hostel and fall asleep.
If you have a secret you can't share with anyone,
whisper it into a tree hollow and cover it with mud.[6]

Next morning I have breakfast (included in the hostel price). I pay for my additional mango shake and leave to walk the market. I buy grapefruit, mango and dragon fruit - pink on the outside, clear marble and small black dots inside, the funniest, cutest and weirdest fruit I ever ate. Apparently the belief here is the first customer of the day brings good luck, so if the vendor gives you a good deal, their day sales will be grand. I find nice tiny flags to saw on my backpack: Thailand, Cambodia, Vietnam, China and Malaysia. The first one I ever put on my bag was Brazil: then Peru, Bolivia, Argentina, Panama and Belize. I go back to the hostel to find the chap returned from his trip. He says he didn't know if I wanted to go. How about ask me?

---

[6] Tony Leung, *In The Mood for Love.*

I go on facebook and start uploading pictures of my birthday. BAD sign. Means I am not getting what I need from present day reality. Oh. My Birthday. Noom DID make a mean barbecue as at least five men flirted with me and one offered to buy me a beer - strange but nice Paul - a Brit who has good taste in islands, movies, entertainment, who calls himself a bum...and looks like a bum.

Noom and I had gone to buy me a birthday cake from the local shop I strolled into the day before we came but could not understand what they were saying. My Thai to this day remains, *sawatdeeka* and *korpkunka*. Gemma brought the cake with candles lit and took pictures for me. Abby gave me a wooden stick with a pink flower to put in my hair...very, very nice touch. I went online to find my friend Alan, the Mormon I made out with in La Paz tag photos of our border crossing...I guess it was his little sign of attention. Lots of congrats and stuff.

Manage to get up at 5 a.m. to get to Angkor before sunrise. It is said to be the most beautiful sight in SE Asia as I ride my bicycle to the admission booth and get my entrance ticket. I ask Guidance as to which turn to take to get to the main temple. I see a path of light forming to my left. I go to the right to test it. I end up NOT where I wanted to be. I park my bicycle and watch the sun rise. I drink water insatiably.

This is the hardest month ever since I left home. I will visit Tha Prom and Bayon where allegedly Lara Croft was filmed. Lara Croft. Lots of praise around the area. They are charging tourists 60 dollars a day to visit a three-foot waterfall which was apparently featured in one of the scenes.

Water and water-gods have always been important in Hindu mythology as naga-rajas (Serpent-Kings). Serpents were venerated also because they were considered emanations of the spirits of rivers and streams. Most temples are made of sandstone and a lot of them had been neglected during the ages. Except the main one of course. I open my camera to take a picture.
It fails to.

In Cambodia the belief of the God-King is prevalent, thus the architectural metaphor. The king of Khmers is in the middle = the temple is physical evidence of his higher power. This mountain-temple served as an abode of the God-King - the Earthy abode - also suitable for heavenly gods.

A local 5th-grader selling postcards explains to me that the Khmer genius was fully expressed in the joining of religious principles and achievements in the field of engineering. As a result, "wonderful temples and fascinating hydraulic buildings appeared, which gave the Cambodian civilization the ability to not only create a grand depiction of the Universe, but also use the water-ways for agricultural needs."

I fall asleep at the foot of Tha Prom - the famous sight most people want to go - thanks to the overgrowth of trees right through the walls of the temple. The trees are hundreds of years old - they support the structure. If one fails...all fail.
In Bayon the underworld is represented by a fish, the symbol of the ocean's depths, placed underneath the temple. The most important one is the central temple as a depiction of the mythical mountain Meru. A moat which represents the great ocean, guarded by a wall - mystical wall of rocks, separating the ocean from mountain Meru - thus, the grand scheme of the Universe.

A sense of vastitude. Look into the galleries. As they are going into space beyond the limitations of the central complex constrained by moats and walls...

It is considered that bridges with water moats, connecting the central sacred space with other clay structures, signify rainbows, often represented as serpents, reaching their heads up to the sky or drinking from the sea.

These serpents appear in the end of balustrades on the bridge and at entrances into Khmer temples.

These ancient balustrades of nagas also remind me of the ancient Hindu myth about the Churning Ocean of Milk when the Gods used a gigantic serpent like a twirling to create worlds out of chaos - a very well-known legend amongst the Khmer rulers. In the center of the temple's tower there is a pivot, symbolizing the king, who provides well-being, taking power from the temple and spreading his goodness by rainbow bridges onto the human world...

...wake up. Camera works. Ride further up. Sure I've made the loop already - no pun intended - as I see the enigmatically smiling face - the Bayon. The mystical feeling is strengthened...

...make a picture and follow the road as it leads me to the last on the list and the highlight and the reason for being here....

....Angkor Wat...

....I approach the main entrance...finally...*like so many times in my dreams*...I revel at the beauty of it...as I bow down...and cross the first bridge.

Place my consciousness out of the 3D - I picture my pin-pointing on Earth. From a satellite. As I zoom out. I see it. The Temple is built with four moats - another example of sacred geometry.

Grand Palace in Mandalay. If I see myself floating on top of it...I delve deeper into the mandala...*unpacking consciousness.*
I glare at the Gallery of a Thousand Buddhas...
The myriads of forms...as a triangle...in a square...and then a circle....all a symbol of love.
Anything you set your mind for, you will achieve.
I leave Angkor Wat tired, thirsty and burning hot in the sun.
Ride back to Siem Reap.

On to Phnom Penh the next morning and meet a Ben from England. Stay at Okay Hostel for 5 dollars each and the rooms are tiny, hot and humid; we eat dinner in a restaurant downstairs. The main reason for tourists to come to this town is to see the Killing Fields - sites of killing of thousands of people during the Khmer Rouge regime - which I refuse to go to. Sometimes the right thing to do is to keep moving. Until you just...can't...anymore...how tiring this is. Past the Royal Palace which is over two centuries old and the present king and queen of Cambodia live in it. My camera...isn't working...as the photos from the temples in Siem Reap are in one of the XD cards....I read in the guidebook that you can fire a cow for 40 dollars - as a sport.
At a local market a woman is preparing to cut a chicken's head off. I run away in despair.
Ben is filming a woman cut a durian open - the spiky-on-the-outside and yellow-and-soft-on-the-inside "jackfruit". Amazing how she handles the thing. As we walk through the dusty streets local vendors are selling us counterfeit-copies of travel guides and major bestsellers. I picture my book illegally copied here: what an honor it would be.
On to visit the National Museum: artifacts, statues and ancient scrolls. But
everyday is torture, everyday is pain.

Djana is
exploring the temples of Angkor amazed at its beauty but tortured by the need to reunite with my other half.
I hope he reads it. Like I read him.
When I saw *him* visit the Temple City.

Hotel Cambodiana. 7 dollars to use pool. Wear pastel blue dress and enjoy Ben's gentleman attention and interest. But this man doesn't NEED me. He jumps into the pool as I read his Rough Guide on Macau. I throw on my sleek black dress...same one I wore for my birthday. I had a long black skirt with me ever since I left the United States. I bought it in Nepal. Together with my blue skirt. I always wear it to evenings or when I feel feminine and sensual. Feeling that way makes me want to be sexual with the right man. But there is no right man. But there is the need to be sexual. Which starts with sensual. So I tried to get rid of it for a few months. And then...on the night of my birthday I sat on a nail and tore it apart. Be careful. Be very...careful.
I suppose it got rid of me before I got rid of it.
So now I only have my sleek sexy black dress to go out in. Ben flags down a rickshaw and we go to *Rendez-vous* as recommended by the Lonely Planet. I tell Ben about life in Miami which he likes the sound of. He makes me promise when I am rich and famous and have published my book to take him out in Miami. Or perhaps he made me promise him to publish my book. Whichever it was...neither him or me remember now...we were too tipsy off of beer Khmer.
We play pool at a nearby bar overlooking the Tonle Sap River. I am ready to leave. As much as I wanted to go to Sihanoukville, I can't take this invasion of European tourists....and frankly I am in a rush to get out. Cambodian girls at the bar call me "pretty girl." Ben and I go to get a massage. Big mistake that cost us five dollars each and bruises on our bodies. We return to the hotel, he

says the past few days had been *amazing*, gives me his phone so that I wake up the next morning to catch my bus to Nam-Viet.

Fortunately...I did not have to run around for a Vietnamese visa as Russia and Vietnam have a special arrangement to encourage tourists from Russia: stay up to 15 days with a stamp. Again I have no reservation and no idea where I will stay. The officials stamp me with the date of entry and a note of *visa exemption* as I request stamps to be put on THIS page, and not THAT page, because I need THAT page for my Chinese visa, whereas THIS page has space from other stamps. He takes care of it no problem and hands me back my passport as we carry our bags through the customs.

VIII. Vietnam.

Ho Chi Minh City: a slap in the face, crazed with traffic. Pham Ngu Lao St. hostel for 2 dollars. Last empty bed. Fruit shake for 10,000 dong = equivalent to 70 US cents. "Same-same,"- says an American expat to the fruit shake girl. Apparently it has become a trend to retire in Vietnam...marry a local girl, set up a small business. Tailors across the street make about 40,000 dong per day: roughly 4 US dollars. Stroll downtown through Vien Van Hoa park. Have I mentioned the traffic is crazy? Particularly exciting! Night market of Ben Thanh, abundant in shoes and ao-zai, the traditional Vietnamese female outfit of pantaloons and silk tunic. Tailors offering their services. Tour agencies selling tours to the Mekong Delta, Ku-Chi Tunnels and the Reunification Palace...watching photos from beach towns of Mui Ne and Nha Trang, I buy an open-ticket which will take me all the way to Hanoi - as I had planned to do so and NEED to do so in order to cross over into China.

Bright and early: bus to Mui Ne = a cute fishing village. Now that I have so much time on my hands I am getting a list of my priorities together. What do I want to do when I return?
I put down activities I enjoy in order to work out the ultimate happiness-strategy: trekking, swimming, dancing, boxing, surfing, jogging and skydiving. I like to socialize, have a lot of people around me, soak up the energy and exchange the energy.
I am good at counseling, coaching and helping people solve their emotional issues.
As 4 hours on a super-comfortable bus are over I am surrounded with 20 people selling tours and hotels rooms. I walk off. My backpack is heavy. I find one hotel, another hotel, they are too expensive as I continue walking on the highway. A motorbike taxi driver stops to pick me up and offers to take me somewhere

I don't know where. He takes me to a bungalow hotel. The main reason to come here is kitesurfing. When I return to Miami after this world trip, I want to live happily ever after, enjoying the sun, making up for the times I've exhausted myself like I am as I am traveling, kitesurfing and laying out on the beach, eating organic foods and brushing my teeth every morning and night with fluoride-containing tap water.

The bungalow hotel costs 10 dollars a night and the receptionist says she will keep my passport. My passport is the only thing I have as my proof in this foreign country and I will not give it to her under no circumstance. She says she will not check me in or give me a room without me leaving my passport with her. Apparently she has to take it to the police office?
Blah, blah, blah.

I give up, knowing I have little option. I relax in my room and change. I take a stroll down the shoreline and take in the beauty of the palm trees, the sand and the ocean. I see kites catching wind and follow their beckoning. I enter the very first beach club, Jibe's Beach Club: part of IKO and run by an Australian man. Fully equipped and I can come watch surfing videos for free. I meet my instructor Jane. She teaches me to inflate the kite and connect strings to it. She explains to me how people who pass by think it is a fun thing - whereas if the strings of the kite touch them - it will cut through like butter. Graphic!

She puts a harness on me and attaches a kite-control-bar with steering lines and explains the three measures of safety: the donkey dick which goes through the chicken loop and the "pistol" - the last resort to release yourself from the kite if you get caught in all the mesh while carelessly surfing out there. She explains to me about the "wind window" from left to right as I see that when I hold the bar straight the kite stays "neutral": horizontal/parallel to the ground. As I feel the power of the kite surfing in the wind in my hands she says after a couple of hours there should be windier for me to try and take it to the ocean and try body-gliding. I am starved, and run to a cafe across the street to get eggs with toast, peanut butter and coffee.

I return to the beach club to swim in my goggles and lay out and top up my tan but it seems the kitesurfing isn't happening as no wind is happening. I fix the bill and leave. I book my trip for my next stop - Nha Trang. I order delicious Vietnamese tea, cream of crab meat and a seafood salad for dinner. Surprisingly enough...or not surprisingly at all, my Russian SIM card has service. I text my dad to tell him I am having cream of crab in a fishing village.

I leave for Nha Trang as the bus rides through beautiful sand dunes. I love how Vietnam is simple and convenient to travel in, thanks to the open-ticket tourist bus system and the prolonged shape of the country. One can also go to Vientiane in Laos on a 24-hour bus from Hanoi and my camera is still not working.

I have been told that Nha Trang is famous for natural pearl, which is grown inside the pearl oyster when a foreign organism or parasite enters the mollusk and stays inside the shell: the mollusk is irritated by the intruder and repeatedly covers it with a secretion of calcium carbonate, thus, forming a pearl. They come in many different shapes and sizes, and perfect round ones are very rare. Thus comes the metaphor for something very admirable and valuable.

This time, I have a reservation at Backpacker's House. Nha Trang: very different from Mui Ne. A major tourist resort town of high-rise hotels, PADI shops, bookshops, clothes shops, cafes, bars, clubs and restaurants. A counterfeit copy of the China LP costs 200,000 dong...just over 10 dollars. I will buy it for 100,000 dong. They refuse so I just sit down and flip through.

The beautiful mountains come up from far out and take me in as I see how high the tide is. So Rio. I book my bus to Hoi An and I should be on my way with no distractions as I have a Chinese visa to arrange for. News has it that a bus full of Russian tourists crashed in the Northern Highlands of Dalat and they all dead. I go to Church to pray for their souls.

A Vietnamese lady says *privet* = *"hello"*. Of Persian descent, born in Moscow, raised in Iraq, educated in Cyprus and living in America. *Privet.*

Nha Trang is very more convenient in terms of arriving and leaving, as the bus station is five blocks away from Backpacker's House. I buy two packs of Oreos for a bargain price of a bargain price and negotiate the counterfeit copy of the China LP for 150,000 Dong. Excited, tipsy, walking to the bus station, sit down, wait, realize I am, as always....early.

Nice couple. *Smile.* I hop on the bus, studying about Yunnan province and popular routes. According to the guidebook the Tibetan world begins a few towns BEFORE the Autonomous Region of Tibet itself. Like Zhongdian (Shangri-La) in Yunnan province...A route to and out of Tibet in between Yunnan and Sichuan provinces is connected by a town named Kang'ding and Ya'an...and the Buddhist Mount of Emei: one of the Four Sacred Buddhist Mountains of China, along with Putuo Shan, Wutai Shan and Jiuhua Shan. Yunnan province was out of my initial route but somebody awaits for my call there.

But...*I don't know that.*

The bus arrives at Hoi An and I give back the little torch I borrowed from the girl I smiled at at the bus station. We grab our backpacks as I notice she has a big flag of Japan on hers along with a few others, just like my backpack. She asks if she can walk with me. I tell her, of course. She lives in Spain and her name is Lora. She has amazing long blonde hair. We share a room for 5 dollars per night, each. The owner offers us coffee on the house. Lora speaks five languages. She has been on the pill for 10 years because she was afraid to get pregnant. She then went off it and now her body is re-adjusting and the hormonal imbalance is right on her face - as she masks it with concealer. She does a good job and looks beautiful. She also wears skirts and espadrilles. Not only me!

Hoi An is a famous tourist town mostly because it is where you would go to get cheap, custom-made clothes. The vendors are persistent and I bargain hard. The very first one offers to make a dress for me for 20 dollars and I tell her I would not pay more than 10 as she agrees after 10 minutes of arguing about how little money it really is...for us.

I sketch a black sleek dress with wider thick straps like Mariah Carey's *Honey* video. I am finally getting the exact style dresses made for *me*. Little girl's dreams come true!

We eat by a bridge in the center of this cute town in a joint called Mr. Chow's. Vietnamese wontons, salad and cao lao noodles. The best food is spring rolls...any time, any day. Lora is drinking green coconut: good for rehydration. Lora is soft but she means business. She tells me I need to get a manicure. I *look* at her, offended. But I *feel* no resentment toward her. Her energy reads clear as her emotional body meant no harm or offense...thus I not need get my defense...this makes me further wonder whether every intention of a person can be through their emotional body instead of what they are actually saying.

We return to the shop to pick up the newly-tailored clothes as I try the dress on and love it...Two more! One in red and one in

white. Both with different style straps as I like variety. All three are a so-called "strict" length, just above the knee.
Very, very elegant.

The tailor woman convinces me that I need a silk dress too. I agree to have a long classy ivory silk dress as she makes sure she has the correct measurements for my body. We leave for yet another stroll down town and meet up with Lora's friend - Olaf from Germany. Lora tells me she started talking to me because I smiled at her. The power of smile. *When you smile, the muscles in your body relax and people feel it.* I try on my new custom-made black dress and love it so much that I keep it on for the night. We go to sit down for a glass of wine and then down to the coffee shop to have cheesecakes, chocolate fudge cakes...life is good. Socialist-star visors!! We get a deal of two for two dollars. I also try on a myriad of different black knee-high boots. They look hot. Especially with the black dress. Somebody call Hoi An Vice.

Lora and I hop on the bus to Hanoi with a quick stop-over in Hue. *Thanks for the Memories.*[7] A woman had a blood transfusion and knows things about a man's life she has never met. Somehow she also knows archaeology and Latin. She finds out that the memory is contained in the blood.......the man rejects her...

As we approach Hue I make a transfer on the overnight bus to Hanoi. Lora and five Swedish guys are coming too. I continue researching my China LP. My initial plan was to enter China from Hekou - in the Northeast of Vietnam right after trekking to Fansipan Mountain North-West of Hanoi. I wanted to conquer

---

[7] A book by Cecelia Ahern I read on the bus.

the greatest summit of SE Asia at over 3,000 meters. Form the energy for my next experience. Go to the Chinese Consulate first thing after checking in. While the visa is processed which I assume to be 5 working days I will go on the trek and to Halong Bay: the highlight of anyone's visit to Vietnam. How many people do so many things!? I tell our Swedish friends about my travels as I finish fried rice and spring rolls in one gulp. As we hop back on the bus I wonder if Yunnan is the right thing to do since it was not my plan...and which border should I cross if I was to go to Yunnan...I would have to make my connections through a city called Kunming - the capital of Yunnan province.

The bus drops us off in the middle of a highway as taxis pick up foreigners for 10,000 dong each. It is 6 a.m. and we are tired as dogs. I made a reservation beforehand for St. Patrick's Day celebration at Hanoi Backpackers' Hostel. I think "why oh why did I not spend 4 dollars on an oil painting of Angkor Wat". *It would be nice to hang it in my apartment in Miami when I return.* It is raining cats and dogs as we pass by the main square and lake in the center of Hanoi. I just wish it was not so hectic. Pedestrians yield to everything.

No. 46 Hoang Deui Street. Chinese Consulate. A huge line of Vietnamese at the door and two foreigners of an Israeli girl and a Finnish guy. I also need to arrange for a Hong Kong visa...so I fill out a separate application as we run to the copy shop next door. We line up and chat as the Israeli chick storms out the gate screaming she was just refused a visa and says she will wait for me to go in to see if I will be given one. The Finnish guy's turn comes and he is refused as he snaps out and starts screaming that they have no right to refuse visa without a reason. The security guard tries dragging him outside the hall as he successfully fights back. The girl behind the window who refused his application says she will take his passport if he does not leave. She hands it over to the guard who walks to the door and the Finnish guy follows him yelling that he will call the Finnish Embassy.

My turn comes around as I pray and believe my application will be miraculously accepted. The official behind the counter stares right through me scanning my truth detectors with her eyes. She asks me "why do I want to go", I tell her, "for tourism." She asks me "where do I want to go", I tell her, "Nanning, Shanghai, Beijing and Russia." She asks me, "why did I not get a visa at home." "Because I have been traveling for a year now and assumed it would be easiest to get a visa geographically closer to China." She takes my application, walks away, comes back and hands it over to me, saying "declined." I ask her "why?" she says they are "not issuing tourist visas to foreigners right now." I ask her "what should I do? Is there a consulate in Vientiane in Laos that issues visas?" She turns her head in a "No" way.

I catch a motorbike back to the hostel as I am ripped off for the ride by 30,000 dong! I run to the closest Internet cafe, skype my mom and dad. Hysterically I tell them how tired I am of 3rd world tape.
Mom tells me to pay a travel agent so they can arrange visa.
I ask three different agencies but cannot decide on the date I want to leave or the border I want to leave from. This is affecting my plans and my mood as it seems it will cost around 100 dollars...for a frigging sticker! It makes me mad as I hate overpaying for services like this. I know because this is what I do myself...*used* to do at home in Moscow. Documents, legalization, notary work and all the bureaucratic paperwork seems to have been my karma all my life. By my work I paid it forward. I helped many people get their papers *in order*.

There is a place in this world where every time you look up into the beautiful blue sky...Angels look right down back at you. That place is South Florida.
Is that why I feel the need to reunite with that place.
Only when you're not there.

I negotiate to pay 94 dollars to have the visa ready in 3 days. I hope they will not lose my passport as I see the delivery man carelessly throw it into the storage space underneath his seat on his motorbike. If he loses it will mean I can't travel and complete the journey. Because of something as little...as a careless motorbike driver?

I research Chinese geography on google maps. Unsuccessful. All names are in Chinese. I only know two characters: one for love and one for truth. I had them temporarily tattooed on my right ankle back when I had my first prediction made....the very first intervention of the spirit world through a medium.....the name of the medium was Arthur...on July 14th, 1999 in Venice Beach....California.

I surf into Sean's Guesthouse in the Tiger Leaping Gorge, connected with a legend of a tiger running away from hunters, leaping across the gorge: hence the name. As I look across the room I see the Finnish guy. I walk up to him and ask him what is up with the Chinese visa. He arranged for it through an agency too. He apologizes he left the consulate without me - he was just too angry and too confused. He is a lot more relaxed right now as we sit down to eat pho bo - a Vietnamese soup - the stalls come out at 7 p.m. every night and cost 20,000 dong. Tourist price, of course. I can't have beef - "pho" - and ask for chicken with bean sprouts and cilantro - pho *ga*. It is delicious but I wonder what is the white crystalline powder they put into the soup. Oh. MSG.

This is what makes me hyper, makes me sweat and want to smoke...the Finnish guy's name is Matti. He is slim, he wears a bandana and has a goatee. He is my soul/mate - he was doing exactly what I was doing: trying to get a Chinese visa in Hanoi. We have ice/cream overlooking the Huan Kiem Lake.

When I had learnt about my Spirit guide I had always prayed and hoped that we can make an arrangement for him to materialize...to stay with me in this timeline...I still pray to this day for him to find me.

If you read this, I want you to contact me.

What hurt me all that time was that I could not reunite with him in this reality. If I could...I would have to give up everything. Risk everything. Put everything on this belief. Trust the Love. And the only things that are justified are the things we do for and out of love. The power of love. I was mad all this time...because when I raised that energy from within myself...from within my Soul...it seems like everything had already been written and said...many times over...and whatever I say now is recycled information.

I take a tour of Halong Bay as the Sun makes its last degree of Pisces. The bus is late to pick me up, so I walk to the agency to find out what's up and they tell me a guy on a motorbike will take me to the bus. I greet everyone in the van and realize that they put me into a bus with a completely different company...not the one I paid to take the tour with. I stress about it as they tell me they will put me with my company later on...once we get to Halong City - the port that the boats leave from. I wonder why the hell did I even go with a tour and did not just take the public bus...and then boat...and I remember it is because I wanted to chillax.

It all *does* begin from within. I did not relax within and thus projected that energy out and my tour is so stressful and anything but fun. A Russian couple with a kid of about 7 years old watch me as I argue with the guide. I scream at him that they will not leave me here alone. The Russians think I don't understand that they are bashing my balls off to how it was my fault and I was the idiot who was late. I am an idiot for not speaking right back at them in our language, mirroring how rude they are.

Halong Bay is a World Heritage Site of limestone karsts and isles in various shapes and sizes. An old legend has it that during war, the gods sent dragons to protect the land which later became the country of Vietnam. The dragons started spitting out jewels and jade, which became islands and islets to form a great wall against the invaders. The mother dragon's landing place was named Ha-Long.[8]

Its beauty is captivating even today as it is gloomy and we hardly see anything. We are given lunch as the boat docks in one of the floating fishing villages. I small-talk to an old French man from St. Maarten in the Caribbean as he tells me how much he enjoys traveling alone but doesn't know
...what it feels like...for a girl...in this world.

The boat returns to Halong City and I ask one of the guides about Vietnamese martial arts. He tells me he does not know of places that train foreigners. I tell him I know muay thai. He tells me he thinks I am pretty. I ask him about the Vietnamese hats. He tells me they are conical charming hats, plaited with palm leaves, extremely lightweight and resistant. They are used to escape the scorching heat or tropical rain. Cyclists, people

---

[8] Bay of Descending Dragons.

working in ricefieldss, rowing boats, selling fruit in the street or elegantly dressed business women...all wear them.

Back at the hostel, Matti tells me to be prepared that in China, nothing is in English, people stare a lot, most of the tourists are *Chinese* tourists, and that when I go to Guilin I should go straight to Yangshuo and stay in Monkey Jane's Hostel. He will be going to China in a few days when his visa is ready, crossing through Nanning, going to Beijing to arrange for his Tibetan Permit, then to Xining, then on to Lhasa...then Nepal....and India...

I book a train ticket to Lao Cai for 27 dollars in 3rd class from the same travel agent that arranged my visa. The price of the ticket is actually 136,000 dong (do the math of the rip-off), had I bought it at the station, but no "same, same", no "speak speak" Vietnamese. As twelve hours on a sick train are over, we arrive to the border town one hour North from Sapa - a village and a popular tourist site. I nervously smoke in between cars on the train as I just realized...the travel agent had lost my immigration card for Vietnam.

I have little choice but to either go to Sapa for the night or go straight to China. *China*. No time to think twice. Just walk. I try asking the locals "Where is *China? China?*" but all I get in return is a clueless look as response when I realize that I don't know how to say *China* in Vietnamese. I perhaps should get some small dollar bills in case I will need help crossing the border. Finally I see a bridge...I am definitely the only white person crossing it. I forgot I have no Chinese money. Damn. I walk to the immigration official and ask him to put my exit stamp right next to the entry stamp. He checks it, stamps my passport and hands it over. I thank him and walk over the border. *Thank God.*

As I approach the Chinese Immigration an official points a line for me to pass through three customs officials. A woman goes through my entire backpack and specifically pays attention to the China LP. She flips through the pages with pictures and stares at a photo from the Sichuan province. Underneath it says *The Giant Buddha Head of LeShan.* "Where was it taken?"
I tell her..."I don't know..."
I was afraid they would take it away as I have read happens frequently....*just not today.*

I ask the immigration officer checking my passport to please stamp me down THERE, where I have space. NOT on an empty page. These pages are worth in gold.

My visa is a double-entry: I will enter now, and then the second time from Macau. How good it will feel if I can get what I want: the World's Highest Bungy Jump. A double-entry visa means I wont have ability/opportunity to deviate from my route: change my plans/flex it/announce I am going to take a ferry to Japan and Korea and back to Shanghai or maybe even Russia's Far East. Reason being: the loop must be stopped and truth revealed by traveling backwards in the world of Buddhism.

IX. China.

The few seconds of entering a completely new place and energy: the border town of Hekou. I am looking for number one: currency exchange. number two: bathroom. number three: coffee. Bank of China - the only one open on a Sunday! They will exchange my dollars at a rate of 6.7 Yuan to 1 Dollar. "Two years ago the rate was 8 Yuan to 1 Dollar!"
I see how nice, patient and friendly the lady at the bank is, shut up and hand over 100 dollars. I find a coffee shop on the main street by the river. I find a bus station which I have been looking for in the last hour just walking around - right by the border gate. Dah! As I get my ticket for Kunming on a bus scheduled to depart at 1 p.m. a local *merchant* approaches me and asks me if I want to exchange money. Thank heavens for him: as he exchanges my leftover dong into yuan and buys my SE Asia LP. He speaks impeccable English, unlike most of the population of Yunnan: the poorest and least educated province in all of China.

As the bus rides through the jungles of banana palms, corn and rice fields, I feel I am just about to touch the peak of my Asian travels. The electromagnetic grid of planet Earth had a wormhole through which I merged with another part of my soul spark in this same area when I psyched for him...tapping in>
I felt him move down South China and enter SE Asia.

Real flowers grow in the wilderness.[9]

Again I have no reservation. The LP guide has hotel names and addresses listed in English as well as in Chinese. No need to

---

[9] Mei, "House of Flying Daggers"

worry. The bus stops for dinner and I eat noodles which thankfully don't make me sick. They cost 5 yuan! I LOVE CHINA. Everyone on my bus is Chinese and the supervisor tells me "WC!" as she points in the direction of the gas station. An "efficiency" right by the gas station.

These notorious...squat toilets. No problem! Much healthier and more natural than Western toilets.
I am reading *Karma for Travelers*. The book exchange would not buy it from me...so I
think of Dhyani. Why did she teach me to be a "macro" person in a "micro" society?
And then leave me.
a true test: to live as a Buddha in the world of lies, deception and betrayal.

After another 5 hours the bus arrives at somewhat of a bus station. I am trying to find it on the map, hopelessly trying to get directions from the bus driver. Can you ever rely on the Universe leading you through somebody who gives you wrong directions? Would it be your own projection of a wrongful idea or is it simply...chance?

you can either trust it or trust your own self.

A man getting off the bus happens to speak English. I ask him for help with a cab. He offers to give me a ride with the taxi he will hail for himself. I tell him I need to go to Kun Hu Fandian. He welcomes me to Kunming and asks me where I am from. I hop out of the taxi, wave goodbye to the kind stranger and run to my hotel via an overpass.

I pay 60 Yuan per night for a huge room with three queen beds. The bathroom is outside in the hallway...just like a hostel. The housekeeper leaves a thermos with hot water on my table. *Xei-xei*. I brew green tea and flip the channels as they are all in Chinese...

I check out the next morning as my powerful intention is to stay in a hostel and make friends to travel with. Enough of being frustrated and lonely. I ponder whether to take my backpack or not. If taking it will affect my choice of hostel or how fast I find it and check in. I decide because it is a beautiful sunny day I will walk around with my day-pack and after checking in: come back for my big pack. I start walking in the direction of the center of town. I see a China Post - the only sign in English.

My emotional body floats out and I catch myself smiling at a cute Westerner walking in my direction. He smiles back.

Good sign. There should be plenty of them here - Kunming is the crossroads for traveling in South-West China.

Walking in the direction of what is supposed to be the HI Backpackers Hostel. After browsing the area for an hour, leave angry, confused with an extremely imbalanced throat chakra.

I can't communicate here...nobody understands English. When they damn should!!

I visit a Yuantong Temple in the center of town and a Muslim Mosque. I have a burger for 2 yuan. I thought I would never do something that would harm my own self. Then why did I eat this burger that I know I can't eat beef? I buy some fried potatoes...it does not take away the hunger or the blood sugar abnormality...whichever it is that is affecting my mood and I feel lost and confused. I *am*...lost and confused. The counterfeit guidebook has a shitty map and wherever the hostel is supposed to be...it just isn't there! Good God had I not come here last night...I start looking for another hostel called *The Humps* as I walk back to my hotel. I just have to be physically moving...ALL the time. I feel like there was something in my life...something in my emotional body that I couldn't travel without...an attachment. A drive. That after all the years of wanting to travel, I finally took off on a one-way flight and I am currently still on the journey to eliminate that emotional attachment.

Fulfill my purpose and dream.

Travel the world.

As I approach the last intersection before the hostel, according to the map - my emotional body is expanded straight - and my eyes meet a pair of eyes in sunglasses - the same guy I saw in the morning. We smile at each other...and say *hello*.

The Humps is on a second floor of a building with a big balcony. It is a hot spot with pool tables, an expensive bar and they are booked for the night. The staff speak English...what a relief! They ask me how long have I been in China. Two days. They tell me not to worry, as "China is very safe to travel!" They show me to go for Internet around the block.

After half an hour of browsing the one corner, I settle down to call home in frustration and anger. Bummer. Even the Internet is in Chinese!

As is skype.

I shouldn't have come here. I wonder if being refused a visa was a sign.

The supervisor of the place calls for a guy who speaks some English to hook me up with an English version of the web browser.

As I start surfing I can't believe just how much stuff is actually...censored. Facebook. CNN. youtube.

I leave the cafe, go back to my hotel, buy a frosted donut which makes me feel ever more bloated. I hate eating. I hate food. I hate coming here. I hate myself for taking so much risk and not booking a hostel in advance. Had I not been angry from the MSG in Vietnam, I would not have been so hyper and quick to leave! Is it all about what I eat!! Is all energy that is affecting my programming......

I check back in Kun Hu Fandian into the same room and ponder how my day would have been different...*had* I taken my backpack. I would have HAD to find the hostel. My internal mechanisms would know I MUST find a place to stay with other backpackers. Oumph. I should have at least talked to the guy I smiled at and asked him where they stay.

I gaze out my window and have a cigarette. I must decide between Dali and Lijiang - the next two towns on the beaten backpacker trail. I go to the train station to find a ticket for a night train to Dali. The bus ticket saleswoman catches me halfway and takes me to the ticket office and I am lost again in my intentions as they offer me ten things at one time: I look in the LP Guide to ask "what time does it leave" and say *jidian kai?* They respond in Chinese. They see the clueless look on my face. They write it down. In Chinese. I can't take it anymore.

But the gigantic prayer wheel I saw J spin in one of his photos beckons me...I believe he was spinning it and calling out to heaven/praying for guidance/support of the higher power/to guide /lead/protect him on his journey=I heard it.

Every time he span a prayer wheel it purified ether sending out a message to heaven...it resonated *as is above, so is below* and I caught it...my head would spin around...and round...and round...
We need to talk. The gigantic prayer wheel and I.
We have unfinished business. I spin it...anti-clockwise...and end the time loop.

I read that the bus to Dali really only goes as far as the town of Xiaguan. From there one must catch another bus. I have no reservation. Perhaps I shouldn't even point it out any longer...I normally just follow the *call* and take a risk. As I get off the bus in the cute town of Dali - cobbled-streets and small wooden houses, four city walls forming a good aura and keeping the energy within the square space....I walk to Tibetan Lodge, where the room is cramped and tiny. The bed is cute and I wonder if the owner who sold it to me knew a legend or a myth linked to this room. Perhaps a spirit lives here that only allows certain people to resonate with it.

I eat "across-the-bridge-noodles": a hot pot of boiling chicken broth, chicken bits, ginger, greens and non-glutenous rice noodles. Legend has it, a painter's wife used to bring him lunch from their house to his studio. So that it doesn't get cold, she would keep the cauldron on a hot stove and put the ingredients when she brought it to him, across the bridge.

All backpackers should come to Dali: I guarantee you feng-shui surrounded by mountains, great trekking and beautiful scenery of the Er Hai Lake.

Speaking of feng-shui. Literally, feng-shui means "wind-water" - the two natural elements. It is an ancient Chinese art of determining sacred places on earth. The breath of life to the ancient Chinese was in the *qi*. By determining the movement of qi in the landscape, the ancients determined the safest or the most fertile places with the most favorable characteristics of the Earth's geomancy. The philosophy of natural balance or equilibrium was considered a teaching of the Dao = the Way = represented by Ying (female) and Yang (male) - which continuously flow into one another.

Some of the qualities of the ying are valleys, moon, water, cold, slow, passive and smooth; whereas some of the yang are the sky, mountains, the sun, fire, hot, fast, active and bumpy.

Thus, the energy - qi - of a place can be determined by the co-relation of ying and yang - for which a special compass, named Ba-gua is used - literally "eight trigrams".

The basis of the Daoist cosmology carries the five elements of Fire, Earth, Metal, Water and Wood. On a metaphysical level, the five elements are not touchable substances, but different emanations of *qi*.

The cycle of creation begins when Fire creates Earth, as afterwards ashes remain. Earth retains Metal, as mineral ores are excavated from underground. Metal feeds Water, as water is retained in metal vessels. Water feeds Wood, allowing it to grow, as Wood feeds Fire, when it acts as a fuel.

A cycle of destruction is anti-clockwise: Wood parts Earth, Earth absorbs Water, Water quenches Fire, Fire melts Metal and Metal chops Wood.

The Ba-gua forms 64 possible combinations and are called I-Jing or The Book of Change. Each hexagram recommends a preferable attitude in order to attain good fortune and avoid bad luck; and is used for divination. Everything in the Universe, including Earth and human beings, is subject to constant change..

In Chinese tradition the forces of nature are triple: the sky, human, and earth. The character symbolizing it is a straight line on top, a cross in the middle, and a straight line on the bottom. Chinese tradition has used geometric symbols to explain micro- and macro-cosmic influences for many ages. The entire world order represents a pattern of situations, resulting from interaction and fight of good and evil, strain and compliance. All changes are considered not as a result of the effect of external forces, but as an internally-inherent inclination of all things to constantly change.

I rent a bike and go around the lake to The Three Pagodas Temple for auspicious reason. According to a legend the town used to be a swamp inhabited by dragons before the humans arrived. Dragons were believed to create natural disasters in order to dispel human intruders, but they revered pagodas, which were built to constrain them.

Dragons ruled bodies of water and were able to show themselves as tornados. Chinese mythology and folklore was the oldest one to utilize the dragon - symbol of prosperity, power, striving and good fortune. They are frequently associated with the number 9.

First, there was nothing.
Not knowing how to call it, I will simply call it "the Way".

On to a small stall of souvenirs selling just about anything and everything jade: green, white and black jade. Figurines of the Three Star Gods who represent prosperity, authority and longevity; wind-chimes, pen-holders, vases, health-balls, tortoise figurines - also symbols of prosperity. The tortoise is also one of the four celestial animals in Daoism, along with the dragon, phoenix and tiger.

Admission is 150 yuan or kwai - as I have learnt the locals call their currency - I skip it and continue biking.

A wave of pain comes over me (must be the wheat pancakes I had in the morning). I *must* find the key to unlock the mystery and conspiracy behind our connection. Where in the world do I need to go to find what it is that keeps me in this pain. When is his face going to fade out of my mind, my heart...what is it in this grid that I have not experienced yet...that I have to find...what is it that I need to know...what is it......

...that I am not finished with.

Understanding others is knowledge, understanding oneself is enlightenment;
Conquering others is power, conquering oneself is strength;
Contentment is wealth, forceful conduct is willfulness;
Not losing one's rightful place is to endure,
to die but not be forgotten is longevity.[10]

.....as I take a break glaring at the mountain tops I start to remember....
Duality of nature that complements each other instead of competing with each other —
the two faces of the same coin —
one cannot exist without the other.[11]

---

[10] Dao De Jing.

[11] A theme from Dao De Jing.

...an urge to connect from my inner second chakra...it is coming to me. splitting into bits and pieces...as I split into an asteroid...a part of my soul cell that is out there in the Universe.

Wo tingbudong = I don't understand.[12]
I need to get to a town called Wase to catch a boat across the lake straight to Dali. I still have over 2/3 of the way ahead of me.

The time of the sun is running out.
Stop off the curb and take a wee next to the lake.

Confucius say,
Man who live in glass house
must change clothes in the basement.

Start pedaling again. If I am fast enough I can get back to town before sundown. But if not...I will have to sleep over...perhaps right here...Could I perhaps sleep at one of the family's houses? The indigenous peoples are very friendly. I see a police office. Should I ask them for help?
I pass by. I ask a taxi driver how much to go back to the city. He tells me 200 kwai. I only have 20! I try catching a minibus but neither driver understands what I need...a ride to the city...for 20 kwai..!
Finally I am out of breath and get off the bike to carry it uphill.
Used up all my chances.
No options left but to hitchhike back. Last chance.
Sun is almost One with Horizon.
Raise my hand.
Please help.
...a truck stops. The driver waves for me to get in. No English.

---

[12] I learnt another Chinese phrase.

Pork Buns (with some soups inside).[13]

Using sign and body language I let the driver know I will ride in the hood of the truck. He "tells" me "no, it is not safe and it is filled with supplies." He helps me put my bike into the hood and I hop inside, squeezing in with the family.

The ride takes 40 minutes as I explain the family that I am from Ou-wo-sy.[14] I understand nothing from what they say but when the mom makes the money sign with her fingers...I get it.
Well...I must get back with 20 kwai which means I will give them 10 to get to Xiaguan and pay 8 for the bus to Dali.
They park nearby their house, I pay them and find the bus station as a young Chinese man tells me in perfect English that I am lucky to be here as the last bus will come in 10 minutes!
I love feeling excited. I love feeling love. I love feeling inspired.

Inspired...

To know and yet
(think) we do not know is the highest (attainment);
not to know
(and yet think) we do know is a disease.[15]

---

13 Today's special.

14 Chinese for "Russia".

15 the Way.

I check into a HI Dali hostel I haven't noticed before - next to the bike rental place. It is clean, spacious with free Internet time. I forgot to let ya'll know that I took a tai-ji class early the same morning. A small Chinese man picked me up from the hotel and took me across the street into the center for martial arts. We practice in a swimming pool...without the water. He smiles all the time as his eyes are as thin as long-grain rice and I hardly see his pupils!

Tai-ji is a meditative form of exercise from which one obtains physical and spiritual health benefits, and an hour of which bores my body.

The true meaning of it is "the ultimate" as it relates to fusion of the ying and yang energies represented by the Tajitu symbol = the fishlike symbol. Thus, taiji is the male-female principle of bipolarity, the most fundamental, cosmic "first principle."

As qi/ji=energy moves through one's body in form of a breath, in coordination with arm and legwork...a few other young kids join us for *another* hour of training. One of them is an American who translates to the teacher that I am *Russky*. The teacher calls me *tovarish*.[16] I run off that minute as I notice how the spark between me and the Americano would lead to a small-talk....and...XYNZ....and

The more you go in search of an answer,

the less you will understand.[17]

I do my laundry, hang it to dry at the rooftop of the hostel and go hiking to the Cangshan mountains.

For hours around the beautiful mountains...all the way to Zhonghe Temple.

---

[16] comrade.

[17] A theme from Dao De Jing.

Past the entrance...but can't escape having to pay the admission fee of 80 yuan.
Shown the way - a whirlwind of a walk through graves, rice fields and farmlands...

Time slows down....<<<<<<slows down....
it is my purpose....to give you my love, my Love.
streaming time....a time loop not over<<<<<<<<<

Let the pain go....Only love shall remain in this heart. <>

The Three Jewels of Dao =
Compassion - Moderation - Humility.
Higherland Inn. Take a break. Eat a papaya. Past the Phoenix
Eye Cave (representative of the *yin*) and on to the Dragon Eye
Cave (representative of the *yang*).

In Daoism the central concept is wu-wei which means "without
action" or "effortless effort".
As "shui" - water - is soft and strong, moves earth, carves stone
and burns flesh. One must learn to appreciate the ability of "still"
water - ice and "fast" water - stream to understand "why".
Shui of becoming still cracks stone,
shui of great speed burns flesh.

Qingbi stream. 50 yuan cable-car back down to main highway to
catch a cab to return at 7 p.m. and check if there are any friends
to be made at the hostel. *Nada. Bupkes.*
Run around naked.

According to Daoist philosophy, the Universe works
harmoniously in its own ways. When someone exerts his will
against the world, he disrupts that harmony.
Daoism does not see the man's will as the primary problem;
rather, man must place his will in harmony with the Natural
Universe.[18]

Unable to sleep, I log on to facebook at 2 a.m.
Biting on my shoestring...the pain is so unbearable.
Idan asks me what is up. I tell him about the man I cannot forget.
He says I focus all my pain and frustration on him, because he
rejected me. He says I chose it. I chose to fall in love with a man

---

[18] The aim of Daoism is to achieve immortality.

who is unavailable. Because people like me want things they can't have. It is a challenge!...He asks me what is going to fuel my fire after I return home from all these travels.

He sends me a link to a song

...Because of you
I learned to play on the safe side
So I don't get hurt
Because of you
I find it hard to trust
Not only me, but everyone around me
Because of you
...I am afraid [19]

---

[19] Kelly Clarkson, *Because Of You*

Lijiang. Get granola bars and whole-wheat cookies at bakery. No bloating, no hunger, as it will give me fiber and fill me in = perfect. Feel tired. Unable to cope with the pain of transition. Can't understand how I am going to get out of the pain. I've have had no explanation for it. Perhaps it is easier than anything I have known before. It is so very simple. Just like Chinese Medicine: bi-polarity. I do love a man I can't be with. I do want things I can't have. I do make myself suffer. How do I get out of this vicious cycle? The cycle of anger, repressed emotions, feelings I can't handle....feeling nothing.

"Don't leave the bus or plane station from which you arrived! Don't be afraid! There are public phones around all stations, find a Chinese person to help you call us and tell us where you are we will definitely come find you!" [20]

I wait for Mama Naxi as I gaze out at the mountains and reminisce. If only my past lives with J could have been surfaced. Could have been opened...by the Akashic records...they would not hurt as much. I have no conscious memory of us. I have no story to tell. All I have is...pain.
Which reminds me...he *did* exist.

Luggage? Mama Naxi throws my heavy big-ass backpack into a taxi which takes me to the guesthouse as a young girl tells me she will be right with me. I sit down on the porch with no energy to walk...no power to get myself up. I feel like the bad spirits are taking over my mind. Yelling at me for coming here. Giving in to the drive to travel. I am wrong. I am a bad person and the world hates me. I'm a slut and went to travel to escape from myself. An old couple sees me sobbing on the porch all alone and invites me

---

[20] Mama Naxi's Guesthouse No. 3 catchy business card.

to eat with them. I tell them no, thank you, I want to remain miserable in my mind with the bad thoughts.

The girl comes back and tells me we need to walk to the guesthouse with dorms. I walk with her as I stop halfway and collapse in the middle of a cobbled-street.

The town is full of Chinese tourists. Who would have thought the Chinese travel China. I get back up on my feet as I grin and bear it...and walk the last 10 feet to Guesthouse No. 3.

I get a bed for 10 kwai a night, shower and fall asleep. I wake up to visit the Black Dragon Pool Park but don't walk inside as the admission is 100 yuan. I walk back through the main square as the town is a maze of gushing canals and brick bridges. After a restoration from an earthquake some years back, the town became a World Heritage Site. Since then....it has been flooded with tourists.

- Excuse me! May we delay your time!

Chinese kids, studying English with a teacher from Chicago. Incredible: a younger generation speaks English whereas it is the old people that don't. Just like...Russia.

They tell me they came to Lijiang to study as they are all from smaller towns in Yunnan Province. They want to get to know me and practice their English as per their homework to approach a foreigner and ask questions. I tell them I work as a translator. They tell me they all want to be translators as they really want to travel. They tell me to try an authentic Lijiang snack: chicken pea jelly. Sweets - Chinese version of cotton candy, made by hand by a girl right in front of me - her face is covered with a cloth and her eyes-lashes are covered in powdered sugar as she rolls up Dragon's beard candy, so called because of the fine sugar strands giving it the appearance of a beard. I get a box for 10 yuan and get lost in this labyrinth of the town as it had gotten dark while I had been chatting with the kids and somehow after wondering around and about I return to the hostel to eat a little bit fried eggplant with rice, having missed the buffet dinner.

Mama Naxi is a fun woman with three daughters, two sons and a husband all working for her guesthouse. Occasionally she would ask "Hungry?" or give out pancakes with honey.

- Mama clean! - as I hear her mutter to herself while she mops the canteen floor.

I meet a cute Israeli guy named Kris, originally from Ukraine. He has just done the famous Tiger Leaping Gorge trail. He says everyone here is doing it and it's very easy to arrange for transportation to go there and back. In fact, he tells me first I catch a bus to Qiaotou, then drop my bags off at Jane's Guesthouse, hike for 2 days, return to Qiaotou to pick up bags and catch a bus to Shangri-La.

Kris wants to go to Tibet as he had just come back from Deqin - the last Chinese city on the border with the TAR. It was closed when he was there. Word is out: it will be opened again April 1st. Instead he wants to go to Tibet through the "back-door" - the Lugu Hu at the border of Yunnan and Sichuan. I am not sure if he knows that....it does not connect to Tibet.

He has finished the Israeli army and has been traveling for six months in North India before coming to China. He says Indian people are the stupidest in the world, but he loves them. He says he was stomach-sick every day of his trip, but he loves India. He says he had to go on antibiotics for a virus which gave him the diarrhea in the first place, and most foreigners get it, but yes...he loves India. He stayed in what is translated from Sanskrit into English as the Region of Snowy Mountains.

He says when he goes back to Israel he wants to pursue a degree in psychology: he wants to help people.

Ying-yang philosophy was put into a system of Wu-Xing: Star of the Elements - five elements, which gives a full understanding of the workings of the body, mind and spirit. The five elements which represents the four seasons, plus the 5th for the late summer. Elements are connected with colors, emotions, taste sensations, sounds, various organs, foods and herbs. The proportion of elements in the person's body determines the person's character. The ideal condition is when all the five elements are balanced.

In acupuncture, using special needles a trained doctor of sacred medicine puts them in special acupuncture dots in the channels (meridians) - are places where the qi is closest to the surface of the body.

Chinese physiognomy, or face-reading, projects the five elements onto the face: the forehead/fire/heart; left cheek/liver/wood; chin/kidneys/water; right cheek/lungs/metal; nose/spleen/earth.
The physical body is built, or more precisely, the energy body builds a physical body on its base.
"The face is the mirror of karma".

The Chinese character for "person" is a straight line. Add two lines around the one - you get "three lines" - the character for "water". The symbol can also mean river, vessel, kidneys or diarrhea.

Dr. Po invites us for a tea ceremony. It is a culture in itself in China, conducted for family and social gatherings. Of the four different types of teas along with white, black and oolong; green tea is the most well-known.

Chinese Traditional Medicine assumes that each person is born with a certain amount of jing, and as we live, it is slowly expended or lost. The lost jing cannot be re-gained, it leaves for good. When the jing is expended, a person dies. Jing is lost when one lives wrong or carelessly. But it can be retained, if one lives in moderation. Movement of vital force of qi is connected with movement of consciousness.

Qi-gong is used for replenishment of jing, also one of the internal martial arts. The word "gong" means achievement.

Jing is responsible for growth, development and reproduction. It represents the potential of a human being for his development and is similar to the Western concept of genetic memory.

Thus, male semen carries the most jing. The Daoists believed that complete avoidance of ejaculation conserves the man's life essence.

Daoists believe a man may increase and nourish his own vitality by bringing a woman to orgasm. The woman's orgasm strengthens her *jing* (essence - contained in the bodily fluids), also considered as one of the Three Treasures of Chinese Medicine, along with qi (vital force) and shen (consciousness).

Shen is often compared to "soul".

It shows itself in the individuality, ability to think, sensory perception and awareness of the self.

In the Daoist view of sexuality men are encouraged to control ejaculation to preserve the vital force, whereas women are encouraged to orgasm without restriction.

After a fascinating lecture with a Chinese doctor, we browse the Black Dragon Pool Park. Apparently Chinese garden design is also linked with Dao De Jing - the ancient text by Lao Tzu which is is fundamental to philosophical Daoism.[21]

---

[21] Dao in its regular course does nothing (for the sake of doing it), and so there is nothing which it does not do.

Enter from a side street, cross a bridge hearing the waterfalls cascade and glare at Meili Snow Mountain - walk back to the guesthouse and buy local yak yogurt for 4 yuan. Eat dinner and magic cookies. Get high as the boys play poker.

Kris explains to me that the dealer hands out cards, everyone looks at their cards and depending on what they have, they either raise the bets or stay. It is a game of illusion and deception as you can try and make someone think you have *high* cards...double-pun intended...when you really have *low* cards. You need to match them to a certain combination: straight, flush, house...

Mama books me in with other people for the Gorge trek. Two Italian girls who study Chinese in Kunming ask me if I am British, as I have an English accent. Mama Naxi sets us off on a minibus as she gives everyone a banana and a "lucky charm" Naxi amulet. The two guys in the group are Mike from Germany and a French guy whose name I keep forgetting.

The minibus drops us off at Qiaotou and we leave our bags at Jane's Guesthouse. I try to use my Youth Travel Card for a discount on admission as I would with an ISIC. Doesn't work.

The trail begins as I make everyone pose for a picture. *The hiking team is so fit!* I glare at the Jade Dragon Snow Mountain, thankful I took this detour and came to Yunnan instead of speeding through the coastal cities of China.

The trail of nearly 15 kilometers will lead on to Haba Xueshan - which stands opposite of the Yu-long Xue-shan, another name for Jade Dragon Snow Mountain.

The Frenchman tells me that *yu* (jade) was considered the "imperial gem" and was used for manufacture of utilitarian and ceremonial objects for ages in China. Artisans crafted scholar objects and mouthpieces of opium pipes, due to the belief that inhaling through jade would increase longevity.

In Chinese folklore, the tiger has always been rival to the dragon, the idiom of "Dragon versus Tiger" is nowadays used in martial arts to describe equal rivals.

Wo Hu, Cang Long

...a truly beautiful tale of love. Wo Ai Ni.

A devoted heart grants all wishes.[22]

---

[22] Jen, *Crouching Tiger, Hidden Dragon*

As we pass the first kilometer I bump into a very, very tall Dutch couple. The French guy shares snickers minibars with everyone as we have twenty-four bends to walk off the fat and sugar we have just ingested. Tomorrow our plan is to walk the Middle Rapids, the Lower Rapids and the Tiger Leaping Stone - apparently THE Stone tiger leaped off. The last city on our route should be Daju.

One of the Italian girls tells me they have been to Shangri-La and will be going to Lugu Hu after the trek. She says that Deqin is the last town on the Yunnan-Tibet border. She says it is a shithole but the countryside is pretty. If I go there...I should go straight to Feilai-Si. Mike calls me a "princess" which makes me lovesick.

I need a romance.
As the rain starts to fall I look back to see I have lost everyone - Mike and the French kid were ahead of the group so I guess they went further and everyone else is way behind me. I walk past a sign pointing to Halfway Lodge. Maybe they found shelter from the rain in it?...

In the old Daoist Sexual Practices, the act of lovemaking was considered a way to make jing. By having as much sex as possible, men had the ability to transform more and more jing, thus obtain many health benefits.
Daoist sexual positions also served to cure or prevent illness as the concept of ying and yang held special importance in sex.

It's NOT funny how the trail looks different when you're walking it the other way. Noone to get directions from. Then I remember...it is a poor agricultural province. Don't blame construction workers for not being able to explain in English.

..I try to get myself together. If my intention to find them is strong enough and I truly need help...it will come.

....but it just doesn't. What am I gonna do?
Walk all the way back? how can I.
What if they all stayed in a guesthouse along the way somewhere and ignored my existence....?

He who knows
(the Dao) does not
(care to) speak
(about it); he who is
(ever ready to)
speak about it does not know it.

He
(who knows it)
will keep his mouth shut and close the portals
(of his nostrils).
He will blunt his sharp points and unravel the
complications of things;
he will attemper his brightness,
and bring himself into agreement with the obscurity
(of others).

(Such an one)
cannot be treated familiarly or distantly;
he is
beyond all consideration of profit or injury;
of nobility or
meanness:--he is the noblest man under heaven.[23]

---

[23] the Way.

...as I make the last turn of the winding trail back through the rice fields, I see the Dutch couple in the mist after the rain.
Thank heavens.
The French guy and Mike run up to me and ask me
Where have I been?
Where have *you* been?
they found shelter in Halfway Lodge and hoped I would figure it out.

May not the Way
(or Dao) of Heaven be compared to the
(method of) bending a bow? The
(part of the bow) which was high is brought low, and what was low is raised up.
(So Heaven) diminishes where there is superabundance, and supplements where there is deficiency.

It is the Way of Heaven to diminish superabundance, and to supplement deficiency. It is not so with the way of man. He takes away from those who have not enough to add to his own superabundance.

Who can take his own superabundance and therewith serve all under heaven? Only he who is in possession of the Dao!

Therefore the
(ruling) sage acts without claiming the results as his; he achieves his merit and does not rest
(arrogantly) in it: he
does not wish to display his superiority.[24]

---

[24] the Way.

...we walk for another mile across a bridge on to Tina's Guesthouse. I have a Naxi milk tea for 8 yuan.

I feel the ocean of milk churning in the stomach.

we go to see the rapids and have to PAY 10 yuan extra each to use the path the locals *built*. The rapids visitation site is full of Chinese tour groups.

I sit by the falls and streams and hope...pray....

Please give me the gift of sharing a romance....
A magical romance...with a guy I would travel with.
...a mental, emotional and sexual connection....

The Italian girls exchange facebooks with us and say goodbyes. The rest of the gang and I walk back up for another half an hour as I insist on staying at Sean's Guesthouse. I only took 150 kwai for the entire trip - as I thought it would just be one night. So I am either going to have to walk back or borrow money from someone.

I shower as I run out wrapped in a towel, smile and say hello to a couple outside the restaurant. I return to sit down with them after changing my clothes. They were dirty and smelly. My clothes, not the couple.

I order a glass of red wine for 30 kwai and a big fat hash brown.
As I flip through the menu I see a shy sign at the bottom of every page....it says
Everything can be made magic for 10 yuan extra.
We move to the TV room as the sun goes down and it becomes super cold. We watch local English TV as I continue a fun, bubbly conversation with Melissa and Josh.

Lights out, I flip through a book on *Ishinpo* Dr. Po gave me.
For Daoists, if sex was happening in a manner when both partners desired it, the woman creates more *jing*, and the man easily absorbs the *jing* to increase his *qi*. Women had a great deal of strength in the act of sex as they had the power to bring forth life, did not have to worry about ejaculation of refractory period.

I roll in my bed thinking of Josh and Melissa in a private double room together on this cold night, holding each other and making passionate love. As their bodies are worked up, warm, moving intwine....

Daoists called the act of sex "a battle of stealing and strengthening" as the woman was referred to as the enemy, because part of the intercourse was assumption of male's dominance of the female's sexual prowess.
He must remain still when she makes sexual moves, avoid her caress if she touches him, employ stillness and relaxation to overcome the woman's excitement and movement, keep his mind detached as it if it were floating in the azure sky.

These sexual methods are like military methods. Cool!
Never use sex as a weapon, or a tool.[25]

I go out at 3 a.m. to smoke a cigarette.
Now I can fall asleep.

I wake up in the morning into a chaos of packing and getting ready to leave. Josh and I negotiate a ride back to Qiaotou. As we get into the minivan he tells us about taking the fast boat

---

[25] Dhyani's voice in my head.

from the Thailand-Lao border to Luang Prabang. He says he was sure a rock could hit him any minute and would have never taken it...had "the person he was with" not wanted to do so.

I ponder the texts on immortality of the Daoist sexual practices which indicated that the sexual arts concerned the first precept, which is treasuring the jing. Treasuring the jing = sending it up into the brain. In order to send the jing into the brain, the male has to refrain from ejaculation during sex.

If this is done, the semen would travel up the spine and nourish the brain instead of leaving the body.

As we wait for everyone to get their bags, the French guy tells me he went to Xishuangabanna province and rice fields in Kaili. He flew into Shanghai and traveled South-East. He also teaches me to count from one to ten in Chinese.
yi, er, san, si, wu, liu, qi, ba, jiu, xi.

We walk to the intersection to catch a bus to Shangri-La: two hours and twenty kwai.
Every time. an end of a month.there is a transition

An hour to find the hostel as the Chinese people understand one word of all the words we ask = hostel. They point us in different directions as I feel we must follow our inner guidance. Mine is absent full-time when it comes to directions. I just want to feel my Spirit Guide's whisper in my ear. *On to the gigantic prayer wheel.*

We find Kevin - the owner of Trekker's Inn - by synchronicity in a cute Tibetan-style cafe. He says he only has room for 2 people in the dormitory. I feel guilty to go with him even though I know

I must follow what is the right for me = my heart. The French man says I should go and not worry about them.

Big white chorten. I still have no cash on me as Kevin's wife, Becky, checks me in. There are three beds in my dorm and the closest one to the window bears a cowboy hat. Shelves are full of Buddhist books and icons. *Hmm I don't know about the cowboy hat.* Everything else works.

*...it begins with a flicker of magic...a hint or a spark of love once found and lost...*I drop my clothes to the floor, wrap myself in a towel and run to the shower.

Out the shower, into my dorm, brush my hair.

- Oops! I am sorry!
- That's okay...

He is mine. This is destiny.

I jump under a blanket and fall asleep. I picked the bed closest to the other end of the room to keep my distance. There is another twin bed between our beds.

- Knock, knock...

I hear him in my sleep.

I get up to meet the gang at 7 at the cafe in old town. I walk to the closest Bank of China to find the doors closed. Maybe I can exchange money with the Dutch couple. I walk back to the hostel and hear the hottie walking behind me, whistling to himself. I continue walking fast. Not now. I want him to be distant. Maybe inaccessible. I will feel when the time is right to introduce myself. I open the gate to the hostel and two huge dogs jump barking at me.

- Yeah, they are friendly...! - says the hottie.
- Oh, hey!..- I say as I notice he ducks his head down.

I run to the cafe to meet the French guy and Mike. I order a carrot cream soup as the French guy has offered to lend me additional money. Mike is stressing out as he has loaned the Dutch couple over 300 dollars in yuan.

- Hey, there they are! - I shout as I see them walking towards the cafe.

Mike is relieved. They tell us they found out the cafe was shit, so they went to a cafe with the same name but 5 minutes walk from here b/c it is a lot nicer. They tried calling this cafe to find us to tell us where they were but to no avail.

We walk to the other cafe past the Tibetan dance at the main square. The French guy grabs my hand as we follow the dance moves.

We walk to Noah's Cafe and I order a glass of red wine all the while looking out the window. I introspect. I like to feel like I am on my way with someone. Connect their spirit to mine. I want to think about him. Another glass of wine. Walk back to the hostel freezing my ass off. I get to our dorm room to find he is not there. I go the TV room.

- Hey!
- Hey, what's up?

My God. So hot.

- Where are you from?
- Moscow.
- What is your name?
- Djana.
- I am Andrew.

He must be over 30.

- How old are you?
- 27.

He sits up as we make eye contact in the light. I like his smile, too. I love his eyes. He looks like he is warm in his sleeping bag. *You're welcome to jump into my sleeping bag.*

- Are you cold?
- Yes, very. I have no warm clothes. This looks like a comfortable sleeping bag.
- Uhm-uhm.
- ......
- Did you just come from the Tiger Leaping Gorge?
- Yes. It was amazing.
- I know...I did it two weeks ago and I loved it. I saw you take a nap earlier. That was sweet! I liked that. Come back from a trek, relax and sleep...
- I feel better now. My friends and I just had some dinner, too. I will introduce you to them, if you like, we can go to eat tomorrow or something.
- I'd love to!
- We just went for a dance on the square.
- I know...I was watching you.

- Where are you from?
- California. San Jose.
- I was in San Francisco for New Year's.
- I am doing a by-correspondence course majoring in Tibetan studies. I came to China from laos. The yak cheese I bought the other day from a Tibetan lady gave me bad gas and I am just recovering now. You are lucky, otherwise you would have been suffocating.
- ...
- So how long have you been traveling?
- Almost a year.
- Did you rob a bank for this or something?
- Or something. What are you watching?
- *12 Monkeys*. Quentin Tarantino. It is really good.
- I am scared to watch it. It's not really my cup of tea.
- You should use some Internet if you want...I have over 20 hours paid for.
- I might add my newly made friends.
- Go on, do your facebook.

I log in to see 20 messages in the last 4 days which makes me feel loved. My Cambodia pics are still in my XD card which still refuses to work. It's been in a coma for a month now. The camera...not the card. The room smells of sulphur and it grosses me out. I stand up, walk out the computer room to our dorm and lay in my bed.

- Hey Miss Djana...
- Hey.
- How are you?
- Tired.
- Hey it's been a while since I had a fun, bubbly conversation with someone. What do you do at home?
- I work as a translator.

- Do you have any aspirations to become anything? Not that working as a translator is insufficient.

I am going to publish a book about the soul's journey, become famous for my psychic transcendental art and continue working as an energy therapist.

- No.
- What brought you here?
- Heartache.
- How long has it been?
- Almost two years.
- How long were you together for?
- We hanged out for two weeks.
- Who is the guy?
- American.
- Okay?
- You remind me of him. He liked trekking. The outdoors.
- So what happened? - as he gets comfortable in his bed.
- I....he....he wasn't ready...I was in love...he wasn't...I was psychically connected to him.
- That is some trippy stuff!
- ...
- Do you stay in touch now?
- No...I stopped e-mailing him. I went to travel. Then in Thailand the memory came over me and I wrote to him.
- Did he respond?
- No.
- How long ago was this?
- Four months. He had nothing to say. After all this time.
- I know how you feel. I have a girl at home..
- What happened?
- We couldn't be together anymore...she was younger and a girl her age should be living her own life, having friends and going to college.

- ...
- We haven't spoken recently.
- Like us. He has nothing to say.
- You wont say his name?
- No.
- I have a lot to say.
- Is that why you don't write?
- This is a woman who really loves me and I have been waiting my entire life for someone to love me. I have been broken-hearted before. But I got jealous a lot...
- Where do you think it comes from?
- The need for love.
- You are so...smart.
- Well the only reason you think I am smart is because you are smart.

I really want you now.
- How do you deal with intimacy while you're traveling?
- I don't.
- ...if you want to cuddle...just lay here with me.
- I am scared, okay!
- I am sorry. I should have felt it at some point.

We fall asleep.

In the morning I see him do tai-ji in the front yard.
He waves *hello*.
We smile at each other. Reality stops. It is time.
He cooks boiled vegetable matter and feeds me.
On to a park nearby as he buys boiled eggs and bread.
Across the road to a dumpling place. He gets a plateful of *carne* dumplings for 8 yuan. I am afraid to even ask *que carne*.
In China it could be roadkill.
- Which monastery did you study in?
- Kopan.

- You're kidding!
- No.
- Wow. One of my tutors recommended I go there for study and research.
- You should, it is a good place.
- Where was the guy from?
- New Jersey.
- And so...have you guys...
- No...we haven't. We met in a monastery.
- That's a very important detail!
- What do you think that's like?
- VERY hard to have good sex!
- That's ALL you ever think about!
- No...but if I am attracted to someone and they are attracted to me...

...as I walk past the dumpling shop through the cobbled streets of the old town of Zhongdian
on to the gigantic gold-encrusted prayer wheel, here I am...here we are...

located in time, yet there is no present moment.

I walk to the temple and sit down to listen to pujas. A treasure vase, one of the 8 auspicious symbols. They are commonly placed upon altars and on mountain passes, or buried at water springs, where their presence is believed to attract wealth and bring harmony to the environment. It represents the spiritual abundance of the Buddha, a treasure that did not diminish, however much of it he gave away.

I start walking back to the inn and see the Dutch couple trying to get a ride to visit Tibetan villages. There comes Andrew.

I introduce them and Andrew says we can go trekking from behind Kevin's Inn, which will lead us to one of the villages. The couple must think there is so much chemistry between us...we look good together...and with a slight trench of hypocrisy, they ask me, *do I like him.*

-   Yes...of course we really like each other.

As we walk out and past the cemetery behind the inn, the Dutch man points to the snow-capped mountains to the East: they are sky burial sites - corpses of lamas dismembered and left atop a mountain for vultures to feast on. It is considered great honor. Past the houses of poor Tibetans, catch a ride back to town, have milk tea and split to meet for dinner at Noah's Cafe with the French guy and Mike as they are staying at International Youth Hostel down the road.

Andrew invites me to meet the Skalsky's - originally from Seattle, living in Shangri-La for 15 years now. Amos and Josiah are two sons of the dad. They run a trekking-supply and travel cafe: Turtle Mountain Gear. When he first started the place, it was a shack. He did all the work to make it look proper.

-   Young lady from Moscow, why is your English so good?

Ever since I was young, Spirit spoke English to me.

-   My family lived abroad. I went to an English school.
-   Oh, ok. Have you guys been smokin'?
-   No...
-   Amos, put some music on, will ya?

I open a skydiving magazine and flip through. It makes me uncomfortable to be here with someone who does not acknowledge my presence: Andrew. He sits with his back upright, posing, as if he is king. I slouch. This man is trying to show that he is very confident and doesn't need anyone to remind him thereof. I am barely in the conversation. I feel sick and want to leave.

- Have you already felt how the Chinese government controls your e-mails?
- Yes. Some of mine never went through.
- Whenever you mention any provocative words like Tibet, it is censored.
- Guys...I don't feel so well. I am going to go to the hotel.
- Are you okay?
- I am just...tired...and cold.
- I am so sorry.
- It is okay, I will see you later.
- Bye! Come back! - I hear the dad.

I cuddle in bed. Andrew comes around and asks me how am I feeling, runs his fingers through my hair and asks me if I want to make out. He says he thinks I am pretty and have beautiful eyes (translation: I am really horny). I am horny too. "Yes, I want to make out."
We lock lips in a kiss.
- Hey...it is already past 7. We got a meet up to go to.
We rush to meet the gang at Noah's Cafe for a glass of wine and head to Andrew's fav place as he orders 5 plates of boiled meat dumplings and 2 plates of fried dumplings. Everyone is excited and in twenty minutes 7 plates are down people's throats into their digestive tracts, their guts, the bile starts covering the chewed bits of cows, goats, dogs, cats...
After small talking and unsuccessfully planning to do something together the next day, Mike hugs me goodbye and the French guy kisses me on the left cheek and on the right cheek. Andrew and I walk together as I put his arm around me. I feel very thin and healthy: glad I did not eat...otherwise I would smell like Chinese spice and all that cow, goat, dog............
just like Andrew. I can taste it from his lips and I don't like the way he kisses. But how am I going to tell him?

If you like the way a man kisses you, you will like the way he fucks you.[26]

We cuddle as he undresses me. He takes off my sweater, my shirt...sucks on my nipples (hate it).....runs his hands on my nipples (love it)...gentle strokes....sometimes hard....*a man should only enter a woman when he has aroused her so much that she cries of arousal*[27]....he runs his hands down my stomach (love it 2x).....and gently kisses me below my belly button (love it 4x)....he really wants to stick his fingers inside my juicy vagina but I don't let him. He hasn't washed his hands...and he has a wart-looking like thing on his middle finger. He asks me if I have herpes that I don't let him play with me. Why does he think it is about me? I am so shy and so careful of not hurting his feelings to tell him he has a wart and I don't want him rubbing against me? It is my health. As he kisses my body I get so hot and wet I try fighting him off but he manages to take off my panties, tickling my clitoris and rubbing inside. He is using his other, right hand. Thank goodness.

-    Djana, what do you like?

You're gonna have to find out...

I am truly opening

wide open

....hands on my thighs, my stomach, my back...

I moan loudly.....slip on a condom as I open my legs wide and I feel him going inside me

.....yes...slowly....yeah

....his big cock slides in and out of my vagina and I feel so good.

....in the dark of the room...with a street light shining on his forehead I imagine he has curly hair...more chest hair...

---

[26] A misconception I heard somewhere.

[27] Kama Sutra

....until I feel a coming to an end
almost about to explode, and then it happens..

...s*o that's what it feels like.*
I orgasm with a guy for the first time.

...I sneak into his bed and start kissing him as I press my body against his. He gets excited, aroused. I want him. He slips on a condom and I want to be on top but he gently lays me down and goes inside me as I sign and we both move up and down as I smile at him...we are making love in the morning. He stops himself after I come, grabs my towel and jumps into the shower while I get my green tea. He will be studying all day and I will be visiting the Ganden Sungtseling Gompa. It is 300 years old. It was destroyed during the Cultural Revolution and completely rebuilt. It is situated 5 km from the city on an isolated ridge known as the Guardian Hill, to which I catch a bus. As I make my way through the main gate I feel I am back home. The white-washed walls, the crimson decorated window-frames and monks spinning prayer wheels. I walk around and take pictures. Yes...my camera is working again.

The walls of this Tibetan monastery are decorated with murals of parasols - one of the 8 auspicious symbols. The Sanskrit term 'chattra' is a reference to its shape. The parasol or umbrella is a traditional symbol of protection and royalty. The ability to protect oneself against inclement weather is a status symbol. The coolness of the shade of the parasol symbolizes protection from suffering, desire, and other spiritually harmful forces...and my favorite has always been the endless knot. Like the endless channel of energy within a group of souls...

...and love in its pure form. Kindness is a daily form of love. But love goes beyond kindness...

All the great spiritual traditions of the world teach that love is the essence of all things and that creation arises from love and is sustained by love. People who have had mystical experiences say the same thing, as they describe their individual self feeling the indescribable bliss of the creative, sustaining love. Ever afterwards their lives are changed by this glimpse into ultimate reality. Many people who are resuscitated from clinical death speak of the same thing, and once again the experience can be life-changing.

Love of this kind is very much more than romantic love: a unifying, life-enhancing love, which embraces all that is and subsumes time and space and all that ever was and ever will be.

Kindness is an expression of love in daily life, but love goes far beyond kindness. The experience can unify all opposites, reconcile all differences and end all strife and suffering.
Mystics say that in the experience of this kind of love all mysteries are revealed, including the mysteries of life and death and the mystery of our own being.

I imagined everything. When I had the chance, the loophole to find out about destinies and reach the Ultimate mystery of our being...the Guardians of Buddhism blessed me with that opportunity.

Destiny is like a river: if you keep resisting your destiny you will always be swimming upstream. If you give in to your destiny, the river will carry you.

Find out what your destiny is.

Buddhists believe in precious human lives. You could have been born a bug, had you had that bad karma. But to be born as human, is already significant of good karma. Thus...this precious human life.

Once you see the future, it changes. Because you have seen it.[28]

I return to the city as I see him going into our favorite cafe. I get off the bus and step inside as he says hi to me and continues talking to another chick. I get absolutely furious but say nothing. I stay in the cafe for a little bit...and walk out. I did not think it would be over THIS quick. It sucks. It is unfortunate. Why are all guys the same. Once they fuck you, they lose interest in you.

- Djana, hey!

He is walking right after me.

- I assume...right now...you are feeling something close to jealousy...??
- You assume correct.

I continue walking. He stands still for two minutes and leaves. I walk down the street to get some wine for dinner and return to Kevin Trekker's to find him sitting on the porch, waiting. I did not think he would be.

- I am glad you did not go far away.
- Well...I am here.

I walk into our dorm. He follows me.

- Djana...listen...can we talk?
- Okay. Talk.
- Look, let me explain myself. It is funny that you think I like that girl because frankly all she does to me is annoy me. I talked to her as I met her in Lijiang and she happened to be at the cafe. When you saw me - I just got to the cafe. I bet you thought I arranged to meet with her and had been hanging out with her for the day. I did not introduce you because she was not important. All I really wanted to say was, *Djana, I am really excited to see you.*

---

[28] Nicholas Cage, *Next*

I know how you feel - I have been there. I am probably the most jealous person ever.

I smile at him in relief.

- So are we okay now?
- Okay, - as I smile and move closer, - thank you.

He holds me in his arms.

- Let's go eat dinner with Kevin and Becky.

Kevin is a die-hard traveler and trekker from Kunming and he is building a bar downstairs. He always wears protective gear and super-warm boots and jacket. His wife, Becky, cooks a vegetarian meal for us as we hungrily finish it.

Andrew tells me we have to be quiet if we want to get it on...as I had been so loud the night before. I step out in my beautiful white robe I got custom-made in Vietnam as he jumps into my bed. We kiss...as I caress his body, he lays on his stomach as I lay on top of him, kiss his neck, run my hands down his back...I want to ride him...as he lays on his back and I get on top...and rub the diamonds between my thighs against the family jewels between his...he slips on a condom and goes inside me as I sign...deeper...and deeper...with my legs squeezing his hips....his back....he puts me down and puts my legs up and hits the spot...as I feel I am about to explode...he stops...and then starts again, having spread my legs wider...as he goes in and out of me...I feel it again...inevitability...the point of no-return...the energy building up...ready to release...as I feel my thin muscles contract.....

I come.

That's so cool.

In the morning I start kissing him again as he lets me make out for 5 minutes and when I reach for his cock he tells me he wants to do tai ji. He says he can't make love every morning. I continue playing with him. I get him hard...aroused...wet...and tell him to go do tai ji. He jumps out of bed and disappears out the dorm.

I drink three cups of green tea after my morning stretching by the chorten. I will be hanging out alone as Andrew has to work on his study...again. He says we will hang out "soon"...right after he is finished with the paper he is working on.

I kiss him. He gets hot. I get wet. I jump on him, he holds me against the wall, presses his cock against me. I moan loudly as he covers my mouth so that the little girl in the neighboring room does not hear us.

I love your sex drive.

- What do you like best?

To come.

He lays me on the bed and asks me if I am wet enough for him to go inside me. I put my hand in my panties...yes I am wet...and hot...and right here...so get your cock out and slide a condom on...and go inside me and move inside me...as he moves inside me...I sign...it feels so good...yes....fucking all day long...it is what I want...yes...oh!

- You're so close...aren't you?

- Yes, yes!

I come.

He stops, gets up and gets dressed.

Don't you want to come?

- No. I feel loss of energy when I do. Now, it is circulating in my system. For a man, it is loss of vital force, when for a woman, you gain the force when you come.

Gain the force.

What a blessing!

Actually three blessings today, and it is only noon.

Andrew told me that his parents were farmers. They were both working in greenhouses and his mother told him the story of meeting his father: they each had a small plot to work on and they were both moving towards the center of the same bed - as their eyes met and his mother knew this was gonna be serious. So she did not speak to him for a few years until they met again, engaged in an affair, got married and had their only child. My interest right now is purely carnal...and my intentions are indecent...as I have come so far away to find someone who would spring this from within me...and having had an orgasm with a man for the first time...one goal for this trip>accomplished.

...I wake up to find a note from him telling me he went to meet up with a professor for his research on soil and agriculture.

I grab a DVD and a thermos of green tea. Andrew returns happy and excited. He kisses me, sits down with me and puts his arm around me. I feel like a girlfriend.

- What are you watching?
- *The Bourne Supremacy.*
- Yes!!
- By the way, the building Jason walks in front of in the twilight after talking to the girl whose parents he murdered....is the building I live in.
- No way!

Way.

We fall asleep in each other's arms after another session of hot sex as he tells me he feels so healthy after we have been having so much sex. Me too...me too.

I wake up to go jogging and stretching in the morning. I watch the gigantic prayer wheel spin in the wind. *How many mornings do we have left?* I return to the inn and find him cooking breakfast. He offers me tsampa - a roasted barley meal - bought from Tibetan ladies in the city. He is eating yak meat - he says he wants to take in the power of the yak. I sit down with him and he

asks me how long has it been since I had sex. *Six months.*
"Wow." I tell him I love sex games as they are exciting. They are
good for people...and everyone has control issues. Isn't this true.
I hate being bossed around in daily life - but when it comes to
sex...I enjoy being controlled...he could tie me up...blindfold
me...bondage-discipline-dominate-submit...tie my hands behind
my back....tie my hands to the bed rail...and go down on
me...open my legs and hold them open when I try to shut
them.....................

- Can I ask you a favor?
- As long as it is not eating yak meat.
- Haha. No. Can you not make out with me in front of
  Kevin and Becky?
- Why not?
- This is a very conservative country. I don't like them to
  think that I --
- I know what this is about and I take it very personally.
- Please don't.
- It's like...I am not good enough for you.
- It is not true...and you being affectionate of me in public
  means they think that all foreigners are easy and just
  have sex everywhere and have no morals--
- Why should I let their morals bother me when I am with
  someone I really like?
- Just please...I don't want them to think that I--
- ...that you have a different girl every night?
- It is not true.
- Sounds to me like it is...if you are so protective of it.
- I am not. I am enjoying you.
- I would think they would be happy for us.

He leaves to go upstairs and comes back down. I ask him what's
up. He says he has work to do. I feel like shit. He doesn't want to
hang out with me. He also tells me he will be leaving for Deqin

after tomorrow - alone. I ask him if I can come with him. He says no. I feel worse than feeling like shit.

I walk out the inn and feel the tremendous urge to eat so I go to have dumplings. Or not. I shall resist and have a box of Oreos instead. I walk past the Public Security Office where people extend their visas, and further down to an orphanage with two dogs barking their asses off at me. I quietly leave to sneak into a thangka painting school: foreigners can take classes.

I walk back to Old Town and into the Stupa Book Cafe, the Potala Cafe and on to an Internet cafe next to Old Town Youth Hostel. I check my facebook and nobody is ever writing to me...I try to find a reason or meaning for this behavior of his. It is all energy. And I have given him mine...was it when I came?

I should have told him I came with a guy for the first time.

But then he would feel special. As if a man who deflowers a girl does. And his ego would need even more nourishment. Arrrggh. I trek up following the vision of the chorten and sit down to listen to pujas: hoping the pain of rejection goes away. I wonder if I am making it up or is this really happening and he is letting me go. I have my mind blessed by a monk. I sit at the temple's doorstep hoping they would invite me to sleep over so Andrew would start to worry where I am and what I do. Why am I not back? What am I doing? Has what he said hurt me?

I go to eat the goddamn dumplings, feel bloated without a hint of energy as my body is recklessly trying to break down the damn cow, cat, dog, whatever. I return to the cafe I went to with Mike and the French guy - and have a broccoli cream soup. Does not help. I return to the inn and find Andrew upstairs and give him an apple a monk gave me. He thanks me and appreciates the Amazonian dreamcatcher-earring I am wearing.

I leave the kitchen and lie down in my bed, as he comes in and touches my hair as I get horny and wet again. I tell him about the orphanage, the thangka painting school, the temple, the monks and the pujas...when a man knows you're busy doing your own thing...he will know you don't need him to be happy or self-sufficient. He says I must be ovulating if I am so horny. If I get aroused quickly. Gosh. Then I am ovulating 30-days a month. Gimme a break. A healthy sexual drive is a good trait...and a *healthy* trait. Keeps you from eating dumplings. saves lives of thousands of cows, cats, dogs, and in this country...yaks.

The poor cute yaks.

I get up, brush my teeth and do my morning exercise. Andrew finds me in the kitchen and asks me if I want to go on an adventure. Yes! He is coming back to me. We **will** be together.

Tashi Delek! People greet us. They seem to greet him more than they greet me. He says it is because he puts out a friendlier vibe. Friendlier *vibe*?

Everyone just says hi to the man, not the woman, when two walk together. It is politeness in this...conservative country.

-   You have made my stay in Shangri-La, you know.
-   Yes! And you have made mine! Thank you so much!
-   Thank *you*.
-   Honestly...I have been hoping and praying to have a romance in Shangri-La...and it just wouldn't happen and I was wondering how can it be, I am open, I am not bad looking, so what is going on?! And then you showed up at my doorstep!
-   I wished to meet a man that I would have an emotional, mental and sexual connection.
-   Do you believe in miracles?
-   Yes.
-   I believe in miracles too. I span the prayer wheel and sent out a wish.
-   Me too. It is magical, you know...

But now you will leave me.
- I will be going tomorrow to Deqin. I want to go alone.
- Why do you rush to end this?
- I become very resentful of the person who keeps me from what I want to do in the first place.
- I know what you mean.

...men leave when they got what they wanted. Qi.
- I wonder if you are going to feel that way about me.
- I already have.
- I am sorry about that.
- It's like...you knew there was going to be a moment when you would give in to hurt me or resist hurting me. Be the first to leave!
- I don't know what you mean...
- I mean you waited long enough to take the energy from me and then when I opened up to you...you announce you want to be on your way.
- No...I was staying in Shangri-La because I was having all the course work to do.

I take a photo of him with the mountains in the background.
- How many times have you been in love?

Hard question. Many times over.
- Perhaps...twice. You?
- Maybe seven. Unrequited. You know...the more I think about love...the more I realize that we fall in love because of timing. If the time is right...you fall in love with the person you're with. If you are ready for love.

When is it going to be the right time for me to love.
- I think it is funny when people confuse love with ego. Love and co-dependence. People say I have a broken heart, when in truth, they have a bruised ego.
- Listen, you are young, beautiful and I have no doubt that very soon...you will find the man you want and need.

173

As we walk the last 200 meters before the monastery I see small prayer wheels for sale. Should I buy some of these for home? I always wanted one. The vendors have really tiny ones for only 10 kwai each. I pass. I need to pee. Andrew tells me to go in the bushes as it is unhealthy to hold it. STOP trying to make me feel worse about you leaving and letting me go.

Just...don't care.

Andrew looks in awe at the depiction of one of the 8 auspicious symbols of the Victory Banner - a sign of victory, an emblem of the Buddha's enlightenment, heralding the triumph of knowledge over ignorance. It is said to have been placed on the summit of Mt. Meru by Buddha himself, symbolizing his victory over the entire universe. We spin a prayer wheel.

He thanks me for bringing him here.

We walk back to the city and drop in for dinner.

- Isn't this the life! Traveling to beautiful places, meeting great people, eating great food!
- I love it too!
- And so do I. I love it that you care about what you eat.
- I love that about you too. That's neat.
- ...and I wonder how likely am I to meet someone like you.
- I think...your chances are high...if you are open to it.

We walk to the inn to find someone's stuff on the third bed and on Andrew's bed. Someone will have to sleep on the floor tonight. Andrew tells Becky he will volunteer his bed and sleep in the TV room in his sleeping bag. Becky refuses his offer and tells him she will give him one of the single rooms. Andrew gets excited, taps me on the head and runs out the dorm. He returns and tells me his great plan: we can make love all night in his room.

- What makes you so sure?

Tonight I will sleep alone.

I go to the TV room as he sits down to watch *Twelve Monkeys*. I ask him if we can talk. He says he is enjoying the movie. *Asshole*. He can't make time for me now? He pauses the movie.

He says he doesn't understand my aggravation over this and asks me if I felt better had he told me he is leaving from the very start.

- For sure!
- This is horrible. It will be a while before I have a fling again.

He says I should e-mail him sometime but he wont be able to go online for a few days since he is going to be hiking. He writes his e-mail address in my red notebook. He also says he is really into the movie and if we are finished with this conversation and turns it back on.

* * *

I love the cold air in the morning is so refreshing. It will be over once I go to the South-East. breathe. relax. Easy.

I shower and throw my jeans on. I clip my hair up and wear my white circle earrings. I go to the TV room to make a call to reserve my bed at Mama Naxi's. I miss her food.

- Hey, Miss Djana!
- Hey!

I run up to him and hold him tight.

I hate letting you go. Can't you love me.

- You are very beautiful today.

Why the fuck are you so happy leaving then?

- Still not good enough for you!
- That's not true.

I wipe the tears away from my face.

- Wait, I got something for you.

I grab the khata I was given by a monk two nights before - and bless his mind for protection to be safe when he is walking in the mountains. He is touched. He tells me that I am very beautiful today. I hate letting him go and if love is not now...then when is it?..

- Andrew!

I wave goodbye as I stand at the gate. He sends me his heart as he gestures around it and disappears on the horizon.

I run to the ticket counter but there are no seats for "Supreme Bliss" Deqin. I grab a ticket to Lijiang, clear away the doubts and feel no pain, no gain, no fear...no thing.

The reason to go back is Mama Naxi and her famous delicious buffet dinner for 20 yuan.

I am contemplating on going to Dali again.

I am overlapping my travel plans...I wanted to travel the Yantze river...on a cruise...from Wuhan to Shanghai...but it means going to Chengdu which I hear is a great city...beautiful city...

Full of pandas....

...pandas?...

in China...?

....China is the LAND of pandas.

You don't know of the sacrifices you have to make when you are living out balancing between realms of empath energy.

Yes pandas. The photos I used to flip through from J's profile were from Chengdu. One year ago it suffered an earthquake. Now I get it. After Lhasa, he must have traveled to Golmud - the last stop on the railroad and then on to Chengdu...and then he started making his way back into South-East Asia.

It seems pieces of the puzzle are coming together the more I find out.

I leave for Dali as the bus ride takes four exhausting hours. I think: after this journey I do not want to travel anymore. I am old enough now to know that whenever a place calls for me it means I have karma with it. I have people to meet that I have karma with. I refuse to follow that call...

...when the truth is...there *is* no call.

If there was one...I would not have heard it.

This is what drives me most about our reality and the big conspiracy *behind* our existence....we strive to *find* balance....we seek the way out of duality into oneness...but the truth is...it will never happen.

...because if it does, our reality will cease to exist....[29]

...so we spiral through the wheel of samsara....a guinea pig in a wheel in a cage. That's what we look like when we try escaping the pull of our program that keeps the system working.

I arrive to Dali at Jade Emu hostel and browse the book exchange shelves. I pick up a self-help mind-mapping life-planning book and "Why Men Marry Bitches." I make a reservation at *The Humps* in Kunming. The book has the truths of men...and the falses of women. According to this one, men like independent women who do for themselves, stand up for what they believe for, push their limits beyond their comfort zones and generally...have high testosterone levels.

Well in that case

I AM THE MAN I WANT TO BE WITH!

I book a ticket for K394 train to Guilin, reserve a bed at Monkey Jane's, grab my bags and catch a bus to the train station. I wave Kunming goodbye and make myself comfortable in the sleeping car. I got a second-class ticket instead of the normal 3rd class and the ride is costing me 375 kwai.

I lie down and listen to my mind as I have been traveling without an i-pod for the last 6 months.

---

[29] Truth

Sally picks me up from the bus station at Yangshuo.

Some things just are. Whether you believe in them or not. [30]

Monkey Jane's is famous for the rooftop bar as hostel guests enjoy beers during happy hour at 10 kwai per bottle.

Cute town. Main avenue of Xi Jie: cafes, bars, shops, souvenirs, earrings and bracelets, all for a bargain price of 10 yuan. Especially special are the Chinese scrolls as the main topic in Chinese art goes to landscape. High-up-in-the-clouds mountains create a vertical, a river or lake - a horizontal. Sometimes, tiny figurines are present. The depiction is flat, deprived of central perspective or depth.

The vendor explains to me, that Chinese artists often depict animals, especially horses, birds and other animals which have symbolic meaning, for example, tortoises, herons and cicadas. In the flower compositions, on the first place shown are the "four noble ones": orchideas, plum flower, chrysanthema and bamboo, which repersents the seasons. Depiction of people - commonly portraits of famous people, or an archetype, like a hermit or a monk. Chinese masters often created simply for themselves, if we are talking about clerks, art was delight of the eye and soul, or, being craftsmen, they aimed to create something new and wonderful. The peak of perfection was however, jade cutting, rock and ivory cutting, as well as calligraphy on rice grains.

I bargain for the scroll from 50 to 10 yuan.

Further down on the main avenue to the Li river: the mind-bending landscapes which occurred as a result of long-term erosion of shelly limestone. Over 300 million years ago these spaces were filled with water. Water has pulled back, leaving limestone residue, and hills formed, underground rivers and caves. Each karst rock has a cave with stalactites and

---

[30] Truth II

stalagmites. Many painters and poets drew inspiration in this region. Cinnamon trees abundant in the area provide factories with raw material for perfumes, essences and treatment balm.

Calligraphy classes are available around the corner as it is also linked with Dao De Jing, Calligraphy (from Greek: "beautiful writing") is is not only a skill to write beautifully, but a special genre of art, allowing the master to fully express his individuality with the frames of tradition.

The "Four Treasures of the Workshop" are used: paper, brush, ink and pumice. Ink in form of sticks is broken down by pumice in a bowl and is dissolved with water. The density is determined by the intensity of the tones - from light-grey to dense-black, the main color of calligraphy. Paper easily absorbs the ink, transferring the smallest hues of color, the kind of stroke, etc. Each touch of a brush creates a drawing, which, in contrast to European art, cannot be changed or corrected. The same applies to hieroglyphs. The idea must be fully ripe in the head of the artist, before he takes the brush.

Calligraphy and art are strongly interlinked as both are based on the same principles and often complement each other. Hieroglyphs strongly remind us of a drawing, whereas paintings mostly house poems and other writing. Traditional painting forms a scroll, up to several meters long, which is opened, and then scrolled back into a tube.

A dream among karsts: gigantic bamboo sticks fluttering in the wind. Fishermen chop and make rafts.
Buffalos, dipping their gigantic horns into the river. Drinking clear water....and this dream becomes a reality.
We are navigating the Li river.

I stretch to the sky as I feel the Angels looking over me. Feel light as rain as I walk back to the hostel past a travel agent selling bus tickets to Macau, Hong Kong and Guangzhou. Both Guangzhou and Macau are little visited by tourists and are definitely out of the backpacker trail. There is one hostel on Shamian Island in Guangzhou but it cannot be booked online so I call them to ask the prices. They tell me a dorm bed will cost 150 yuan per night due to the Trade Fair week.

I also try and get hold of the Immigration Office to make sure I can get a visa on arrival for Macau. According to a travel webpage a visa costing 100 yuan is issued at the border. I can't reach a representative so I listen to their answering machine...in Portuguese! I might have a chance to speak some I still remember from Brazil, as Macau used to be a Portuguese colony.

I surf into a Lodge in the center of Macau for a reasonable 10 dollars per night. Geographically it is a peninsula with two small islands, Taipa and Coloane.

As I picture myself standing on the tip of the bungy ready to jump down, let go and release my fears and doubts

It's just once...and what is 4 seconds in a lifetime?

Bike rental shop. Maarti from Finland and Lourens from the Netherlands. Only eating green tea. Everyone gets deep fried greasy food my stomach cannot digest. Michael hands me a piece of the deep fried thing so I can bite from his hands. I tell him no thanks but he insists. I tell him, does he know what it's gonna do to their stomachs? It would swell them up and make them curl. I take a bite, chew it and then for my own good...spit it out on the street and run to get some water to brush my teeth. Michael smiles at me.

Maarti tells me that Fubo-Shan ("Wave-breaking mountain") goes back to a legend where during the Han epoch, an army leader was sharpening his sword on a mountain, which had such strong power, that all enemies ran off in terror.

According to another legend, once upon a time, in the "Cave of the Returned Pearl" grotto a dragon kept his pearls. A fisherman found it and stole it. But when he found out who it belonged to, he returned it.

Michael introduces me to a French girl Marie whom he met on the Trans-Siberian train, continued to travel together and currently shares a double room with. I don't know how she manages to not sleep with him...because if I was sleeping in the same room with this man...I would be jumping him the first night. There's something irresistible about him. He seems very shy and polite...but a man that hot...wearing white slacks and a white shirt with *Rich and Famous* embroidered in crystals.

As we ride bikes through the gorgeous karst scenery, Marie tells me about trying to get a job as an English teacher and that her relationships have been nothing but a control issue. She does not like someone liking her: it turns her on when someone does *not* like her. "Which is perhaps the reason I've never *had* sex!"

Maarti is going to Hainan Island next: definitely off the beaten path. Michael is going to Macau right after this to do the World's Highest Bungy. He entered China about the same day as I did and needs to leave to have his visa cancelled. I tell him I am going to Macau to do the World's Highest Bungy and we should hang out when we are there.

If you want to find metaphysical friends, you will find them doing exactly what you are doing.[31]

We return to the city and eat at a *cheap* place hidden in one of the narrow streets off the main drag. I spill food all over my white dress. We return to the rooftop bar to smoke, get high and happy in good company. I blow into Marie's mouth as we kiss as the boys watch us, loving it. *Someone's immense attention and interest.* But this man is too hot for me to handle...he will be too distracted by too many girls to just focus on one.

The next morning I book my ticket for Guangzhou and have breakfast alone. I meet the kids at the hostel - as they went out the night before. Michael says he might hop on the same bus as me...as it is always better to go *with* someone. Marie keeps the room to herself.

We eat a late lunch and get to know each other. He likes to spend on himself - he does not count money. Every time he eats he probably spends about 100 kwai - what! As I eat my fried rice at a restaurant in the center of the tourist district he eats a pizza with a beer. He tells me they came to this restaurant a few nights ago, had a blast, made friends with the waitress as she offers him beer on the house. Good job. He steals some rice from my plate and counts for the amount of beer I drank equals to the amount of rice he has taken from my plate. Cheap bastard. Rude and bad-mannered. He says it was rude of me to get my ticket without telling him as I knew he might be going as well. We

---

[31] A psychic from Brooklyn, NY.

smoke weed, drink beers, grab our bags and walk to the bus stop. I stay focused and keep myself centered and in control. I buy oreos, peanuts and banana chips for the bus ride.

Michael gives me one of his earphones to listen to All Saints tunes on his i-pod. He closes his eyes as he lays in his bed and the corners of his lips widen in a cute smile.

Our emotional bodies are talking

While closing your eyes, let ice-cream slips with water-mouthing moment. Feeling of silky touch as some cozy jazz,......[32]

A young Chinese guy taps me on the shoulder letting me know to get off the bus in the middle of a highway as apparently the bus is going PAST Guangzhou, not TO Guangzhou. We need to catch a cab to the hostel as the driver quotes 50 yuan and I bargain down to 20 which Michael pays for.

Money is nothing but energy.

As the sun starts to show on the horizon of the Pearl river the cab drops us off at the hostel. The lady behind the desk tells me they don't have my reservation and they are booked for the week. She offers us a double room for 600 kwai per night. I refuse, yelling, "No money!"

Michael asks me if I want him to do anything about it.

"No."

He says he will pay for the double room and I can just give him 150 kwai as I planned to spend. We make it a deal, check in, I go to shower as Michael puts a tune on...

Stranded in this spooky town...

Stoplights are swaying and the phone lines are down..

This floor is crackling cold...

She took my heart, I think she took my soul...

---

[32] Jinsong Foods Banana Chips Bag

Running shoes on as I love to run and feel muscle happiness. Power. Strength. I see a bunch of people on the main walk by the river doing tai ji. I watch the sun rising higher and higher. As I return to the hotel the music is still playing; I shower and doze off.

With the moon I run...

Far from the carnage of the fiery sun...

We get ready for exploration of the city and I figure if we catch a train to the bus station we can then hop on the bus to the border town of Zhuhai = and walk across the border to Macau.

Catch a subway to Renmin Park in the center of town and slowly wander through the city into the shopping mall of Beijing Lu. Michael is hungry for some roast duck as we stop at a siu laap joint (meats fried Cantonese style).

On to visit the Temple of the Six Banyan Trees.

I grab incense sticks and light them as my offering and pray **for the benefit of all sentient beings.**

I give Michael incense sticks so he can make an offering as well.

-    Am I really doing this?

-    Yes.

We walk out the Temple and I get a soy bean drink for 2 yuan. I give him a taste.

-    One for me, as well. - he asks the vendor.

We walk further on the main street and inside the small lu's to the Guangxiao Temple with a statue of the laughing Buddha.

On to the Temple of the Five Immortals. Michael pays my admission and I pay him the 5 yuan back. The temple is Daoist - according to the legend, right here, five goats each carrying a celestial being landed, each wearing a colorful robe and carrying a stem of rice in their palms - signifying the end of famine. Hence the nickname of Guang-Zhou (Fast-city): Goat City.

We return to the hotel and pop the cork of the wine I bought for 40 kwai. Michael rolls up a joint. He tells me about his decision to call his ex-girlfriend to come and join him in his travels. Michael tells me his ex-girlfriend choose a property he was against, as he is a realtor. She then had a girl who sub-rented a room in the house she was renting. I tell him about the sub-tenant in my apartment and start dressing up for a party. He is very easy...he just follows me.

We walk the boardwalk as he is checking me out. He buys me a drink at 2-4-6 bar. We are offered a game of dice by the bartenders. One who loses - drinks! Michael plays as my turn comes, I lose, drink and realize it had been sweetened bottled tea!

On to Babyface to be greeted by loud music and a bar of young Chinese people and old foreign suits. We dance for three hours until the alcohol is gone from our systems. We walk back on the river-front and stop for a kebab.

Driven by the strangled vein...
Showing no mercy I do it again...

As we get comfortable in our separate beds, Hhe puts on Kung Fu Panda on his ipod. A cartoon about a panda who likes Kung Fu whose father is a chicken who owns a noodle shop and wants him to take over the family business but the panda wants to do kung fu. I crack up and doze off.

The next morning we pack up and leave to the long-distance bus station, grab our tickets for Zhuhai, the rain starts pouring down, as we drive out of Guangzhou and I say goodbye...listening to my new favorite tune...

Open up your eyes...
You keep on crying, baby...
I'll bleed you dry...

186

Closer by Kings of Leon. It fits my dramatic mood and the setting of driving out of the amazing trade/import/export center of South East China.

As we get to Gongbei Port, we line up at the immigration to be stamped out. I am a nervous wreck as I wonder if for any reason I do not get a visa for Macau I will have to return to China the same day and this will cancel my existing visa for the second time and I wont be able to go to Macau and do the world's highest bungy jump...as I relax and hand my passport over to the girl behind the window.
She flips the pages and looks at my immigration form.
- Where is the visa?
- I didn't know I needed one.
She hands my passport over to an official and after 20 minutes of questions why am I going to Macau, how much money do I have and how long will I stay, they issue me a visa valid for 10 days for 100 yuan.
We catch a bus through the Portas de Cerco to go to Edificio Kamloi. The skies are blinking at me...
I see a storm bubbling up from the sea...

Little people know that Macau's Cantonese name is Ou-Mun meaning "gateway of the bay." According to the LP, there is a legend of a girl named A-Ma who was looking to get from Macau to Canton - nowadays Guangzhou - was turned away by wealthy smugglers and picked up by an old fisherman. A storm began and blew off the smugglers but left the small fisherman's boat untouched. After returning to the harbour A-Ma walked to the top of Barra Hill and ascended to heaven in a form of a white light. In her honor the fisherman has erected the A-Ma Temple. The name Macau comes from A-Ma Gau - literally "Bay of A-Ma."

We run to an ATM to get Hong Kong Dollars and Macau Patakas for payment. Less than little backpackers come to the Las Vegas of the East - and those who do, normally come on a day-trip by ferry from Hong Kong. I probably wont be able to go to Hong Kong after all - as my visa had not been arranged for.

Both Hong Kong and Macau are SARs: Special Administrative Regions which for a backpacker means two things: double-entry Chinese visa, and couchsurfing, if you're staying in Macau overnight, unless you plan to stay the night at a casino or pay 200 dollars a night in one of the casino hotels.

Tonight I will wear my red custom-made dress for the first time. I am excited as I neatly slip a pad into my panties as the last drops of the cleanest blood from my body is absorbed.

- Wow.
- How do I look?
- Very nice.

Michael put 3 shirts on my bed so I can pick one for him to wear. I pick a white long-sleeve shirt for him as he looks absolutely HOT.

We walk out the Lodge on to Avenida da Almeida Ribeiro to the Largo do Senado - the Main Square - and into Boa Messa restaurant.

We order a big jar of red house wine and smoke Marlboro Lights.

I go to the bathroom, tipsy. I look at myself in the mirror. I love how the eyes shine green and match the red dress. *I love you baby. I can't wait to be with you in the flesh. Soon I will be yours.* As I realize the beauty of already being here and being able to do what I do.

I love it. I love life.

I love the woman looking back at me.

I return to the table to find Michael watching ballroom dancing on TV. He has just paid the bill. I thank him as he smiles, we walk out the restaurant to explore the streets leading to Casino Lisboa and into the MGM Grand. We walk into the Casino area, the poker and roulette halls. Michael bets 500 HKD and wins back 1,000 HKD.

- You look stunning in your dress with all the fancy shit.
- :)
- I feel like Bon walking through the Casino with a hot chick.

The receptionist tells us to go to D2 club in the Admiral Hotel two blocks off of Avenida da Amizade. Archangel Michael and I walk hand in hand under our umbrella and into the club. He orders us Flaming Lamborghinis as I savor it and feel tipsy. We listen to music and the waiters cater to our needs as Michael orders a Long Island for himself and a Margarita for me, followed by three glasses of red wine....four glasses of beer....as the lights blind me...we are playing dice and he orders tubes.

...I've had a little bit too much...
All of the people start to rush.
Start to rush babe.
How does he twist the dance?
Can't find my drink or man.
Where are my keys, I lost my phone....

- Let's dance!

...What's go-ing out on the floor?
I love this record baby, but I can't see straight anymore.
Keep it cool what's the name of this club?
I can't remember but it's alright, alright...

A silk show begins as Russian acrobats performing in Cirque du Soleil at the Venetian are giving a cameo: amazing as I get to meet Dmitry - Star of the Show.

Michael and I spin in a crazy dance as we have been drinking so much and I love watching him in the flashing lights of the club...I love how hot he looks...as he moves to the rhythm of the night and smokes at the same time. He spins me around and moves closer...as I feel his boner.

Out of the club at 3 a.m. and back to the Lodge. I wake up feeling Michael's hand moving slowly down my pants as I slide away and giggle. I have a horrible hangover having drunk so much and not made myself sick the night before. I am allergic to alcohol...excuse me. I go to the bathroom and after resultless trials to vomit I empty myself from the other end, feel lighter, drink a liter of water, take a shower, change and return to bed. Michael asks me if I need him to come closer and comfort me. I tell him, "yes." But he just sits there. Something is stopping him.

Open up your eyes...you keep on crying baby I'll bleed you dry.

Mid-day. I feel worse than feeling like shit and I swear never to drink ever again. Michael brings me alkazelser.

We go to a sports bar on Avenida da Dr. Sun Yat Sen, Michael buys me a natural spring water as I sit down, relax and enjoy the atmosphere. He apologizes if his hands were going places they were not supposed to that morning. Back at the Lodge, we sleep in our separate beds.

The next morning he is on skype with his girlfriend getting a flight to Hong Kong in a week. The Philippine receptionist tells us we need to check out as they have no beds for tonight. Or we can sleep in the hallway on fold-out beds.

We go to the tourist information office and on to Avenida da Praia Grande to the Macau Tower. In my mind I am singing *Sleep With Me* by Pretty Ricky. It is my new favorite *r'n'b tune*.

The huge sign of AJ Hackett Adventure Sports looks at us. Along with the bungy jump, they have Skywalk X and Mastclimb.

The receptionists tell us they have all done it. They have 30 people jumping every day. Michael puts the charge on his credit card and disappears into the elevator.

The Macau Tower is also used to telecommunications and broadcasting, the height of it being 338 meters. I look out at Taipa island which is said to have a black-sand beach.

Michael comes back from his jump wearing a Macau Tower Bungy Jump shirt which matches his blue eyes and he looks plain hot. I jump on him with a hug.

He gets his free beer - which comes with the jump - and shows me framed photos of himself diving in. He says he let go of his fears. He thanks me for bringing him here.

I jump up and run to get *my* adrenaline and excitement. I pay the charge of 200 US dollars which includes a video of the jump, 2 photos in a frame and a certificate with my name on it. Nice accompaniment for Miami when I return...;)

As I take the glass elevator to the 61st floor panic takes over me as the buildings become smaller and smaller//the higher the elevator goes.

- Holy fucking shit! I can't believe I am doing this to myself! Not again!

My weight and height are checked. The camera starts rolling.
It is actually posted on
http://www.youtube.com/watch?v=XsG5syfNvWA
I paid 200 dollars for this so I better feel excitement, not fear.
Feel excitement!
Holla!!
I am fucking scared! And very excited!!
As my legs are tied together with a towel and my body strapped into a safety belt which makes sure I fall straight down and come back straight up, not go swinging around the tower - I face the

inevitable - the height as I see all of Macau - at my fingertips. *3, 2, 1 Go!*
Ohhh My God.....

Aaah...
As 4 seconds of free-fall are over...I swing up...and down again...and up...and down again...I am taken down and untied. I run to Michael as he claps his hands in my praise.
Like an Angel, falling from the sky!
I run to get my photos back to the 61st floor. *This is to certify that Djana Fahryeva officially has what it takes! World's Highest Bungy Macau Tower at 233 meters. Jumped on April 20, 2009.*
I run to get my free beer. It is hot as I feel tipsy and take off my top. Michael is watching me. *We should go swimming.* We catch a cab to the beach on Taipa across the bridge. As we drive away from the Macau Tower I wonder if maybe going to the beach is the right thing to do. *We end up snogging and making out in the water...*but I have just finished my period. Something else.
Race karts.
- Michael?
- Anything *you* want!
...as tipsy as can be on a mellow afternoon in Macau.
Michael says he is searching for somebody to inspire him. He wants to find someone who makes him feel good. He left home to find true love. He is calling his ex-girlfriend to come out and meet him in Hong Kong to see if they can travel together. If they can make it work in a different environment other than home in Nottingham. I think Robin Hood, I think the Prince of Thieves. I think Noble Knight and Lady Godiva.
Michael wins the race. I could not keep up with him. He is strong and I love how he can be calm and relaxed but determined

and stubborn at the same time. Nothing sexier than a balance of power...and vulnerability.

We relax after racing and catch a cab to go to Rua do Cunha past the Venetian Casino. We find a place to eat as Michael lets me order - rice, fried chicken, nuts and vegetables. I run into a souvenir shop and grab a postcard. He asks me if he has any vegetables in his teeth. *No*. He asks me if I want him to check my teeth for vegetables. *No*. I am embarrassed. He says there is nothing wrong with showing him my teeth. I hand him the postcard of the Macau Tower. He writes his home address and I put it into the mailbox. I think he finds it new and romantic. He gives me freedom. I do anything I want. He trusts my choices. He lets me lead. Happy to pay.

But No. 77 is going back to the city across the bridge. We jump on it and wave *hello* at the Tower. We jump off bus at the exact right stop in front of the Lodge. Michael gives me a high five for the good job.

He logs into skype and calls his dad telling him about the jump. We watch his photos and my photos. He calls his girlfriend. She is getting on a plane to HK in a few days. Michael is overly excited and tells me he thinks we really should go out.

We were told that Casino Lisboa serves free drinks. After half an hour the best free drink we get is coffee with powder creamer. We head on to Rua Cidade de Braga - supposedly the bars and clubs street. We find an arcade on Avenida da Amizade and have fun *racing and shooting aliens*. Michael goes on and on about his girlfriend and how they do not connect anymore. I should cut him off but let him go on and on and on. He needs to find out what it is that he wants.

- Look I'm going to say something...I just...don't want you to feel...
- I don't feel.

- Okay. I don't want you to think that I am sticking my nose into your business.
- Okay.
- Ever since I met you, you have been pretty restless. That's what I picked up from the first day of hanging out with you in Yangshuo.
- You're right...I am thinking whether Carol is the right person for me.

We walk through The Sands Casino into Xanadu Bar.

The guy is amazed at the fountain deco and says he wants an installation like this in his house - when he is rich and famous - and at the top it will say "Micky."

We sit at the bar and watch the live show of Chinese dancers and singers.

- Can I pick a drink for you?
- Please.

The bartender hands me a glass of champagne. *How did he know? This is exactly what I wanted.*

Classy men just read classy women.

- Thank you, Michael.
- My pleasure.

He drinks sangria one glass, comes another one and another three. At 1 a.m. the Chinese band is changed by a troupe of slim, beautiful couples dancing salsa, jive and cha-cha-cha. *They must be Russian.* No other country trains dancers like Russia, and no other country trains gymnasts like Ukraine.

They are beautiful and move to the rhythm of
Oye como va, mi ritmo,
Bueno pa' gozar, mulata...
Oye como va, mi ritmo
Bueno pa' gozar mulata..[33]

---

[33] Santana, *Oye Como Va*

194

I am mesmerized as my eyes meet the eyes of dancers and...*they know I am Russian, too*. Pride for my country = :)

At 3 a.m. we are drinking beers. I run to the bathroom to throw up as Michael is sitting by the roulette tables...winning.

- You always win when I get sick! - as I give him a big hug and he holds me tight.

...we gamble until we can't take it anymore - or more precisely, until Michael loses all the money he bet - as I stop him, exchange the last chips worth 1,000 HKD and drag him out of the casino outside where the sun is already out.....it is 6 a.m. and we need not worry about sleeping late. I walk by the fountain in front of The Sands and dip my head into the pool...play in the water...splash some on Michael...challenge him into jogging to the Lodge. He runs for 2 minutes, stops and hails a cab. I pass out in the backseat. Our beds are made in the hallway by the reception desk; as we fall asleep in two fold-out beds, Michael holds my hand.

I wake up to the noise by the Philippine housekeeper. It is past 12 p.m. and she wants us to either check out or check back in but in different beds. We get up, lazily, both hungover. I shower to return to our dorm and Michael has settled my bill for the night. It feels easy with him. He would not argue about money. I love it about him. I love his generosity. I love it that he does it because he wants to. I love it that he does not expect my affection in return. He hands me his i-pod and puts on a tune for me to listen to *Blinded by the Lights* by The Streets.

And I'm thinkin'...

(Lights are blinding my eyes)

They said they'd be here, they said, they said in the corner,

And I'm thinkin'...

(People pushin' by, then walkin' off into the night)

The song is about a guy who goes into a club, takes E, feels happy for two hours and miserable for two days. We eat toasted sandwiches for 10 HKD = 1 US dollar and walk into the facade of the remains of the Church of St. Paul - the biggest monument of Christian culture in Asia and the Museum of Sacred Art. Past romantic Portuguese architecture which reminds me of a colonial neighborhood of Barranco in Lima, all the way to Fortaleza de Guia - the highest point on the Macau peninsula.

I lie down in Michael's lap in the Flora Gardens as I listen to *Under The Bridge*.[34] A cop passes by and tells me I can't do this here.

Do what? Sleep?

Back to the old city's cobbled streets for fresh mango shakes. I see a shiny black dress on display in a store, but you cannot try anything on until you buy it.

?! So we sit by the fountain on Leal do Senado watching people watching us watching them watching us trying to discreetly take pictures of us. Michael tells me a story from his past about how an ex-girlfriend blackmailed him that he had been father of her child - whereas she had been pregnant before they even got together - because the real father was a nobody whereas Michael's family had been quite wealthy - she tried to get benefits and the girl's father tried persuading Michael into supporting her and her child. He took a DNA test and the day he got the results in his office - a sheet of paper with a whole bunch of writing - and the last line - the only line that made sense

DNA does not match.

...he *phewed* about it but never got the apology of the girl's father, *or* the girl.

He asks me if I had ever fallen pregnant. I tell him no. He tells me his sister is 20 and she has a kid. First, she got pregnant when she was 16, had an abortion, got pregnant again at 19.

- Don't you guys know about condoms?

---

[34] by All Saints.

196

- Condoms...I know condoms...they are fun to inflate and make figurines.
- Michael!
- You have quite long blonde hair, the body of what a woman should be like: your C-cup is the perfect size, you know how to move your body. What has hanging out with me been like?
- It's been...very...interesting.
- Do you find most guys you meet expect something more physical from you?
- Yes.
- Shall we get some food?
- What would you like?
- I feel like junk food.
- Me too. Then *wine*.

We eat Big Macs, fries and sodas. Michael goes to get a shave while I buy profiteroles and we return to the Lodge. We change and head to a club in Edificio Hoi Fu, as mentioned by the LP guide. The cab driver speaks not one word of English as we try explain to him where it is we need to go. He drops us off at building "Hoi Fu" and leaves. We find no club. We walk for an hour, as Michael has no idea where he is going. We catch a cab and return to Rua Cidade da Braga and go to MP3.

- We should have come here from the beginning!
- Well we are here now. Cheers! - as we drink our favorite red wine.

We finish two bottles and a pack of Marlboro Lights, listening to r'n'b and hip-hop.

- So here I am...with this beautiful Russian girl.
- Let's go to a strip bar or a pole bar...I will give you a good time.
- Okay.
- Okay. - as we put out our cigarettes.

Red wine is circulating through my system: on to MP4 club with a stripper pole. Michael sits down and orders a cocktail. I get my ass on stage as Nina Sky and Wisin y Yandel come through the speakers....

...the DJ announces....*tonight we have a special guest....*

...as I swing around the pole in my nikes screeching. Michael is watching me, sipping his cocktail. I forget where I am and dance away to the beat of reggae and ton.

and run to the bathroom to throw up.

Michael hands me a bottle of water.

- The way you move on that pole...girl...you got the moves.
- Damn right...I got your moves.

...out the bar past the prostitutes lined up outside I raise my hand trying to hitchhike for a ride back to the hotel. I love Michael's praise and attention...past the MGM Grand Casino as I bend over backwards to dip my head in the water in the fountain...rise out the water, like a mermaid...Michael has a hot and bothered look on his face.

...closer to the Lodge he watches me walk towards him...as I swing my hips and move around a light post...bend over and tease him...I approach him and he smacks my ass playfully but harshly...

I just had to do this.

...to our dorm and in my bottom bunk. I take off my jeans. I kiss him and he kisses me back.

Michael...I want you...I want you so bad...

...he kisses my body and puts earphones into my ears...

...and it's coming closer...

....he kisses the insides of my thighs and I push him away as much as I can, completely out-of-control drunk. Two other guys in the same room with us, sleeping in the bunk bed next to us.

Michael...I want you so bad...

...he takes off his underpants I ask him if he has condoms. He says "no." He was going to fuck without one? I reach into my bag and find the condom I stole from Andrew when I left Shangri-La. I slip one on him as he goes inside me and one, two three, four, five thrusts, he comes, pulls out of me as I see the condom has broken.

- Did you just come inside me?

Scared/puzzled look.

- Oh shit.

I run to the bathroom and wash myself. If only I had my douche bag with me I could wash out all his sperms. I try to at least wash myself on the outside. I return to bed. Still drunk. Fall asleep. Wake up in the middle of the night from a nightmare of burning inside. This is the first time a man has come inside me. Burning sensation. *Sperms die.* Body rejects fluids. *Throw up.* Log on and search for emergency contraception. Levonorgestrel is predominant in the morning-after emergency pill. It stops the female hormone being excreted in the amount needed for the fertilized egg to grow into a fetus. It increases the level of male hormones.

I try to find an article on the Internet which would convince me I have nothing to worry about as just 2 days after my period there is nothing to fertilize - the egg is gone and the new one is not developed yet. Another article says if a man released his semen inside you - you can get pregnant anytime of the cycle. Shit.

- Did you see what I was reading?
- Yes.
- What do you think?
- I think...it is always good to be cautious...
- Yeah. I will go and get it right now.

I run to the pharmacy next door and a kind lady in a white apron behind the counter gives me Postinor. I remember Postinor. Fooled around with it in college, when I was paranoid you could get pregnant from a blow-job. Take the first pill now, and the second pill 12 hours later. Worry about nothing, get your period in 5 days. Bad imbalance....very bad for the system. I wonder if maybe if I don't take it...I will just feel weird for a month...and then...I will have the answer...no...I can't do this to myself. The stress I will put myself through will be worse than the hormonal intervention the pill will do.

I take the first pill, come back to the Lodge and fall asleep in Michael's arms. He asks me if we have accommodation booked in Hong Kong. WTF?

- I....can't...I don't have a visa.

He offered me to go to Hong Kong with him? Spend time with him until his girlfriend arrives?...

This is the first time a man I am involved with is asking me to come with him. And the Universe just had to do it...when a man asks me....I can't go because of paperwork. Classic.

I lay on Michael's chest and wait until 12 p.m. to take my second pill. We eat dinner in a cute Chinese restaurant at the main square as he orders chow-mein and I get rice with chicken and cashews. I wrap my arms around him.

- Do you mind...

I kiss him hard on the lips and hold him tight.

- ...public displays of affection?
- No...but...easy.
- I knew you would get shy if I did this to you in public.
- It's not that! It's just...if you are rubbing too close to me things start to rise like the Macau Tower...
- That is the sweetest thing!

As I sprint back through the narrow streets of the old town of Macau Michael catches me at the door of the Lodge and kisses me hard, pressing me against the door. As night kicks in, I put on my white nightgown and lay on his chest. I love his muscular body as I kiss his neck...there are four other people in our dorm pretending to be asleep.

- I just...wanna do it with you all day...
- Let's get a room tomorrow...in a hotel...
- Okay.

I continue making out with him as he kisses my breasts, runs his hands over my stomach and presses his cock against me. I kiss his hard-on through his pants. He does not pull it out in my face which turns me on even more.

- Tell me what do you like...Michael...
- ...you're gonna have to find out.

Such a turn-on.

I yank his cock out his pans and starts sucking it. Up and down, and around, in my mouth, he signs as he comes...his jizz fills my mouth...I spit it out on the sheets. I get up to clean my mouth, brush my teeth and return to bed to take my second pill. Michael has a cigarette and we fall asleep in each others' arms.

The next morning he brings me coffee in bed and tells me we are leaving. It is the same if you spell it forwards and the same if you spell it backwards: we will be the first backpackers to stay at MGM Grand. I will fuck his bones so hard for having put me through the morning-after pill. I have all these male hormones in my body that will make wanna fuck like a nympho. His cock must have been too big for the condoms I had.

I log on to call my Hong Konger friend Marco I went to college with in Sydney. I tell him I wont be able to make it over...but he should come to Macau. He says he will try...otherwise we meet in Shenzhen. I call my dad and he tells me HK and Russia are signing a visa-exemption regime in 2 days which shall enter into force come July.

As we check out and walk to the Casino Michael asks me why am I sad. *We are parting our ways*. But I wont cry and he wont see my tears. He says he doesn't want to see me cry that is why he is giving me THIS: for our last day together and for the great week we had...we will celebrate tonight.

At the reception desk he is asked for his reservation number. He reaches for the little sheet of paper from his pocket. He says he learnt this travel tip from me. The check-in guy gives him the key for the deluxe ocean-view suite. He is really spending big this time. I feel like a million dollars.

I am the One to be in a hot 5-star casino resort with.

We gaze at the view of the ocean and Taipa island through the gigantic glass windows from the ceiling to the floor. I love the bathroom with the huge bathtub, shower gels, cool gadgets and a shower cabin. We can have so much fun here....I want to do all the dirty things with him. A guy so well-mannered and so diplomatic is such a turn-on.

I jump on him as he is relaxing in bed.

- Did you know that the cock is made of the same material as the clit?
- Yes.
- Spongy tissue and erectile tissue.
- Yes.
- Michael, can you control yourself?
- Yes...
- What I did with the pill...so bad for me...I am going to have two periods in one month...we have to be very careful.
- Okay..
- Go buy condoms.

I flip through the channels. He does not come back for 40 minutes. I wonder if he had just changed his mind and went to eat Chinese food instead of eating me. I put on my red dress so when he comes back...he will take it off...then take off my red lace bra and red panties...

He comes back having bought 2 boxes of extra large black condoms with a horse on the cover design; 3 beers, a box of Pringles and a pack of Marlboros. The "gentleman" case, so-to-speak. I wonder if this is really going to end tomorrow and secretly hope he will decide to stay a few more days so we can have more sex, enjoy each other more and then when the time is up...the time is up.

- Do you like bath-salts?

I walk into the state-of-the-art bathroom as Michael drops down his shirt and his jeans. He hides his cock in between his legs as he sits in the bathtub. I take off my dress, my panties and my bra. I feel the warmth of the water take my body in as I lean over to kiss him. He runs his hands on my breasts as I reach for his cock. It is big and wonderful. He plays with my pussy as I lean backwards. We wrap ourselves in towels and lay on the bed. He plays with me as he wants to return the favor for me giving him head the night before. He wants to lick me but I don't let him. He plays with me as I moan in his ear...jump on top of him: ride him; he grabs my hips and fucks me up and down and around and faster and faster as I come once, pulls my hair as I can't control the point of no-return, twice....as I scream, yes, yes! feel the muscles inside me contract and wrap Michael's amazing cock tighter and tighter as I get off his cock he pulls my hair and...puts me on the dresser, opens my legs as I moan harder and harder I feel so much fucking is so healthy and I have given in to this right timing and I just want him to fuck me all day and all night and then go to have wine and food and dance and then fuck again and then sleep and then everything starts all over again. He comes as we relax and lay down for a cigarette.

I jump into the outdoor pool overlooking Taipa like a bomb.

- Can you feel when I come?
- Yeah...it's...tighter...

...we race who's faster to get to the other end of the pool...

- Ah! This is the best week of my life. Every time from now on, I will be looking back thinking this was the best week of my life. I had to live until 25 to have the best week of my life. I don't know if this is a good thing or a bad thing. Can anything compare to this?

...we shower and I wear my red dress again. The highlight: soon everybody will refer to me as *the girl in the red dress*. We walk out of the hotel to an Italian place and Michael orders a bottle of wine and a pizza. He says this has been the best week of his life and thanks me. I tell him this has been interesting. He tells me he is looking for someone to plan and to think for him.

I gave you that. Didn't I give you that?

Tomorrow I will leave for China as he will leave for Hong Kong. I will continue on my way and this will remain a memory, *a great sex time in Macau.*

- I will be honest. This was the second time I came from a penis-suck.
- Gehe.
- I have to tell you, I have been asked many times if I am on a honeymoon with my wife during our time together.
- I told you we're hot.
- It's all about you. You are making me look good.

I bet if I got really mad, the only thing he would say to me is *You look so sexy when you're mad.*

I love how somebody so genuinely hot can be such a good boy in life and such a bad boy in bed....

- ....it's when you first danced with me - I knew I wouldn't be able to just let it go...so I...surrendered my soul to you.

So sweet of him to refer to his hard-on as his soul.

- ...forbidden fruit is sweetest.
- I know...that is why I am extending the time right now before we go back to the hotel...I am so horny right now.

-   ...me too.

Have I mentioned that it is amazing to have someone as good-looking, calm, generous, hot, well-mannered, as the man right in front of me? And he just called me an Angel again.

He settles the bill and we walk on the main avenida overlooking the bay. Michael holds my body and kisses me hard.

-   I bet everyone is thinking right now...why can't I be like this?..

We sit down in MP3 to watch a live band and drink wine as Michael asks me why wouldn't I let him go down on me. I tell him I won't discuss this in a bar...as he tells me I am very different from all the other girls he has been with. He says he has been with hot girls before but I am something different: mysterious and fun, easy to hang with and do things for.

We return to the hotel bar and sit in the very front of the live band.

Can't read my, can't read my, no he can't read my poker-face...
She's got to love nobody

Michael befriends the singer and the sax player as they run for their cigarette break.

-   I want this band to play at my funeral or at my wedding - whichever comes first!!

As *Rhythm is Gonna Get You* comes on I grab Michael's hand, lead him to the dance-floor and twist myself in salsa. We are free. We are young. This is our last night. We sip our drinks and he asks me how was he in bed on a scale from one to ten and how his cock felt compared to other guys.

-   You're drunk.
-   Why did you not let me go down on you?
-   I am not ready. I can't.
-   You have to let me do it.
-   I can't. I am not ready.

- Why not?
- It's just...too personal.
- Why did you go down on me the other night?
- Because I wanted to.
- You have to feel the texture of my tongue on your..

Shrug. Ewww!

- I can't.
- So you are saving that moment 4-the-1-U-give-UR-heart-2?

He jumps up and moves like John Travolta in Saturday Night Fever, humping the sofa as I crack up watching him, clap my hands as he moves *closer*, kisses me on the lips, slides his hand into my panties as I push him away.

He leaves to the bathroom and comes back to tell me a guy from the bar who was taking a piss at the same time kept asking him what his plans were for the night. He told him his plan was to go upstairs and make some marks on the windows. The guy asked him *with who? the girl in the red dress?* he said yes. He said he will give her some English cock.

Casino: Michael loses and I make sure he does not spend his last money as he puts his hand over my shoulder, kisses me, and calls me a real diamond.

We walk up to our deluxe suite as he puts on *Closer*, sinks into the couch and lights a cigarette, I slowly move towards him in a slow, hot lap-dance. As he takes off my red dress, my red lace bra and silk ribbon thong, he leads me to the bed and kisses my stomach...I switch the adult channel on, as we sex like porn-stars until the sun shows on the horizon...

Open up your eyes...you keep on crying baby I'll bleed you dry
I see a storm bubbling up from the sea...

...get up at noon and shower together, he puts rose gel on my breasts and gently massages them. Mmm....feels good.

I stand before the mirror.
Should I stay here one more day and do the mast climb?

Michael says this had been the best week of his life...which he will not be able to tell anyone about...as he is going to Hong Kong to meet his girlfriend. We go to McDonalds for coffee and cigarettes. He is buying everything on the menu as he wants to spend the Macau patakas. I will stay for a few more days and do the mast climb. I also want to see Zaia in Cirque du Soleil at the Venetian.

I make a quick call to a Hospedaria to make a reservation.

We stand outside the MGM Grand waiting for the bus to the port.

You, shimmy shook my bone...

Leaving me stranded all in love on my own...

...we kiss as Michael puts an earphone in my ear and keeps one in his...he whispers...

"I'll never be able to listen to Kings of Leon again."

What do you think of me...

Where am I now? Baby where do I sleep...

Feel so good but I'm old...

2,000 years of chasing taking its toll...

He gets on the bus and waves me goodbye. I walk to my sleezy motel. I hate it the minute I get there. I hate choosing to stay here longer the second I start walking alone. I rush to an Internet cafe, desperately trying to get in touch with Marco. At night I grab some dinner at the place Michael and I went to: rice, chicken with cashews and beer. It does not taste the same. I hate being here alone. I wear my Macau Tower Bungy Jump T-shirt and walk to the tower to watch *Knowing* with Nicholas Cage. Freaked out, return to the hotel and never shut my eyes for one minute until the sun comes out, hearing the neighbors fucking as the rooms are separated by cardboard walls which aren't exactly walls as they do not reach all the way to the ceiling.

Overcast, rainy and my plan to run on the boardwalk flopped. I catch a bus to the port and grab a ticket for Shekou, China. On to Xanadu Bar to buy a ticket for Zaia and return to the hotel.......Marco says he is not able to make it to Macau....I get an e-mail from my dad as he tells me the court rule is in and the now ex-tenant had left the building. I rave in excitement as I go to watch Zaia and sip on a frozen Margarita, astounded by the silk acrobatics return to Xanadu Bar, inspired to see the Russian ballroom dancers perform again.

Next morning I rush to the ferry to China: tired, sleepy, blood pressure driving me...I had reserved a bed in a hostel I found in Shenzhen - the border of China and Hong Kong - I will take a bus from Shekou to get to Shenzhen and stay one night and relax...and then...hit Shanghai. I get off the 45-minute ferry and ask the immigration woman to stamp me RIGHT HERE right next to the last entry stamp as she cancels my visa. This is it. Last entry into China.

Kao-ya, rice, Chinese cabbage : hop on bus.

"This is Yangshuo!" - a kind Chinese girl taps my shoulder.
After the bus from Shekou to Shenzhen....after not finding the hostel I DID NOT call that morning, I took the subway to the last stop before Hong Kong. Bought a ticket for 400 renminbi (another name for yuan=literally "people's currency") to Yangshuo on a 12-hour bus. Shenzhen was a major trade town: countless, endless stores of shoes, clothes, CDs, electronics...
Walk on Xi Jie, trying to shove off all feelings of nostalgia. Wont stay at the same hostel, understandably. Check in to HI Youth Hostel. Miss feeling like a woman. Adored, loved, wined, dined and made love to. Wash hair. Wear black dress. Get a haircut.

Take a Chinese cooking class and learn to make kung pao chicken and braised tofu with mushrooms. The teacher takes us to a fresh foods market outside the tourist ghetto and introduces us to a myriad different greens and stacks of firm tofu. Chinese "doufu" it is made of coagulating soy milk, pressing and making soft white blocks. In the West it is also known as bean curd and known to be a rich source of protein, thus a substitute for vegetarian diets.
The name "Kung Pao" comes from the Qing dynasty times and an official whose title was "Gong Bao" i.e. palatial guardian. Bite-size-shredded-chicken, carrots, cucumbers, raw peanuts, stir-fried in a wok in chili peppers, garlic and ginger, with oyster and soy sauce. Served with a bowl of rice into which one must never stick chopsticks vertically into. It is a sign of the food for the dead. Also never suck on the tips of the chopsticks, pierce the food with chopsticks, or point chopsticks at another person (considered disrespect).

After booking a ticket for Shanghai to arrive after 33 hours on the third class train on May 1st - Labour Day

- Did you sleep with Michael!? - Marie jumps on me in the middle of the walking street.
- No.
- Oumph.
- He has a girlfriend.
- So what, he is a man!
- ....
- But did he try?..
- No.
- That is so strange...especially with you...how did *you* manage?

On the day of biking to the countryside with my cute roommate from Belgium, I get my period. Alexander is only 20 years old, driven, cute, with gorgeous long-Tom-Cruise-style hair: he reminds me of my brother. He tells me about visiting Xiamen where they saw a freak-show with a gigantic octopus. As I lay in my bed in my white nightgown (dress) from Vietnam he moves closer and shows me his gadgets - a solar-powered stereo he is going to take with him for the camping outdoors by the river for a few days. He puts on a nice beat by Lamb which, as he tells me, is trip-hop. A break-beat like in hip-hop but instead of the rapping it is mixed with mellow down-tempo sound. He tells me I should know that diamonds are cut in Antwerp, the capital of Belgium. And that they speak Dutch in Belgium, too. His birthday is November 21. He tells me about the volunteer work he has been doing for a project in Haiti a few months back. He is studying sociology. He excuses himself and leaves with a Chinese girl out the dorm for a drink. I login to skype and call my mother to tell her about the Macau morning-after pill as I could not confide into anyone yet...and I need to. She tells me I shouldn't have been keeping it all to myself...and should never been ashamed to tell her anything.

K860 train to Shanghai. To realize my full potential I make a list of dreams, goals, values and actions to achieve those goals.

Active sport, singing and dancing, living with my twin soul in the flesh on a Caribbean island, complete and publish my book, become known for my art, perfect eye sight, smooth underarms, no second chin, no nail-breakage, no mood-swings and balance as my dreams. My goals are to find and successfully settle in a career, beneficial for both body, mind and spirit, counseling work, helping teens, working with sign language, settling in with a soulmate and forming a rewarding relationship. My values are appreciation, praise, gratefulness, togetherness, passion and love. This is supposed to make up for a **complete blueprint**. I also make a simpler list, for simple things. Things I want every day: good food, good digestion, morning jogging, good sex, healthy teeth and eyes, sunny weather, ocean and swimming.

The book says that if you want something, you go and get it.

If you "try and get it" you are setting yourself up for failure...inevitably.

When you go and do it you succeed.

The train arrives to Shanghai's South Station as I feel excitement of being in a new place again. As these days I do not keep a journal and my story is written from memoirs when I had already moved to Miami. As all of this...are memories from the future...

I check into Shanghai Youth Hostel, shower and feel

...all alone, on my own, again.

I have a glass of wine in the lobby of the hostel and buy a pack of cigarettes, nervously smoke and...find a food joint: tofu, mushrooms, tofu, bean sprouts and tofu into my boil. 10 yuan. Eat soup fast. Burns my tongue and my throat. IT IS HOT!

Check my facebook. Message from Michael. He is asking me why did he rush to Hong Kong and tells me it is so expensive. He congratulates me on the tenant eviction. He tells me maybe we will meet again sometime soon.

Now that he is about to meet his girlfriend...he is trying to secure his position with me......?

Shanghai, literally "By the sea" sits at the mouth of the Yantze river and is China's biggest city of nearly 15 million people. A major trade port and "Paris of the East" was never a major cultural or tourist center, not to mention backpacker-center. The famed Ming Hiker's hostel nearby the Bund is booked out so my first place of interest is Jing'an Temple or the "Temple of Tranquility": Chinese Buddhist which dates back to Qing and Ming dynasties. Locals make offerings as I smell incense burning. Visitors make donations as this is a popular place to pray for financial success.

I walk across the street from the temple into Jing'an Park, sit down and smoke a cigarette. The skies are waning on me. I get a sprite to balance my tummy. I run to the bathroom for 5 yuan. It is funny...as I never thought it could be in any other country. I am used to public bathrooms to be *public per pay* bathrooms.

Back in the day there was even a joke about it...in the Soviet times, it was always a problem as to find a place to eat and a place to shit. Honestly...*this* is no joke.

I continue walking West on Nanjing Lu aiming at the Chinese fakes market - said to be very good. Indeed...tourists buying everything they possibly can - this is a circus - just like the *mall* in Shenzhen. Fakes are neither a moral, or a legal problem for the Chinese as I negotiate for a fake i-pod and bargain down to 150 yuan for an 8 GB nano. It must be some sort of trick...it can't just be that good. Next!!

It Either Works, Or It Doesn't!

I get to People's Square for a bowl of spicy soup with tofu, mushrooms, bean sprouts, rice noodles and more tofu. As I wonder and ponder the meaning behind my affirmations. How many times have I wished for something...and there it was - right in front of me. Why can't this happen for my twin soul??

I drop into a mall halfway between People's Square and Jing'an station. I watch *The Fast and the Furious* in a movie theater. Films like this always inspire me.
I realize...I did not make an affirmation to meet my twin soul...not once!
It never felt comfortable. It never felt as my...true desire.
...another morning jog kicks off my day and this time I only have coffee for breakfast from the canteen. Still haven't made any friends in the hostel. Too sprawl. Showers are amazing though. Walk-in showers...lock the doors...go crazy with a hot guy.......
...all the way to the Bund - riverside avenue of banks and administrative buildings. Modern and art-deco European architecture. On the opposite side of the Huang-pu river are the Jinmao Tower and the Oriental Pearl Tower which, along with the Trade Tower, form the infamous Shanghai skyline.
Oriental Pearl Tower is 468 meters with an observation deck at 350 meters, a revolving restaurant at the 267 meter-level, and it contains exhibition facilities, restaurants and a shopping mall.
Jin Mao Dasha means "Golden Prosperity Building" and like the Petronas Towers of Kuala Lumpur, the building's proportions revolve around number 8, associated with prosperity in Chinese culture. Stainless steel, glass and granite form the curtain wall of 88 floors; criss-crossed by a complex latticework cladding of aluminum pipes..
Many hostels in China, part of the YH or HI networks are full of Chinese students. Many speak English, they are humble and uptight.

I guess they would find me pretty...amusing.

Bund Sightseeing Tunnel: catch a ride under the Huangpu River. "You are very sexy!" - yells the ticket-checking girl. As I get out of the tunnel, I run across the road as an angry Chinese cop stops me and waves a 5 yuan note in my face. *You learn one thing, and you forget another thing.*

It is official...he is writing me a fine. I was not supposed to cross here!!

Whenever there is intervention from the powers that be - not that this man is one of them, however, even still - I feel the Universe itself is telling me I had done something wrong and it is stopping me - as means of constriction and control. **For my own good.**

As the cop yells at me in Chinese (Mandarin, I suppose) I yell back at him without the slightest trench of anger - having a fun time.[35] I tell him I only have change which makes up about 3.5 yuan as he sends me BACK to the side of the road I came from. As I turn around I see 3 other idiots attempting to J-walk.

I walk into the underground crossing and emerge on the opposite side of the road. "You have beautiful hair!" - yells a local man.

I walk to far-out alleys: guaranteed to have food stalls with mi-fan (steamed rice) and kao-ya (roast duck). Back to hostel.

Logon to facebook and put my earphones in

Open up your eyes..

It's over, kiddo.

I open my hard drive and try to get some thoughts together as I flip through my photos from Nepal, Tibet and Moscow. I miss family. There had always been a connection between Tibet and Russia...perhaps an even stronger connection than Tibet and the U. S. as the Trans-Himalayan Brotherhood of Light, Great Russian people, Nicholas Roerich - the painter, Helena Blavatsky

---

[35] Deny everything, admit nothing, make counter-accusations.

- visionary and channel, spent years in Tibet. Progressives...non-conformists....those who could not be held down by the constrictive Powers That Be = the Government.

Growing up in Russia or even more so having Russian citizenship is something I was born with - and according to the laws and theories of karma and reincarnation - I chose this. I really...really chose to be born in Russia in 1985. Not to mention that my mother had almost miscarried me three times...as perhaps my soul did not want to enter this lifetime...and she told me many times the story of how I was supposed to be born 2 weeks earlier than I was...and then right before the doctors wanted to start artificial labor for her - I got scared and got born. She always jokes about this being the major trait of my character.

In working with past lives I had come across one where I questioned where the food aversion comes from. Immediately the vision came through from this lifetime - where the first drop on my lips was not my mother's milk - but my mother's poop. As the doctors hadn't cleaned very well after giving her an enema. Thus comes the aversion....feeling that anything I taste will make me sick. I used to have it harsh after college. At the same time, for a year or so, when I was getting ready to either leave home for work or leisure - I felt I was about to poo anytime - and thus had to stay home and constricted. When I had the out-of-body experience after the food poisoning just as I came back from Nepal: my body relaxed and let go. My spirit flew high up in the clouds to see J and be with him where *he* was. The poisoning of my brain from the food my body rejected, helped me stay grounded in the physical body as my spirit left. The way to keep my body rooted in physical reality was through the muladhara chakra....means of control...any means...worth having *you* under control.

I stroll to the French Concession and into a Hair Salon to have my hair washed, cut and blow-dried for a bargain price of 15 yuan. I step out feeling like a million dollars and buy a banana which gives me cramps as I hate I bought it and go back to the hostel to somehow subside the negative effects of the starch.

The rumbling in my stomach reminded me of the times in junior school. It was after my first trip abroad with my sister. It was the bad eating patterns in our host family that caused me to have bad indigestion and my stomach rumbled so hard and so loud - that I had to leave class because I was so embarrassed. My mom calls it "musical accompaniment." In 8th grade the reason for my attention deficiency was not only my drained spirit searching for connection...it was also the diversion of attention from my head to my stomach. I had to leave class and sit somewhere with loud noises.

After years of suffering from this, I learnt to control it - just counted the time it will take from the time I eat to the time the food goes all the way into my gut and starts sending hellos to everyone around me in form of loud distracting churning noises.

After college I was finally ready to question the reason for this. Once again, a past life memory came through....when I was tied and tortured in a camp, unable to move...the sound of the footsteps of my torturers caused the response of my nervous system.............my body still remembers it......

....however as I got older this memory was not enough explanation anymore.

I close the hard-drive as the system tells me the information will be lost as it has not been disconnected properly.

I panic that my book is lost, the majority of channeled writing; talking to my Spirit guides and typing away are never to be found, the world will never know about this work of art, it will be like it never existed....

.....I run to one of the boys who works as tech support and designs brochures for the hostel. He saves my hard drive.
The night before tonight, I uploaded videos from Moscow into my profile on the Russian version of facebook: vkontakte.ru. I feel like this is my way of saying to my family, *I miss you!* As I am watching videos of you and making you understand
I miss you!
I had been wanting to visit Qufu - birthplace of Confucius and home to a Temple, Cemetery and Kong Family Mansion which have recently been listed as a UNESCO World Heritage Site. But it is hostel-free and I would have to make 2 connections to get there. Skip it and go to Qingdao, a beach town on the coast, a seaport, naval base and industrial center. It HAS a hostel. AND a Babyface Club. AND it is the town of beers - Tsingtao is a German brewery the Chinese inherited.

Well. Western Peace. Or, Xi'an, afterall. Had doubts as many backpackers told me it is over-touristy. Figured it will eat me until I DO go there and see the infamous Terracotta Army. Not only that. I realized when I deviate from the backpacker route - I *don't* have a good time. Will hop on train to Xi'an//be there in 22 hours. Now, hostel choice. Xi'an is packed with hostels.
Explore the Dr. Sun Yat Sen Mausoleum: a major attraction and THE reason to be in Nanjing, two hours West of Shanghai. Sun Yat Sen was a revolutionary and political leader and the first provisional president when the Republic of China was founded. His legacy resides in developing a political philosophy known as

the Three Principals of the People: nationalism, democracy and people's livelihood.

Pass by main entrance gate//find small alley that leads to the main steps of Mausoleum. *Hopefully, Dr. Sun Yat Sen will not turn in his coffin when he sees us enter the park without paying admission.*

The visit to the Mausoleum is a pilgrimage. The tomb was built in Ming style - it lies at the top of an enormous stairway with over 500 steps. It is white, blue and my Chinese friend takes a picture of me overlooking the old town as we get to the top of the stairway.

We return to the hostel and go online into hostelbookers.com to book my stay at Shuyuan hostel. Of all the hostels listed, it feels like the one with the right vibe.

We explore the Fuzi Temple around the corner as it is lit at night. Fuzi was the mythical creator of the ba-Gua: Tradition has it, that he defined in the curls of hair on a dragon's back (another version has a tortoise's shell) firm and broken lines, he further took out binary combinations, and thus, eight combinations of these lines...

The admission into the nearby Confucius temple is 100 yuan so we hang out by the free fair area. Leo Nardo, as my Chinese friend calls himself, tells me that Confucianism advocates a structured society in which people are bound to each other by moral ties of the five familial relationships. Confucius was a thinker and teacher whose philosophy of family obligations and good government is based on the principles of ren (benevolence) and yi (righteousness). The main basis of his teachings were to seek knowledge, to study and to become a better person. Social harmony: the great goal of Confucianism results when each individual knows his or her place in social order. *When the prince is prince, the minister is minister.* Filial piety[36] was also implied into the Chinese law.

Chinese *qi-pao* dresses. Traditional Chinese silk attire. Chopsticks and small triangle tops with nothing but two thin straps on the back - mom calls them s*lyunyavchiki* - to describe a piece of cloth you cover a baby's neck when they are fed - so they don't spill their own food on their clothes - they are tiny and triangular. I believe the English word is *bibs*.

We return to the hostel to watch the stupidest movie ever - "Reno 911" as I crack up and reminisce life in Miami - I can't wait to return to worry-free life in Vice City. Apparently everything has been taken out of the condo. There is no furniture, only fixtures, I doubt there are...jalousies. Oh wait. This is a Russian French-derived word. The American word is *venetian blinds*.

In China I have learnt that if you want anyone who does not speak English to understand you, you should SHOW not TELL. When I can't say *Where is the Train to Xi'an, please?* I just show the ticket with Chinese characters and they show me the way. *Xei-xei.*

My train is ultimately going to Lanzhou - almost touching the Northern Tibetan plateau. The Chinese people on the train are very friendly as they share their food, ask questions in Chinese which I never understand so I just smile in return and nod my head. A girl sitting next to me is eating pot noodle.

Everyone on the train is eating pot noodle, now that I paid attention to it. Except for me. A guy across the table is fasting for the entire trip. The girl next to me offers me raw cucumbers. I shake my head *no, xei-xei.*

---

36 Veneration of ancestors.

Hua Shan - one of the Five Great Daoist Mountains of China along with Tai Shan, Nan Heng Shan, Bei Heng Shan and Song Shan as they correspond to the Five Cardinal Directions of Daoism: East, West, South, North and Center.

"Paying respect to a holy mountain" is the Chinese way of pilgrimage. Rain falls down as Train arrives at Xian and I walk to Shuyuan hostel.

When I graduated college, a psychic from Brooklyn, NY who had been reading me for years had told me that once I get into my twenties, I will move through the healing world and the healing realms...at the time I had no experience in conscious energy work and was not aware of the fact that I was an empath. At the time...the power of that suggestion...had been enough means of control and constriction...to keep me at home...stay in my comfort zone, feel abnormal....have my Spirit guide channel messages recorded in my diaries...as I remember writing that I will meet my man and marry him in 2008...my first child will be born June 20, 2010. This would mean I must have sex in September 2009. I wonder if any of this will make sense anytime in the future. I have such a long way to go.

It is important *how* you find something - how you are led to it. I was led to my Rei-ki teacher, when I cried to heavens for help after the sensation of dying. This goes way back before my decision to take exile. I did not find her in a newspaper. It was my need: to heal. Then I gained the ability to see past the choices I make...and watch a life happening right before my very own I's.

...it is...in fact...the night of the full moon. I watch the sky from one of the parks in the center of town and wonder. As is above = so it is below. The body reflects most skies. Many tiny moles.

The stars and constellations in the sky are imprinted in my body as moles. If you look at yours, you will see them too. Each mole - especially one carried on from a family member - is a connection to a myth, or legend and a constellation. They are moments...in time and space...of deep appreciation.

The mole on my back I am very careful of - had been passed on to me by my mother as we are linked with the constellation of Orion. In my research of ancestral astrology I found that these moles are passing on of their karmic program. You are not here to live your life...but living off their karma.

Karma of your ancestors.

The hostel holds a dumpling party every Friday. I make dumplings since I am a kid. They are probably the most famous dish after chicken noodle soup in Tatar culture - filled with beef, pork, carbs and other indigestible matter. As a kid, I loved them - and ate A LOT so perhaps that is the reason for aversion and allergy now. I demonstrate how to make dumplings Russian style - one more step after finishing the Chinese style dumpling: hold the flat circle of dough, put the meat or vegetables inside, half-fold, clip the ends together and close the Chinese dumpling by connecting the two ends of it into a "hat."

The Army of Terracotta Warriors was excavated about 30 years ago by accident during a digging on the site by a local farmer. It is over 2,000 years old and was initially built by the Qing Emperor to guard his tomb. Each figurine was made by a master and ten of his assistants. Masters would leave an impress of their seals: thus, over 1,000 people participated in making the Army. The statues have a massive clay base, which were "clothed" with "clothes" of the same material. The bodies were made from clay rollers or ready-blocks, to which arms were adjoined, etc. The statues were burned in a furnace at 1,000 degrees centigrade. The Army makes up over 8,000 figures of life-size soldiers, archers, horses and chariots. Not one warrior is similar to another; each one is in strict positioning according to the ancient book of The Art of War written in the 6th century BC.

One of the oldest and most successful books on military strategy, it influenced business tactics and beyond.

Sun Tzu, the author, thought that strategy was not planning in working in an established list, but that it required quick and appropriate responses to changing conditions.

Speed is the essence of war. Take advantage of the enemy's unpreparedness; travel by unexpected routes and strike him where he has taken no precautions. [37]

The Museum itself is a covered area and it is nothing of a romantic cave-like scene from *Tomb Raider* or our imagination. I can see why most backpackers were disappointed with it. You can't touch *one* statue :((

---

[37] Sun Tzu, The Art of War

The best victory is when the opponent surrenders of its own accord before there are any actual hostilities... It is best to win without fighting. [38]

A military operation involves deception. Even though you are competent, appear to be incompetent. Though effective, appear to be ineffective. [39]

However a military handbook, it also gives tips on how to outsmart an opponent so that fighting is not necessary. Thus, it has found application as a training guide for competitive endeavors that do not involve actual physical battle.

Subtle and insubstantial, the expert leaves no trace; divinely mysterious, he is inaudible. Thus he is master of his enemy's fate. [40]

Rain continues to fall as I find shelter on a bus back to hostel. Relax for an hour of deep-tissue with a doctor advertised at the hostel. Shower and go downstairs into the lobby to have a beer.

Peeps are playing poker as I sit next to a red-haired guy. *Deja vu*. Loud and clear, vibrant, energetic, sipping bai-jiu ("white liquor") with orange juice. He is going out to a club tonight. Alone. He says he is drinking because he does not want to be shy in a club.

---

[38] same-same

[39] same-same

[40] same-same

I can't make out whether he is gay or just flamboyant as his mannerism confuses me. He says he just got a 3rd class ticket to Beijing on a train for tomorrow night. I ask him why is he traveling third class, he says because it is cheap and he likes adventure. It is not boring. Haha. It is taking me all these massage sessions to make up for the third class ride from Nanjing.

We catch a cab to a club. Harry from Boston, MA buys two beers and I buy another two. He tells me I look hot. Everybody in the club wants to talk to me. He says we should pass by the VIP Lounge and see what happens. Guys will be inviting me in. We pass by and a guy invites both of us in. He offers us to buy a bottle of vodka for 600 yuan.

We pass....laughing in each other's faces.

On to a club next door and he tells me I should be dancing on the pole. I enjoy the attention, and I am surprised at how confident he is. He is absolutely *physically* unattractive. He pulls my hair as I dance on him in the center of the dance floor. He touches my breasts and puts his hands on my hips as I swing them. He tries to kiss me...as I turn away. I feel drunk. We dance...we have a great time....as he tries to kiss me again and sticks his tongue down my throat as I stick mine down his.

He continues to dance alone as I now I see that he sucks as he moves like a...geek. A nerd. He comes to me and makes out with me again. As we get tired of dry humping in the club, we walk outside as I hold his hands in mine and spin....and spin....and fall down....as he catches me....

We eat chow-mein as he enjoys this scene - he says it is a lot like Korea - where he lives and works teaching English. We return to the hostel and make out in the hall as we sneak into his dorm and I take off my pants and my top, climb into his top bunk and in the dark he runs his hands all over my body...my arms...my stomach...my hips...as I sign...and try to stay quiet as there are 4 other people in the dorm with us...

He would put my hands up...while I lay down on my back...and run his fingers from the tips of my fingers into the palms of my hands...into my wrists....and the inner sides of my arms...this used to be the most sensitive part of my body. I imagined it so many....many times...and Harry happens to do it...in the dark...I can't see him...I can only *feel* him....

- You're beautiful, - he whispers.
- You can't even see me.
- I can *feel* you.
- I am going to have to go to the bathroom and get myself off very soon.
- That is so hot.
- ...otherwise I can't sleep.
- I can get you off...just let me...

...as he slides his hands and tries to reach for my warm pussy, I push him away.

Been through drunken sex in dorms already with 4 other people..." sleeping".

I feel his tiny cock as

- Guys...could you...find another room?

a girl on the bottom bunk switches the light on.

I get dressed and disappear out the door. Thank God for the girl.

Next morning I go to the Chinese-spice-market: star anise, cinnamon, cloves, chili peppers and fennel seeds; along with herbs: mushrooms, wolf-berries, ginger and ginseng all used in accord with the Five Elements in Chinese Medicine.

Mosque on Hiajie Xiang. I avoided Harry in the morning.

I hoped not to bump into him.

I visit the Drum and Bell Tower = another local tourist attraction. Apparently there is a history museum and an art museum. But who of the backpackers really cares about 'em? Not this one...I just want to be on my way...know what I'm doing. I go online and e-mail Qianmen hostel in Beijing asking for availability for tomorrow night or the night after.

See Harry. Says he has been looking for me. Says he wasn't sure how I felt and didn't want to pressure me or make me talk to him if I did not want to. We go to play pool.

- ...hey do you have a boyfriend?
- No, of course not. I'm traveling.
- ...you could be in an open-relationship.
- I don't believe that. You are either with someone or you're not with someone. Not to mention...If I was happy I would never leave.

I light a cigarette.

- I love girls who smoke!

He kisses me and tastes the tobacco off my lips.

- Will you come on the same train as me?

I'll take a chance.

- Listen...before you get on that train...I need to tell you that I am in an open-relationship. My girlfriend is in Korea.
- Oh. Why did I need to know that?
- Because...I would hate for you to go 20 hours standing on a train...for me.
- ...I am not going for you. I am going, because I am. We have fun. Actually, I wont go. I wont go *with* you.
- I understand.
- How can you say your girlfriend, when you were ready to fuck me last night?
- Oh, no. I would have stopped you.
- I had to push you away so you would stop. You were gonna go down on me, remember?
- It is okay in my rules. In my rules, you can go down, make out, kiss, touch and get off, as long as you don't penetrate.
- What?! This is ridiculous. You are not being true.
- How so?
- Just think about it. You are anything BUT in an open relationship. You *think* you are. But you are really only making up excuses b/c you think penetrative sex is so important that you cut it out. You think you are loyal and it is ok?
- I used to think that love was all black and white. You meet someone, you love them, you marry them. I just don't think so anymore. I changed.
- You were so gonna fuck me last night. You're so full of shit. *I will* go tonight because what you said doesn't change anything between us.

We catch a cab to the station with a Canadian girl, Brandy.

They are indeed sold out so I get a standing ticket and picture myself sitting for 20 hours on the floor leaning on a door connecting two cars. We grab rice, broccoli, tofu and peanuts.

I sit down next to Harry. The ticket-man checks my ticket. I wait until the one who has this one seat assigned comes along and takes it. Nobody does. Sometimes...miracles happen.

Harry says he really loves broccoli. I tell him, I do, too. He calls me a kindred spirit. He tells me he has a friend who is also very metaphysical, knows astrology and energy, back in Boston.

- I really like you.
- I really like you too.
- You want to get a room together?
- What?
- We don't have to have sex. We can just get a room and stay together in private.
- What do you think we are gonna do?
- Just relax in the quiet of a private room.

I listen to music on his fat i-pod and doze off on the table as we arrive to Beijing West Station. It was a jiffy. Brandy, Harry and I catch a cab to Qianmen Station. Brandy chews on a banana and tells me she is trying to get over a relationship. Isn't everyone, who takes off to travel?? What a drive. A trigger. You attract complete opposites - that's the name of the game.

What if...everyone who ever comes into our lives and leaves drives us to leave in a search. Our inner mechanism activates when someone takes our energy. We need to get it back.

We walk through the hutongs - narrow, dirty ghetto-like streets inside bigger avenues.

And that instant I question myself: would it be so very...very hard for me...to face the fact that I am by myself: and happy this way.

228

Instead of being like Brandy - who just told me the story of how she lived with a man for 7 years and then he just left her (aka their karma was over aka the sex became boring aka she became boring as her sex drive was low because she was on the pill) so she took off to travel and live in Scotland (who the hell goes to Scotland????) for six months...........

Men...make...women...messy. Quote: Rene Russo. Source: The Thomas Crown Affair.
Courtesy: Columbia Pictures.
As we get to Leo's Hostel, my eyes meet a familiar girl. Something is different about her. She looks at me, puzzled. Where did I see her last?
-   You bitch!!
-   Hey, babe!! - as I run up to her, realizing it is Nomin, with short hair. She cut her dreadlocks.
-   You fucking bitch! Do you ever check your e-mail!
-   I am so happy you're here! Unbelievable!
-   You fucking bitch! Get out!
Harry offers to get dumplings - *jiaozi* - for breakfast but I refuse. I get my coffee, whole-wheat bread with peanut butter and sit in the lobby.
-   Excuse me, miss, may I introduce myself!? - Nomin comes up to me.
...we walk outside as she goes on about how much she hates this city because of dust, dirt and narrow *hutongs*. She asks me what has been up in my love life. She says I see the world through *pink glasses*: looking for a prince who will come in to make everything perfect, be there for me forever and ever. I tell her it is not true as I just had two affairs in the last month. For her FYI.

We walk through the Qian'men Front Gate to the Tian'an men Square and the Mao Mausoleum. She takes a picture of my sexy posing by the gigantic Mao Portrait and we walk to Wangfujing Dajie - the main shopping street of Beijing, into a bookstore, as we joke about missing class in school.

We used to go to the Red Square in Moscow - two blocks away from our school - drink pepsi and bitch about our hard lives. She was depressed, just like me. She moved to Virginia for school but came back to Mongolia.

As we walk past Chinese medicinal herb shops to the hostel to ask the receptionist where to get a good massage, she sends us to a parlour right next door from the hostel where for 50 yuan each we get our feet rubbed.

We eat kao-ya in a fine restaurant served with wheat *pancakes*, cucumber slices and oyster sauce (which should not be legal).

Back at the hostel we smoke our assess off and get drunk off local beer. She books her flight to Xi'an. She has a Dutch boyfriend from New Zealand. She really, really likes him. She says she does not want to love. Love hurts.

Love hurts. I show her J's picture. She thinks he is good looking. She has no idea.

We get beers and comfortable.

- I was in Bangkok before coming here. I watched this incredible cartoon on youtube, "Ezhik v Tumani." [41]
- Where did you stay?

---

[41] *Hedgehog in the Fog*: an old Soviet cartoon about a hedgehog who lives in the woods and thinks interesting thoughts and philosophical truths to tell the world as he flows in the river of life.

- Near Siam Station.
- Alone?
- Yup.
- I hate staying alone.
- I feel more comfortable. You know what I adore about my boyfriend Vince?
- His big...Dutch...
- Yes his big Dutch cock. He is also so good to me and he takes care of me. I can be myself with him.
- You of all people I know have the most beautiful heart.

As she sips on her beer I notice scars on her left arm.

- Where are those from?
- High school times.
- ...
- Sometimes you feel down. Things in the family...dad was going to divorce my mom...I had nobody to confide in. So at the time I only had my dog. She understood me. I could confide in her. She would never let me down or betray my trust.
- It is beautiful. But you know she is not conscious, right?
- She understands everything.
- No, she doesn't.
- I don't agree. I have given money to charity so that a homeless dog has a porridge to eat.
- Moni...your heart...is so beautiful.

Tears fall down my face.

- Why you crying now?
- I've just...been through so much pain....and ....I don't know...if anything is worth it.
- You know what I realized? That life is just one big fat joke. So why don't we just laugh?..
- I've lost the will to laugh, love, smile. I can't. I don't want to.

- Djana, listen to me. You have everything. You have it all, you have to take it. Just think of the people around you and understand how lucky you are to have IT ALL. I was thinking...maybe in 20 years our kids will be sitting like this and chatting about us. I can hear 'em saying, *You know, that old bitch of a mom!*
- Hahahaha!
- Whatever this force that brings us together every time...will bring us together again. Also since you are going to Mongolia maybe you should go to Hohhot first. Get to the border by bus and then by train to Ulaan-Baatar. I've been there 10 years ago. You can explore Inner Mongolia as well.
- Good idea. What is UB like?
- Tiny and gloomy. Trust me...you *wont* like it.
- Anything to see?
- The Parliament House and Budweiser Bar. If you're there, tell Dave I said hi.
- Ok.
- I would invite you to stay at my place but I got somebody living there right now....and my parents live in yebenyakh.[42]
- I don't really care...I would love to see it.
- Trust me.

Harry passes by to tell me that tomorrow himself and Brandy are going to see the Great Wall. I want to sleep on the Great Wall. So tomorrow I will be hanging out with Moni.

---

[42] Can be translated into English as a close equivalent to "Far the Fuck Out There".

The next morning we go to see the Workers Stadium and drop into Hooters. It is funny how Chinese girls are skinny but look busty wearing tit-pads. On to Sanlitun Market: clothes, counterfeit brands, cosmetics, shoes, accessories...in the area of the same name, famous for them bars and clubs. Jess tries on a white woven hat and falls in love with it. Oh, I am used to calling Nomin Jess - her nickname from high school. She says she is from Japan when a vendor asks her where she is from. She used to tell people she is from Scotland. She lived in all these places and sometimes has difficulty identifying where she is from. If I say I am from the United States and it calls for less questions than if I tell people I am from Russia, why not?

I try on a white silk dress. Then I try the same model in scarlet red. Moni tells me to buy it as it looks beautiful. *Duoshao qian?* As I bargain the asking price of 200 yuan down to 70 yuan. The saleswoman gets mad. I walk away. Find the same dress for the asking price of 150 and compromise to buy 3 dresses of the same model in different colors for the asking price of one. I look in the mirror and feel like a little princess again. Angry, drop the dresses and run away. I talk Moni out of buying a somewhat shirt/dress the sales woman wont take Moni's price for. She is seriously bargaining over 10 yuan.

We leave the marketplace to walk back to the hostel. I tell her I had a pink dildo and ben-wa balls: especially-made balls with a misplaced weight-center. When you insert them into your vagina, you move around, move up and down and come, come, come. But China is a very conservative country and so far we have not even seen a strip bar. We manage to find a shy "sex shop": a tiny window in a residential building. Dildos, vibrators, rabbit vibrators, rabbit vibrators with pearls, handcuffs, straps, garter belts, boas, but no ben-wa balls. After we return to *the hostel*

..Moni's cab disappears in the dusty streets of downtown Peking.

I throw on my running shoes. I run. Out the hostel.
Free. Temple of Heaven Park.
Altar of the Sky.

That's when I feel pain. I feel hurt. So hurt that having all this...I can't do the most important thing...[43]

The emperor rules by the mandate of the Sky.
Thus the Temple of Heaven was a way to communicate with Higher Realms.
The monarch was supposed to annually affirm legitimacy of his power and ask the Sky for a rich harvest.

I rub my sore feet as *time is standing still when I'm not moving. Should be moving physically. Constantly. It is the only way.* The only way to keep up with moving in time.

The past, present and future collide...in one moment of the ending of July // beginning of August. *Stops* time. *In those dates...time is non-existent as we know it. It is not linear. In that time...we can make a choice.*
Having seen the future.
And having come up with a decision...for our learning.
The best decision.

---

[43] ...I can't give love to the man who sprung it.

I stretch in the kids' park and buy a bottle of warm water. You are 80% water, thus you are what you drink and it is most natural for the body to intake liquid of the same temperature. 36.6 C.[44]
...past shopping malls, cafes, around the Ming City Wall and back to the hostel. Feel hot to get off. Alone in the dorm. Fall back in my bed. Put down the Brazilian flag. Take off my shorts. Touch my stomach, my thighs, as I rub my clit and feel the hairs on my lips...I open my legs and sit on a deodorant stick and move on top...up and down...forward and backward...as it hits the spot...I ride it, and ride it...make myself come in 5 minutes as I let out a sigh and a moan......the shudder...the noise in my ears...the sense of losing gravity....I lay down and relax....sign. then relax. As I get myself together from the ecstasy I had put my body through, I shower...and eat kung pao chicken, string beans stir-fried in soy sauce from across the road.

The next morning I meet a couple from Canada: Judy and Jason. I tell them I want to sleep on the Great Wall as they tell me they will be trekking it in a few days.

I leave the hostel to explore the imperial gardens of Beihai Park and discover the gardening technique and style of the architectural skill and richness of traditional Chinese garden art.
By ferry on to the Pavilion of the Five Dragons to a Nine-Dragon Wall with beautiful depictions of 635 mythical animals. The most beautiful part is of course the white Tibetan stupa given to the Dalai Lama as a symbol of peace during his visit in 1651. This is officially the first Tibetan *chorten* I see in China. It is also the biggest one in China outside of Tibet.

---

44 Do not drink chilled water - it shocks the body.

As I enter the Forbidden City from the "back-door" Gate of Heavenly Purity, I stream through the halls and living rooms of the Qing and the Ming dynasties. It had been closed from visitors for years: hence the name.

There are 9,999 rooms and the concept comes from the principle of yin and yang: the key of all Chinese design. The odd numbers are associated with the male energy - the yang - the emperor - and nine times nine is especially lucky. The color red is abundant as it represents prosperity and happiness. Brides wear red, not white, as white is associated with mourning. A giant screen is playing a video of the restoration of the palace as I pass through the Gate of Supreme Harmony - statues before the buildings represent the ideas of happiness (crane), longevity (tortoise) and justice (rice-measuring provision); into one of the five marble bridges through endless stalls of souvenirs, farewell the guardian lion statues, or foo dogs, symbols of mythic protective powers; and out into the Meridian Gate to the main square.

Backpackers' meeting point. Man wearing shirt with Moscow subway map. Is he Russian? He does *look* Russian. We both turn away as our eyes meet.

Lama Temple West of town. The hall of the Wheel of Law with a statue of Tsongkapa. I sit down by a prayer wheel. Feel no pre-determination. Feel...it is up to me. I can stay at the prayer wheel, or leave. I can ask someone to take a picture of me - or not ask anyone and have no pictures from here. I feel jaded.
I feel...James.

I exit the pavilion as a sandalwood-carved image of 500 scholars of the Buddha made of gold, silver bronze, tin and metal farewell my visit.

Across the street on to the Confucius Temple: the largest outside of his birthplace in Shandong province. 198 stone tablets with 51,624 names of the advanced scholars...and the Master's statue.

In the afternoon I make a run to the shopping mall next to Wangfujing street - famous for the live scorpions and raw anything and everything that crawls - and find the dress I had been looking at buying with Nomin. As much as I love white and scarlet red, I buy blue for a change.
I get a beer and sit down at the lobby. Need a romance. Quick shower, put fresh yogurt into my hair for nourishment.

Mongolian visa application to the Consulate wearing a black dress from Vietnam and my flat shoes which are officially torn apart.
Bright and early: I have been told they only accept applications until 11 a.m. I apply for a 5-day transit visa.
No more stories of encephalitis ticks from the deserts of Gobi. I just want to visit monasteries in UB. Then be on the way home to Russia: the first time I enter my home-land over-land.

I bump into Judy and Jason as they tell me they are ready to go to the Great Wall. Tipsy from beer I see the Moscow shirt guy again. I walk up to him. His name is Philip, he lives in Las Vegas, he just came from Mongolia on the TS train. He is old and bold. He must have major hard feelings. He keeps to himself. Hard to get to know. He has a look in his eyes...a kind look. I offer to grab kung pao chicken together. We laugh and cheer. He leads me into the hutongs, gets lost and a kind Chinese man speaking a few words of English shows us the way back.

The next morning I check out and Judy, Jason and I go to Dongzhimen station to catch our bus. Simatai section of the

Great Wall: as it is said to be a lot less touristy than Badaling. My initial idea was to get to Jinshanling, trek 10 kms to Simatai - and catch a bus back to Beijing.

As we get to Muyin we charter a minibus which costs 20 yuan each - and will take us right to the entrance at Simatai. Jason controls the situation. Expectable for a guy of four feet of height. Judy has bad acne. No wonder Jason controls her. She says they have been together for 10 years...since high school. Jason is the type of guy who has nothing to show the world but his control over this girl. She is pretty...but very unfit and beer-bellied...just like Jason.

Take Nothing But Photographs,
Leave Nothing But Footprints,
Keep the Wall Wild and Beautiful![45]

We catch a cable car to take us to the wall so we can start the hike. The Simatai section is very steep. As we walk on the wall, it breaks - and I tell the guys to turn back because it is unsafe and crazy. They tell me if I think it is crazy I can just walk back alone. I continue walking with them. We go past the sign which says *Enter at your own risk.*
This implies that if anything happens to you, nobody but you, is responsible. This is also true for everything else.

---

[45] Note at the Entrance.

The Great Wall was constructed during 2,000 years. It is over 6,000 meters long, its construction was complete during the Ming dynasty when the Mongols were extruded from China and the gigantic defense would stop them from hitting again. It starts from Shanhaigu'an pass and ends at Jiayugu'an pass, looking like a gigantic dragon, twisting from hill to hill: it can be seen from space.

We "get comfortable" in one of the watch towers and Jason takes a picture of me sitting on the wall, glaring into the valley. We watch the sun go down. *Tell people you work in counseling.*

As I lay down hearing indistinct conversation, thinking how nice it would have been if Philip was here too. We would cuddle in his sleeping bag, kiss and make love. It remains my fantasy to this day. *Make love on the Great Wall of China.*

Sleepless and annoyed, I start reading through the Trans-Siberian guidebook Philip gave me. I will enter Siberia from Mongolia - a border town called Naushki on to Ulan-Ude - the capital of Buryatiya Autonomous Republic. Then to Irkutsk - a major tourist stop-over in Siberia because of Lake Baikal. The lake is very significant in Russia...and to the world. Not only does it hold 1/5 of the world's fresh water reserve and is hundreds of miles long, it holds the secret of our existence.
Its depths have had numerous divers looking to find living Lemurians. And they have...once. The underwater caves...hold preserved foundation of humankind....in the state of samadhi...
...they are able to breathe under water as they amphibians...and their noses are formed in a little twirl which allows them to be amphibians....just like the Nepali number "1"...their eyes are looking down, half-open with the top lids covering the upper

halves of the eyes...as they inhabited in partially infra-red light...[46]

The lake is part of the Tea Road, by which Buddhism came to Russia in the first place. Tibetan Buddhism. I can already feel my powerful anchor...the juniper in the monastery...the oil lamps...the chants...I have a special mission there.

In Ivolginsk Datsan - the biggest *lamasery* in all of Russia - bury my treasure vase of memory of the powerful soul connection and love - give it back to where it belongs.

"...human's torsion fields are twisted anti-clockwise by the forces guarding entry to the caves...

...causing extreme pains and willingness to leave" [47]

The LP Guide has little tips on Novosibirsk - the biggest city and the Capital of Central Siberia. Same goes to Barnaul and Altai - the mountain range in the Southern part of Central Siberia which borders Kazakhstan....also a Unesco World Heritage Site.

As the sleepless night is over with the first rays of the sun coming up on the horizon I walk out of the watch tower with my back sore from the rocks. Lol no...I won't be attempting to jog today.

Free spirit...but a grounded, stable base is important. *Freedom within frames*. Powerful Moon in natal chart signifies family ties and emotional security linked therewith. Moon in Gemini - Sun in Pisces - communication is important, as are short travels, and all kinds of media = all the traits of Gemini. When I have children, I will have twins. *When Moon progresses in fifth house.*

---

[46] Muldashev, Ernst. "Ot kogo mi proizoshli?"

[47] Ditto

240

Sun in Pisces = men I am attracted to are mystical, spiritual, introvert...and highly-chanced mental patients.

It all just goes together.

Do not listen to predictions...they only trickster.

The kids get up and we walk to the exit. Past the zipline and out the park I can see a path onto the horizon leading to Jinshanling.

It turns out it is illegal to stay on the wall overnight but everybody does it anyway as the private drivers facilitate us.

We switch to a bus to Muyin at Beijing. Shower, change and run to the Mongolian Consulate to get my passport and visa. It is now time to get paperwork in order: ticket for Ulaan-Baatar. Stay in UB Guesthouse, as recommended by Philip. The word is out the ticket to UB costs 200 dollars and the only place to buy it is at the International Hotel, next to the Central Train Station. This all seems like a bad dream. I am not spending 200 dollars on this ride.

I return to the hostel and see Philip...checking me out. Why doesn't he do something? He introduces me to his friend who wants to buy a China LP Guide: Niall from Ireland. I invite him to join us for dinner. We buy kao-ya for 20 yuan, rice and fried string beans. We drink cheap beers from the hostel's bar and I get tipsy as fuck. I change into my sleek black dress. Philip and Niall stare at me. Oh. The desire to be seen. Who did not see me for my personality? So that I use sexuality to gain that recognition?

Philip is the type of sad who keeps it all to himself. What it is he is sad about? We get comfortable on a couch next to my dorm. After ten minutes of sucking on each others' necks, Philip jumps up to get a private room. I sober back to my senses and tell him to forget about it and about J. I tell him...I understood him more than anyone ever has...and he had to fuck up and betray the most important person in this life. I retracted, withdrew, abused the teachings because I fell madly in love. Which I hadn't been able to feel ever since - as the chemical high is gone. No relationship lasts because the sex drive = the chemistry fades off. Philip says it is not about sex. He tells me of a woman he dated when he was young who married somebody else and left into the blue. She came back after 8 years....but he had no feelings for her. She died for him. I tell him it is not fair...as love is stronger than pride.

- Eight years, darling. Eight years.

I wander off to the Summer Palace: a garden where the royalty escaped the roasting summers in the Forbidden City.
Gigantic, beautiful Kunming Lake. Cute Marble Boat.
Garden of Virtue and Harmony.
Glare at the lake. Sip on a soy bean drink.
Higher decisions are not even made in 3D - they are made in the higher soul frequency of the color blue.
Temple of the Sea of Wisdom.
Take in the energies of the people who lived here...loved here....who were born here...who died here....and I feel.
Dizzy.
... out the park. Through the Hall of Happiness and Longevity. Energy of the vague sky...the clouds setting in...almost about to rain. Drum and Bell Towers.
kinky Chinese man. Tries to take a picture of me. *Turn away.* I've hated taking photos and been conscious of other people taking photos of me...since I've seen how in rural villages of Russia people use photos to manipulate energies, intrude into a person's energy field, cast a spell on them, put a hex on them...very...very popular trend in Russia. Comes from the ritual purification from sins, also called baptism with holy water. Slavic Aryan Vedas say all re-ligions originated therefrom.

242

Love has been the most amazing thing that has happened to me and it has been the worst punishment.
Love was the strongest drive and the weakest link.
Love was the trigger for my search.
A trigger to work out karma with someone.
It saddens me...that somebody so beautiful...intelligent...had such a bad experience.
It saddens me...but
I feel nothing. In truth...I feel nothing.
Whatever happens next....will only trigger me to work out more karma.
More pain.

No more pain.

I feel like a girlfriend now that I have someone waiting for me and I doubt Philip had been up to anything the entire day but siting around. Eating chicken and cashews. I stop at a bakery and grab a dessert of strawberries with whipped cream. Mmmmm.

I see Philip sitting there all day, doing nothing. Just sitting around. Eating his chicken cashew. Putting on weight. He almost jumps on me, restrains himself from kissing me on the mouth. An Israeli chick bums into our privacy without a hint of diplomacy. I stand up and sit next to the TV. Philip comes by into a chair next to me and puts his arm around me.

- Had a good chat?
- No. I don't care about her, - as he kisses me hard on the lips.

Niall buys my LP Guide for the asking price of 35 yuan. YAY! It is full of advice, tips and true things about places I visited.

Philip and I get drunk from the beers I am buying all night. I get mad at myself for doing all the work and I am mad at him for being okay with it. He does not realize there is anything wrong. We start making out as I rub against him in our new favorite spot = the couch upstairs in between my dorm and the bathroom.

- It's been too long for me I guess. Like a year.
- I hope you're not hoping to find true love while you're traveling.
- No...but...how long has it been for *you*?

None of your business.

- I never really orgasmed with a man until recently.
- Never ever?
- No. Not during intercourse.
- Oh. I have a friend who never orgasmed.
- Ever, ever?
- Nope.
- Weird. I orgasmed...I know my body...I know how to get myself off.
- I have this friend at work at home, Cassie. She got a dildo with a suction cup and said, *I ain't leaving the house for a week!*

I have one of those too. Which is why I never *left* the house! Lol. Philip goes on to check his facebook as he received a message from a Brazilian friend living in his apartment while he is not home. He says she acts really interested in him, but he is not into her, because the only reason she likes him is because he is *different*.

I went out with a Brazilian guy and I felt he only liked me because he thought I was *different*: looked like Anna Kournikova.

- What is the story with you, Philip?
- Stacy. I was with her during high school. I met her when I was 17.

- She was your first?
- Yes. I was her first, too.
- See...that's a very important detail.
- She went off to marry someone who got her into religion and she said she was in love with him...
- ....sounds like religion and love, something I went through.
- ...she called me 8 years later and said she owed me...said she wanted to see me...she realized nobody treat her like I did...
- ...and...?
- I said no.
- Did you have sex?
- She offered...she said she owed me...but I refused.
- I've thought over and over again how can you love someone like I did...having never had sex with them. I wondered if I loved him so much because we HADN'T been intimate.
- Djana, love and trust. It is all about love and trust.

...and all that time I thought I was hurting because I still loved him.

....and when he didn't respond I realized I was hurting because I was still so hurt.

...out the hostel in the hutong past the dumpling shops as a hologram of Philip materializes before my eyes. Great.

- Hey!

How do I get rid of him.

- Hey. I am going to the Liu Li Chao bus station, do you want to come?
- Yeah!

Can't he just do his own thing.

The ticket clerk tells me I can't book the bus earlier than 24 hours in advance. The bus leaves at 6 p.m. and arrives at 4 a.m. at the border-town of Erenhot.

- What am I gonna do at the China-Mongolia border at 4 in the morning!?
- Perhaps it's better to just take the train.
- ...
- But it's 200 dollars.
- Let's go to the train station and see what is really costs.

Ticket salesman says train 23 departing at 7 a.m. on Sunday costs 150 kwai to Erenhot. It is a sleeper. No question about it. But maybe it's some mistake, no?

International Hotel. CITS Office. Price for Beijing-Ulaan-Baatar Train 23 departing at 7 a.m. on Sunday is 1,900 kwai. I ask them for a quote on the Beijing-Erenhot price but she says she cannot give me one.

- Same train, but a difference of 1,750 kwai? - asks Philip.
- Apparently so. But what will I do at the border?
- Can't you catch a bus or a taxi to the border?
- Why did you not do it?
- ...my friends and I chickened out.

I run to the post office to send a parcel home. I pay 300 yuan, it is 99% hot lingerie I never wore and very unlikely to need in the middle of Mongolia....I figure if I have no hot clothes to wear - chances of finding a decent man are higher.

I buy my ticket for Erlian = Erenhot. I plan to get to the border and catch a taxi or a bus, cross the border and catch a train to Ulaan-Baatar for 20 dollars as I had been told is what it really costs. That way...when everyone else is paying 200 dollars for the trip...I am paying 50...tops.

Philip shows me a video of *khoomii* (throat-singing) in Gobi.

As night kicks in...we drink and make out on *our* couch. I see a guy who reminds me of someone...from some movie. He has blonde hair and he is very focused on his computer. I need to have his attention. I wonder where he is from.

Back to Philip: his hard-on is about to burst.

- I want to eat you out.
- I wont let you. It's too personal.
- I am REALLY good at it.
- No guy is good at it.
- I always have been. I ate Stacy for 3 years.
- ...
- We've never had sex.
- You've never been with her?
- No.
- Sounds weirder than I thought. Like me. Religion, no sex.
- I really like to..
- ...no guy likes it.
- I love it. I love watching a woman come.
- ...
- You say that because you don't like to suck a dick.
- That's not why I say it. I think it's gross.
- Cus you don't enjoy sucking a dick?
- How long will it take you?
- Ten minutes.
- You're bragging.
- Do you have any tattoos?

- No. Never will. I hate tattoos.
- You don't like body art?
- I don't like the idea of needles on my body.
- I have a tattoo.
- Where?
- On my ass.
- What is it?
- Your name.
- Haha.
- Really. It says, *Your Name.*
- It's funny. I don't think you have had the time to tattoo my name on your ass in two days.
- Do you want to see it?
- No.

He jumps and pulls his pants down.
- No!

What the fuck is wrong with this guy sticking his ass in my face?

The guy promises me he will wake me up by kissing me in between my thighs.

I wake up early, go jogging, come.back and start.packing.

Philip comes into my dorm, flushed, excited. He smells like smoke, stinks, still wearing the Moscow subway shirt. He sits in my bed. I should say, "get out of my bed, you smelly nasty dirty thing."
- Can I focus please? I need to get things done.

He quietly walks away.

I find him downstairs on his computer and ask him if he wants to have breakfast. I make whole-wheat sandwiches with peanut butter and banana slices. He eats it and continues watching TV. Annoys the shit out of me. Where is his "thank-you, Djana for the lovely free nutritious yet savoring meal" ??

I say nothing and continue bubbling inside.

-       You want to go to the amusement park today?
I do. Since money had been such a big thing for him, he is not going to pay, so I say,
-       No.
I leave him and change.
My last day in Beijing I will go to the Olympic Stadium and run. Run the anger out. Alone.
-       Philip, do you want to go see the Olympic Stadium?
-       Well...I actually wanted to see it at night-time.
I go to the Internet. I yell at a Chinese cop supervising the calm abidance in the cafe for bumping into my chair. I get so mad, frustrated and I feel everyone is using me because I am so nice...and I cannot help it...cannot help but want to help, teach, protect others, neglect *my* needs. It sickens and saddens me. I put on my running shoes, take a bottle of water and catch the subway to the Olympic Stadium. I get out into the street. I see it: it is a Bird's Nest.
-       Can we take a picture with you!?
-       I am not a model!
I run. run. and run. I sit down on a bench. Everyone wants a piece. Everyone wants energy. But what about me.

What about me?
....It is within my innate nature to want to save another...at the cost of my own. How long is this going to go on for.
I stretch my back, my legs, my arms. I reach for the sky...
I did not find you. This is my last chance.
This is my last day in China and I cannot find you.

My journey has no meaning. Slowly but surely...I fucked up. I failed to find you.

Why can't he just be here with me.

...I sob...through the palms of my hands...I try to wipe the tears running down my face...
I throw off my top and run in my sports bra...I gasp...and sign...out of breath. I drink water.
I had been losing moisture excessively....sweating *and* crying.

I stop. I reach to the sky.

Angels...Angels...

This man who is always with me...but never really with me.

I come back to the hostel and finish packing.

Shower, wash hair, fix braids.

Feel *so* good. Muscle happiness. Right here. Out the hostel for kao-ya...steamed rice...broccoli. It is all for me.

Sit down, eat alone.

- Hey! - the Israeli chick smacks my head to get my attention, - what's up?
- Don't you ever fucking touch my head.
- Are you serious?!
- Does it look like I am joking?

I love myself. It feels amazing to take care of myself and no-one else. No longer co-dependent on other people's happiness. Finally FREE...finally ME.

- Hey! - Philip sits down next to me.

Always the moment for idiots. He couldn't get the energy from me so he is doing everything he possibly can to get it.

- I've got a lot of food here...if you want some...

He grabs a piece of duck, chews it and throws the bone back into the bag.

- The bag for bones is over there! What is wrong with you!
- You disappeared. Did you go to the Olympic Stadium?
- Yes. I ran for three hours. I thought I would have needed more nutrition than normal since I lost so many calories. But I feel quite full now. I would really love some red wine.
- The store is closing now if you want to get some.
- I paid for last night. I would really love some red wine.
- JESUS CHRIST! - as he runs off.

Unbelievable. So easily manipulated. He comes back with a bottle of wine and two plastic cups.

- I am glad you are not drinking fast tonight. You get hot and make out with me.

- Okay, I wont make out with you.
- It's just that you get hot and in the morning...communication is lost. You get so distant. It's like...if anything happened between us, next morning would have been horrible.

Change your clothes! Don't sit your dirty ass on my clean sheets!...and

- I gave you breakfast and you did not even say THANK YOU!
- Is that what this was about? About me not saying *thank you*?
- That, yes, and other things.

Guys flip out about gratitude all the time.

Now it's my turn. How does it feel!

- Thank you, Djana.
- Whatever! I am always the giving one and I never get anything back.
- Well usually I am the one doing that and you know, that night...things were really hot...
- ...
- ...maybe you are more used to situations like this.
- Stop trying to make me think that you're in love with me.
- I'm not in love with you.
- So stop trying to make me think you are.
- ....have you ever had a broken heart?
- Is this your way of saying you had an erection?

...and until you fuck me, you can't forget me.

A movie I am not paying attention to is on.[48]

- Are you absolutely sure you can't have it?

---

[48] ...if I know for sure that the most important thing in my life...I can't have. One thing I want that I can't have.

Am I absolutely sure that my other half cannot be with me in this timeline in physical form?

- Yes.

A young couple sits down next to us: an ugly fat British beer-gutted football fanatic with a cute French girl. They have been together for four years. The girl asks me why do I not have a boyfriend.[49]

- I haven't found the right one for myself. And...I am unavailable. I can't be with anyone.

The pain of rejection has blinded me as I stream across the world in vengeance.

- Men find unavailable women attractive.

Which is why J ran away just as I confessed.

- Love and trust, Djana. Love and trust.
- With unavailable women they can pretend they want something more. If they believe hard enough in it. In truth they know, consciously or unconsciously, that they will never breakthrough this electric-wire of a defense. Guys like you pick women like your Brazilian friend: not good enough for them - making sure they don't get tied down.
- You're talking about yourself now, Djana?

I am

- talking about you.
- Djana...
- Philip.
- Djana.
- Philip?
- Do you have any idea how beautiful you are?

---

[49] I do. He just...can't take me out so that you can see it. When I feel horny I get myself off and he mentally comes with me too.

I suddenly realize...from all this talk from this 40-year old guy who has not lost the urge to get married and have a family one day...he had been stuck in this relationship with one girl. I remembered him. I had seen him before. A lifetime. I was his. He was not mine. I don't trust him anymore. We lived in a gher. He betrayed me for a herd of sheep. And he is trying to teach me about trust today.

I realized....how can this truth be so simple...here it is...right in front of me...

Ever since I remember....everybody had somebody....a girl, a boy, a love from childhood, a past memory they hold on to....I had noone.

I had nothing/nobody to show for the reason for my pain....

Karma in soul groups. Is what binds people in this 3D drama....

And I did not have to do it anymore...when my two barren years in Moscow working as a translator for my father's company....was *closer and closer to my dream. CLOSER>* to waking up to the memory. EMPTINESS.
Remembering my lifetimes with my twin soul.

It was times when I watched so much drama unfold before my eyes - and I was so happy to be free from it. I knew I would never face anything like everyone else around me was going through - girlfriend/boyfriend/husband/wife drama. Wife nag/kids bitch.all that bullshit.
Because to me...it did not have to happen. I had all been tied to my twin soul who stands with me every moment of my existence and witnesses my failures and my successes.

But he can't hold me. He can't make love to me....he can't wash my hair while I shower... massage gel into my breasts....play with my clit and rub the walls inside my vagina.

But it is our karma. It is the best way out of this story.
It is the only way out of this story.

Over-writing it in *this spooky town*...

....and that's how I knew....

...but the reason for not having anyone to fall back on in my memory was that my twin soul, the one I have the most karma with, had not been incarnated in flesh, here, with me.

He shares a parallel with me. he cannot be with me.
how am I going to explain this to the world.
I live with the man who loves me more than anything else in the world...and because he does...I feel he can only let me know so much...at a certain time....and keep the rest from my mind's eye...for my own good.....
....and I never find him.

He is never here. He whispers.

Once he yelled at me. In the crowd.

It starts with a hum....

As I ran through the crowd as I couldn't take the energy....I recall him...in Disneyland in Orlando three years ago. I was going off a ride. I felt the pain. He yelled at me.

we were separated....we were separated....

5 a.m. Get up, brush teeth, drink water. Hungover from the wine the night before. Take my backpack. Check out. Hail cab to train station. Pay 20 yuan. Line up for train. Hot Israeli guy. *Sucker for the long dark hair, blue eyes, dark hair, blue eyes....*
...on to train No. 23. Get into cargo car. Will be disconnected at border. Wheels of train>changed.

....fall asleep...being alone always shifts where I belong. It is times like these...that I fall asleep...and then wake up in a different place. the journey is almost over.
we are almost there.
I have carried the pink crystal from the Himalayas as it symbolized a medium carrying memory of the love I touched when I met another part of my soul living in the same timeline *when* I thought he did *not*. A purple sand-clock given to me by my mother. The highest metaphysical color. I put them both into a white handwoven bag I bought in Mexico City.

China-Mongolia border. Dark and chilly. Looking for a taxi cab or ANYOne who can in anyway show me to Mongolia. Nobody speaks English. Writing in Mongolian. Scared shitless. Taxi drivers point back to train station. Wait for ticket saleswoman to open kiosk. Only open only 2 hours daily: morning when train passes through to Beijing and at night - when same train goes to Ulaan-Baatar. 750 yuan for the train that will take me through the border and on to UB.

"Can I buy a ticket to get across the border?"

"Yes". Then I will have to buy the ticket to UB from the car supervisor.

Think fast.

Go to supermarket, exchange 100 USD. Buy ticket into UB. Saved 70 dollars on trip.

Sit in the waiting hall with a group of foreign travelers. Israeli guy writing thoughtfully in his journal.

On to the immigration office. Hand my passport over. Ask to put exit stamp next to entry stamp.

- Russian? - an officer asks, not even having looked at my passport.

I am not...Russian. I was born in Russia.

- Yeah!! How did you know??!

This has to be the most romantic station I've been to so far.

Can't we just have some fun once in a while...it doesn't always have to be so serious.

I hop back on the train and my neighbor is a Mongol kid who offers me sticky sweets. I thank him, but no thank him, and brew my cream of broccoli soup. It has to be the most nourishing thing while you're train-traveling. Starch is better than crackers, that's for sure.

Well...right here, right now, anyway.

X. Mongolia.

The Mongolian immigration officials step on the train, wearing protective masks, keeping themselves safe from the "swine-flu". I filled out my declaration form in which I indicated that I am brining 200 dollars with me. I ask if the entry stamp will be put on my visa or a separate page. The official tells me, "no problem, yes it is put on the visa, not on a separate page". I hop back on the train and we are in Zamyn-Ude.

The foundation of karma in a bloodline is formed...for the actions of people...which shall protect their children, grandchildren...the positioning of the planets at the time of birth...your complete blueprint and course of destiny...<u>here.</u>
....*I never want you to say anything that does not belong where you belong. I feel you had been here so many times before...and when the time comes for you to get married and have children as it is your destiny to continue the bloodline and be the first - two powerful children - as psychic as you are....love will give you the will and the desire to live, love and give birth to two lives. Two boys. Two twins.*

I wonder if I should or should not call the hostel people to pick me up. How is the journey going to differ if I get to the hostel by myself VS. have them pick me up? Would I meet different people? Would I get angry and upset after walking to the hostel when I could have been going by minibus without worry?...
...not as adventurous...but simpler....easier: call Bobbi who confirmed my reservation. I ask the *provodnitza*[50] for a cell-phone and dial UB guesthouse.

---

[50] Car-supervising lady.

- I have a reservation for today. Train 23. Car 9. Can you pick me up?
- Thank you for calling, yes, of course we will pick you up!

There we go. See? Easy. No stress.

The writing is on the wall: Ulaan-Baatar. Mongolian is similar type to Russian - but that's the only commonality.

E.g. hello = *bayeyarlaa*.

I get off the train and thank God I called and asked for pick-up.

Into the minibus: good-looking blonde guy with a dark-haired friend. Where have I seen him?

In Leo Hostel. While making out with Philip.

- Where are you guys from?
- Michigan.

YAY! Americans!

- I live in Miami. I am from Russia.

Love the energy of getting to know new people.

Excitement. Such a drug.

- I live in Moscow for 1 year I study in MSU, - says the blondie.
- Oh really, *govorite po-Russki*?
- Da, govoru.

Love the accent!

UB guesthouse is 3-apartments-joined-in-one in a 1960's building. It's clean bathrooms and a small kitchen.

Streets of Ulaan-Baatar: average-ish suburbia. People understand Russian. I ask about paragliding in a travel agency as the agent laughs in my face and tells me tourism in Mongolia is only starting out, whereas paragliding is a few steps up> *very* dangerous.

I bump into Brandy while shopping for toilet paper. She is chewing on a banana, just like the last time I saw her in Beijing.

- Hey! What are you doing here?

- I am...buying toilet paper.
- I came back from a Gobi desert trip for 5 days...it was fun..but I got a big tick in my ear...
- They are very dangerous.
- Yes, I am going to see a doctor now. It is bleeding...
- Go now!
- Hey where are you staying?
- UB Guesthouse.
- Get out of here!

Okay.

Gandan Khiid. *Mongolian* for Gandan Monastery.

"The Great Place of Complete Joy."

I had been warned it might not be safe to walk to it...so how was I supposed to get there....by flying?? or maybe....paragliding??

I walk to the entrance.

I spin the prayer wheels.

Walk to Sukhbaatar square on to the Museum of Choijin Lama. The statues looking back at me. I return to the hostel to make myself a chocolate pudding. I bring the milk to a boil. I put the mix in and stir vigorously to avoid any lumps. The meditative and consciousness-relaxing process of stirring in clockwise direction makes me go into an altered-state as a memory comes *through*...

- What are you making?
- Chocolate mousse.
- Soon you will be making baby milk mousse.
- Luis Felipe, don't joke like that!

...from a Mexican novella *Marielena* about a woman born to Cuban immigrants literally during their escape to Miami. *On the boat* to Miami. She had a simple life in a poor neighborhood.

She grew up, went to college, got a job in an advertising agency, fell in love with her boss who was married to an older, richer woman - the owner of the agency. Their affair ended in Marielena's pregnancy and murder of the boss's wife. Marielena married an older guy out of guilt as he had lost eye-sight after an accident while driving with her in his car. She is a strong, genuine and loving woman...she is Lucia Mendez.

Her heroic figure lingers. Could there be a connection between mine watching it as a 12-year old kid, forming an image of what a woman should be?

I wonder.

Am I heroic...never allow anyone to help me. I am the one thinking of others and putting others first. Always help others. My honor. My integrity. **For the benefit of all sentient beings...**

I put the dessert into the freezer and steal a slice of pizza. I go out to the street to get some fresh air and *suutei tsai* - Mongolian tea. Greasy and warm. Sour taste.

I book my tour to Terelj National Park outside of UB for 40 dollars/day. Ticks are abundant in the area and I pack some cotton wool to put into my ears. Generally you are supposed to protect all the cavities in the body. I've always been scared of the ticks. It goes back to my childhood when my cousin and I went trekking in the woods and a tick climbed into his belly-button and they had to extract him.

A minibus takes us all the way into the park. Its gorgeous mountain and valley scenery takes me in as we get comfortable in a *gher* and have lunch. It is a beautiful sunny day. It is Mongolia.

And in Mongolia, you don't ask what meat it is. Normally it is pig, dog, cat or even camel. Just like one of those that runs past us as everyone chews their fried rice and pigs. I just say, *bi makh i dej cha dakh gui* meaning, "I can't eat meat." I chew on my rice and vegs. I trek up the mountain as the wind blows in my face and past my ears as I hear Spirits. I fall down and get back up. *Time goes fast.* Was I just in Brazil, thinking the same while kayaking down the Amazon river? I felt this journey will bring me some form of...illness...or disorder. I just come back home with it...Since I've gone through so many changes already. And what about my family? How have they been? With my calls from Thailand telling them I am on the verge of dying from a puncture wound.

How much time has it been? 30, 40 minutes? an hour?

I come back to the camp and we get ready for our horse riding. It's been 5 minutes.

I jump on a horse and trot, gallop and then walk while sitting in the saddle as they are tamed and they know their way in the valley. They shit, too. They have big black cocks. The horse's was hidden in between its buttocks when it bounced down as if it was a hose and started pissing.

- Pisayet kak slon! - exclaims Jeremy, the blonde Michigan guy.

I burst out laughing.

He says that the horse is *pissing like an elephant.*

- Your horse is not pooping the right color! - yells Eric, the brunette Michigan guy.

(Darkish green).

We ride through the valley. My consciousness drifts away again.

We return to the camp.

Three hours later and gassy from the dog/pig/camel insides that must have gotten into my *vegetarian* meal from earlier. Quickly finish some cookies. I wonder of the rotting processes going on inside the gut. I always felt the relationship between the gut and the head - or the mind, the emotions. The chemical processes...that is all is what it is about. The chemistry...

- Hey, wanna play volleyball! - a Swedish girl screams.

-    Yay! - I scream back at her and throw the ball.

Running around screaming, playing ball for an hour, we sit down and relax to watch the sun go down. The boys working at the camp collect 1,000 tugruks from each one of us for beers and we sit warm by the furnace inside the boys' gher.

The family that takes care of us and the horses live here permanently - their ghers have power and light, and even a satellite dish. They need to bring water from elsewhere. The ghers are on a very stable cement base - strong...made to withstand the winds that happen here occasionally. After some urban legend story-telling, we call it quits.

Bloated, I lie down in my bed and try to sleep. I restlessly move up and down until 3 and wake up just before 5 to watch the sun rising.

Back in UB Guestouse I book my bus for Ulan-Ude for 950 RUR: Russian Rubles. I will leave at 7 a.m. and arrive to the Russian border at Kyakhta at 1 p.m., cross it at 2 p.m. and arrive to Ulan-Ude station at 8 p.m. I arrange for a bed and pick-up in Baikal Ethnic Hostel that Bobbi recommended. It will cost a 450 Rubles - roughly 15 dollars.

One chilly morning Eric, Jeremy and I go to the fakes market. Eric buys himself a traditional Mongol *kaftan* - a warm coat, decorated with gold-thread and blue cashmere. I buy myself an incense burner and a bagful of powder juniper. I picture myself cleansing the space and invoking the Spirits of Tibet into my bedroom when I arrive home. I split from the boys once we have eaten lunch in a local restaurant that makes our bodies want to expel of the excess baggage.

I walk to the Zanabazar Museum of Buddhist Art and the Museum of History, past the House of Parliament. I notice the *Budweiser Bar* on the way...I wave a *hi* to it in my mind. Past the Naadam Stadium = a festival that takes place every July: it is a family reunion, a nomad horse race, archery and wrestling fair.

My English is not so very good at describing this...forgive me....but that is the point behind the book. Not to mention...the Pleidians have brought us the message....English language was chosen to channel messages...from other realms.

- Young lady, let me see your passport. - says an official as I line up be stamped out at the border-town of Kyakhta.
- Here.
- You travel a lot. How did you come to Mongolia?
- From China.
- And to China?
- From Vietnam.
- Wow. You've traveled a lot. Here you go.

I hand my passport to an extremely hot officer behind the window. Beautiful face and big shoulders. I feel an affection and passion. Visions of a life together.

What?!

- Excuse me, I was wondering if the exit stamp is put on the visa or next to the visa?
- Ehm...we put it on the visa.
- Thank you. - as I smile at him, he stamps me out of Mongolia... - Dosvidaniya.

XI. Trans-Siberian Express.

Flag of the Russian Federation and a sign "ROSSIYA".
The three horizontal colors associate white with bright future,
blue with clouded present, and red with bloody past.

- What have you been doing in Mongolia?
- Trekking in Terelj, - I respond, looking down. That split
  second I realize that immigration officials, warriors and
  psychologists interpret *eyes down* as hiding or insecure. I
  look back up.
- How did you come to Mongolia? Oh, I see the stamp,
  you flew from Moscow out of Sheremetyevo Airport.

(The stamp of leaving Moscow is last years' ;).

- Here you go.

I carry my bags through customs.

I want to point out, that even though I named the chapter "Trans-
Siberian Express", it is not to mean there is a train with the same
name.
The railway is the longest in the world at 9,289 meters from
Moscow to Vladivostok and branded trains take 7 days.
There are also two other routes, namely Trans-Mongolian and
Trans-Manchurian. I am, of course, of the Trans-Mongolian,
which began at Beijing. The Trans-Manchurian line connects
Irkutsk with Manzhouli and Harbin in China.

In astrology, the tooth cycle is linked to the mythical Selena - the
White Moon. In ethereal terms it represents the Guardian Angel
as it is physically non-existent: a mathematical *point* - the apogee
of the movement of the Moon through a sign. Its cycle is 7 years.
Milk teeth fall out when a child is 7 years old...new ones grow...
...then I think of the connection between the teeth and the
stomach. If you can't chew or eat properly, you can't digest

properly, you can't shit properly. The system goes kaput. The stomach area. The navel. The subtle strong connection with significant others is through the navel. Astral body of emotions.

The bus arrives to Ulan-Ude to the main square of Ploshad Sovetov with the biggest Lenin's Head Memorial. A little girl comes to me and asks me if I am going to the hostel. I tell her, "yes." She is strangely ballsy for her age as she leads me to the car with her father and her mother smiling nicely at me. He tells me they have a Sofia arriving later tonight - he will go to the train station to pick her up. He asks me what religion I am. I tell him I am Tatar and I come from a Muslim family.

- So you're a.....*magometka*.
- A what?
- Magometka. Comes from the word Magomet.
- If you're referring to the Prophet (May Peace be upon him), his name was Mohammed.
- Same thing.
- It's not the same thing.
- All foreigners know it!
- So stick with foreigners!

As we arrive to their enormous house five miles from the city - the mom shows me to my bed.

- Would you like some dinner?
- Yes please. I really want to get some potatoes....where can I get them?
- You know what they say in the village? You don't *get* potatoes, you *store* them. - as she reaches into the attic and pulls out a sack of fresh season's potatoes.
- I like it that you like potatoes. Foreigners...they just don't geddit!
- I know...but I am from Russia.
- Where?

267

- Moscow. But I haven't been home since a year.
- How many countries did you visit?
- Maybe 15...I didn't count.

Tatiana is so nice, humble and welcoming.

- Many people here are mix breed - as you have noticed. My daughter Alina is a half-breed of Buryat and Russian blood. The Buryat indigenous group is the biggest indigenous group in all of Russia. You should try some *pozi* - lamb balls in dough. Like dumplings. They are served at a poznaya - the canteen for pozi. There is one right by the bus station.
- In the city?
- Yes. Are you going to be here over the weekend?
- Probably not.
- You could come with us to see the Lama. Any questions we have. Moreover, here in Siberia, we are all-religion. We can light a candle for someone's health at a Christian Church, we can ask for well-being prayers from a Muslim Mosque, or have our minds blessed by a Buddhist monk. It is all the same.
- Mmmm-hmm.
- You should visit the *Datsan* while you are here.
- Ivolginsk Datsan?
- Yes. It's named after the village called Ivolga. You can catch a minibus from Ploshad Ofitzerov. From here, catch minibus 22.
- How much is it?
- 20 rubles.
- What is special about it?
- It is the oldest in the area. You know the Tea Road?
- Briefly.
- Dashi Dorzho Itigilov, a Buryat Buddhist lama of the Tibetan tradition is there in his "life after death."

- Lama Itigilov?
- According to the story, Itigilov told his students to exhume his body 30 years after his death. He sat in lotus position, began chanting the prayer of death, and died, mid-meditation. The monks followed Itigilov's directions and his body was was interred in Huhe-Zurhen, which means "Dark Blue Heart" in Buaryat language. 30 years later they exhumed his body and were amazed to find none of the usual signs of decay and decomposition. Itigilov looked as if he had been dead only a few hours, rather than three decades. Go to the datsan early morning - be there at 9 a.m. to listen to the morning prayers.

"The red teaching"was coming to land in 1927 and Khambo Lama said he will return in 75 years so he went to "sleep." As the cultural revolution in China, religion was proclaimed "opium for the people." Fearful of the Soviet response to their "miracle", the monks reburied Itigilov's body in an unmarked grave.

Reminds me those who had a second opinion: artists, writers, leaders, were sent into exile by the powers that be into Siberia - we could not have access to it. Now we have found the "backdoor" and sneaked into it from Mongolia. jaja.))

The Datsan. Vendors selling tiny prayer wheels.
Into the park of the monastery.
Walk clockwise.

...please stand by me.
I spin the prayer wheels made of old tin cans. The paintwork is slapdash, naive, tacky. Burial site for soul lesson?
- You came from far away?
- Yes!
- Take off your hat.

Khambin Temple.
Lama Itigilov's body covered by khatas.
Preserved, whole muscles and inner tissue.
No signs of physical decay.

Limbs flexible, the skin elastic.
The corpse will bleed if punctured.

SYSTEM: VOID

s u n y a t a

Eyes closed ><
Walk 10 feet to the magical stone
Touch center with left hand.

...make a wish.
Speak to a lama.
Put me in for a month of pujas or so.

Museum of Buddhist Art. Explore the endless collection of wooden and bronze sculptures, medical treaties and their painted illustrations. A display contains pages of a beautiful atlas illustrating the Tibetan knowledge on medicine. The museum keeper and lecturer is particularly passionate and eager to explain that the first page of the atlas is a diagram of the Universe in the form of a Mandala.

Buddha is sitting in a lotus position, his body is blue, he is holding a Myrobalan flower in the left hand, representing treatment. He is the teacher of medicine. Smaller scale figures surround him, then on another circle, plants are very precisely represented in the medium they grow in - mountains or plains.

The illustrations were used as reference to spread the knowledge of medicine as it is both a vulgarisation and a pictorial translation of the knowledge.

Another page shows the development of the embryo before birth. It's like a comic strip: the first scenes show the soul of a person in the 49 days between death and life, it has the form of a six-year-old transparent child.

He is there when a man and a woman make love and he tries to penetrate the man's mouth. If all goes well, if there's good karma, the woman becomes pregnant. She is then depicted with an embryo inside her stomach. It develops in three phases: fish, tortus and pig.

Sentences accompany the schemes telling, that the inner organs of the child are given by the mother and that the skeleton comes from the father.

The snow blizzard...The blue tones....*hummmmmm*

...a connection arising....I quickly leave.
My 84 train will go on the circumbaikal railway - overlap the lake on its South Coast...symbolizing the end of the time loop. Buddhism teaches that if you are in pain it means you are resisting something. But what is worst than pain is resisting pain. If you don't resist pain but accept it as a part of you.
Let it run through you

Into a
CATACLYSMIC SYSTEM CRASH.

I catch a minibus to the hostel and get lost in the little streets of the settlement of Poselskoye. After an hour of browsing the goats and geese pathways I get to the house to find the doors locked. I bang on the gate and Tatiana comes out to open it.

- How was your day?
- I went to the datsan.
- How did you like it?
- I didn't.
- Did you have an astrologer do a reading for you? Or a palm reading?
- No....
- Why not?
- I've been through psychic intervention already.
- He is a lama..he could have helped you.
- He wasn't there. I just don't want anyone intruding into the course of my destiny with suggestions. I take such things very seriously.
- We've had a lama cleanse the space of our house before we opened it up to backpackers.
- I sense it.
- You have to be very generous with these people, you know.
- Yes.
- They can clean family hexes and curses. A lama cleansed me when I was pregnant: someone was jealous of me and I was having difficulty in labor. Alina only came out half-way and they had to save the rest of her.

Sofia and I sit strangely calm but embarrassed at the same time.

I memorize the hex put on my grandma by relatives envious of her husband. They had poisoned and cursed a towel - it was meant for grandpa, and they shoved it into their bathroom. Grandma took it and wiped her face with it. She was 25 years old. It became covered with hydro-cysts. She lived with them for

49 years until the day she died at 74 her face was as clean as a newborn child's.

- I wont tell you one story...but I will tell you...I do not believe any of it.

Denial is a powerful protection tool.

- ...we need to pay you for the nights. We both leave tomorrow.
- Yes.
- How much do we owe you?
- 450 per night, each.
- So 900. I will bring it right down to you.

At 25 million years old, Baikal is the world's oldest, cleanest and deepest lake at 1,637 meters. It is home to nerpa - funny looking seals found nowhere else in the world. Its water is drinkable in most places and to this day, it holds Russia's 80% fresh water reserve and one fifth of the world's surface fresh water. Baikal had been proclaimed a Unesco World Heritage Site 15 years ago.

Most tourists visiting the lake go to Listvyanka - a small village on the Western shore - one hour from Irkutsk. Other tourists, who know anything about tourism in Siberia and...most backpackers....go to Olkhon - an island in the lake - closer to the Western shore and reachable by routed minibuses from Irkutsk.

200 kilometers through woods and villages on to a ferry station at MRS for 10 minutes and another 70 kilometers on the island into the settlement of Huzir. Most backpackers stay at Nikita's Guesthouse and I will probably do so as well.
Depending whether I can find someone to go with...as staying alone in a beautiful place all alone would be so boring.
Downtown Irkutsk Hostel. A nice lady welcomes me. I let my guard down.
- Govorish po-Russki?
- Ya Rossiyanka.
Rossiyanka - as differed from "Russkaya" meaning "Russian by nationality" means "Russian-citizen."
I am Russian by citizenship, *not* I am Russian by ethnicity.
I shower in the spotless bathtub and receive a text from Eric as he tells me they arrive to Irkutsk tomorrow afternoon. They will be staying at Admiral Hostel for two nights and visiting Listvyanka - however they are heading to Krasnoyarsk - and wont have time to visit Olkhon Island as two days are needed to go there and come back. Spending at least one full day on the island makes it a three day trip. I, on the other hand, have time.

274

I stroll the city into a bookstore for the right read for my train and pick out the last of the four books - by the Pleidians - actually the first of the four books that I was reading...during writing the first ten chapters of the first part of the story in front of you. Also Emmanuel's Book II. Sit by a fountain nearby a soccer stadium and sip on *kvas* - a fermented beverage made from rye bread, poured into plastic cups from a gigantic tank - perfect thirst-quencher for a hot June afternoon.

Eric and Jeremy arrive with Leonid, manager of Admiral hostel. We sit down at the dining table as they recently renovated everything. As my senses are telling me...they recently did a blessing "baptism" here, as well. Russians...they have to bless the house with good energy so that it attracts prosperity.

Here, I have to note, that superstitions are prevalent all over Russia, not just small villages. Along with having peacock feathers in the house being considered bad luck, wearing pearl is considered bad luck, as well as when leaving the house and coming back if you forgot something is bad luck unless you look at yourself in the mirror. Passing something over to someone and shaking hands over a threshold is bad luck. Sitting at a corner of a table is considered you'll never get married. Also if someone steps on your foot, you should step back on theirs, otherwise you will have a fight!

Altai: next time...when I can take it all in. I wanted to go, but Russia is so not-travel friendly....makes me want to do what most backpackers do: take the train straight to Moscow. Three nights. I might visit some family in Kazan, a wealthy town about a thousand kilometers from Moscow. If I go there, it means deviating from the classic Trans-Siberian - well, Mongolian, route. The railway splits into two roads at Ekaterinburg. The head of the family is Rakip.....but I am not sure how we are related? So I call dad. He says his mother was the last of the 10 children her father and mother had. Because of such an age difference, when she was born the oldest child in that family was already 40 years of age. They all had children. Rakip is a cousin of one of my father's mother's brothers.

Huh?

In Russia something like this is described as "sedmaya voda na kisele": *seventh water on kisel*. Kisel is a jello-like sweet drink on a starch base with a fruity flavor. VERY far out there. Rakip has a wife, Alsou, and two sons of my age - Rafael and Damir. They named their first son like my little brother...how sweet. I figure I give Rakip a call, pick up the energy and go from there.

- Hello? Rakip?
- Yes, it's me.
- This is Djana, I am a daughter of Zigli.
- Yes, hi.
- I want to visit you for a few days.
- Sure, of course. Who is this?
- Uhm....Djana.....Zigli's daughter....from Moscow....
- Yes, yes, Anyone from Zigli is welcome.
- Ok....I will give you a call in a few days....when I know exactly when I am coming.

Mom says he is very determined and clear. Amina says he is very funny...kind of like our daddy. Alsou cooks well.

Ohh she got me hooked right there!! Kazan it is.

I wonder what is on the agenda with Eric and Jeremy. They might be going to Listvyanka.

I buzz in the intercom.

- Hey Djana. Wanna come to the Decembrists Houses?

Four guys raiding the kitchen. Two of them are hot.

Can't remember where I had seen them.

- Where are you from?

- Los Angeles.
- ...nobody's *really* from Los Angeles.
- You're right! We live in Manhattan Beach. How do you...?
- I went to school in the San Fernando Valley.
- I see! That's how you know. Cus you lived there. Where are you from?
- Moscow.
- Are you actually FROM Moscow?
- Yeah. My family lived abroad a lot. What's your....ethnic background?
- Egyptian.
- Are you Muslim?
- No. Copt.
- What is Copt?
- Christian.

A British kid is cooking pasta, tomatoes, sausage and cheese.
- ....pasta and sausage....for breakfast?
- We are starving. We just came from a 3-night train from Moscow. It is basically one non-stop train ride without fresh hot food.

Suddenly, I have a vision.
- What are you guys doing today?
- We are going to Listvyanka.

Wrong vision.

8 a.m. next morning we catch the minibus to the island. The ride of three hours to MRS, then ferry, then another hour-drive.
A car pulls in the driveway as the driver jumps in his seat,
- A woman driving, is like a monkey with a grenade!

Sherif, the older brother, guides the way to the Fisherman's Lodge. We wander the streets of the cute village of Huzir on to

No. 3 on Lesnaya Street. Cute wooden building with the toilet and shower outside, a cute courtyard with tables.

Olga, the housekeeper, and I sit down for *chai s vareniem* - tea with berry preserve.

- Did you know the island is 72 kilometers long?
- Wow.
- You should go to the Shaman Rock, it is right after Nikita's Guesthouse. It overlooks the Little Sea.
- Is it...magical?
- Yes. Shamans who come to the island go to the Rock. But be careful: do not take anything from there.
- I will bring an offering.
- You can bring an offering but if you take something...the spirits will haunt you and you will get sick. It happened a few years ago. Urban kids stole change from the offering space. They went back to their town and one of them got sick for no reason. The other kids' car broke down. Another broke a leg. Don't ever take anything from there.
- I wont. By the way I also want to have a puja done.
- A what?
- A prayer and blessing with a shaman.
- Ehm...from what I know....there aren't any on the island.
- Are you sure? Because I was told they are *here*.
- What did you want with him? If you have a problem and need to talk it out you can do it with a therapist.
- It's not the same.
- Where are you from?
- Moscow.
- And the boys?
- American.
- But I am not...*Russian*.
- What are you?

- Tatar.
- So am I! Yes! *Olga Hassanovna.*

Hassan was her father, as Hassanovna is her patronymic.
When respectful to an older person in Russia, address them by their first name and patronymic. Many Tatar names were Russianized for simplification, like my aunt's name was Hayulia and when she entered primary school the head teacher nicknamed her Olga, and so it stuck to her, nobody calls her her real name anymore. Same thing with my uncle, his birth-name was Zohedi, and he was nicked Gennady. How the relation comes through, I have no idea. By the time the last kid went to school, my grandma made it clear to the teachers that they will stay with her birth-name - Djamilia.[51]

Names carry vibration, meaning in a bloodline and in the person's life. I can't picture a person's life unchanged after they change their *coding.*
Code name.
I felt odd during junior years in Russian schools as people confused my name with the Russian name *Janna,* which has nothing to do with Djana. After years of feeling odd and at times shameful....
....I understood how important my name had been in my life.
Before I officially started going by Djana, I used Jana....for simplification. I felt comfortable with the vibration of the letter J. However I found Jana was only working for my teenage.
Djana, as powerful, as I grew into a woman.

Truth is...you are unlikely to meet another Djana.
My mother made this name up.

---

[51] Beautiful, in Arabic.

Splash!
I dive in and a surge of frost runs through my body.

I hurry out the water as my feet get numb.
I run back to the guesthouse and get dressed. Feel so healthy.
- Did you just take a plunge?!
- Yes.
- You're crazy girl!

We have tea, *bliny* (thin pancakes) with *vareniye*. I grab a few *pirozhki* (small pies) with cabbage for a picnic by the lake and get ready to trek for the day. Fulfill an important mission here...to find and give my precious offering.

We walk out the village and on into the fields. Olga told me about hikers who got lost in the woods. She said these woods make you very confused. Your head spins....

As I turn around...

This land has taken my treasure vase.

So be it.

thank you.

One who finds it will do the right thing with it.

The brothers stay to lay on the beach as I walk off into the long winding road and find a path that leads to Cape Khoboy. I take in the beauty. The snow-capped mountains on the mainland across the island are breathtaking and reminiscent. Magical. I dream of having a home here. A house on the lake. Move here and start a trekking company for foreign travelers. There are more foreign visitors here than Russian visitors. I am not surprised.

The vegetation is dense as I break through the spiky bushes and on to a pathway past a long stream and a gigantic mansion. Before I left the guesthouse, I asked Olga to run a *banya* for us. A Russian banya is a sauna. Every self-respecting Russian man has a banya in his backyard. I picture Amir spanking me with a *vennik*, a broom made of birch leaves. They are "brewed" in boiling water and used to spank a person's back.
I lie down overlooking a tiny island I can swim to in ten minutes - if it wasn't as cold as it is. Cute snow-white pelicans. I pick a rock: marva - only present in Baikal. I love the name and symbolism of purity. It is almost like marble, its grace reminds me of my mother. A snow-white piece of rock.

For memory....

I return to my friends, take another plunge and walk to the Shaman's Rock. A sign post says that one must not bear unclear intentions past the point of entry. One must not speak, either. I climb from the sandy beach all the way up into the offering space between two gigantic rocks. East and West merging and in between, there I am. I pray to Gods and I feel at ease. I attune myself to *see past your choices>you free yourself from the pull of karma.*

We walk into a supermarket as I wonder if I should buy some pryaniki - a dessert-type sweet cake with cherry filling inside - and decide I shouldn't as the sugar and the wheat flour will make me sick. Olga is chopping wood in the backyard as the boys and I jump into the sauna. It is steaming hot...boiling hot...as I feel my desires and fantasies back from college returning.....I brew the vennik and spank Amir's back. Sherif gives me a good spank as I lie down. Dead cells start peeling off my skin is a good scrub and exfoliation. Throwing off my old skin... like an iguana. Shower and jump into my jeans.

Olga calls for us to sit down for dinner which consists of omul cutlets, a fish only present in Baikal. Apparently the entire surrounding area gets water from the lake so the tap water is safe to drink. A French guy sitting at a neighboring table indecently intrudes into our conversation referring to me as "she" in my own presence. That does it. *You're in my country!!*

I storm out the kitchen and eat alone. I go to the store around the corner to buy pryaniki. I normally used to have them with *kefir* - now world-famous fermented sour milk but back then a modest and yummy favorite of my childhood. I would have died for it. Bad news is....now I am allergic to it. I guess *I had a little bit too much.*

I bring pryaniki to the kitchen and feel the guys' fear.

I spread butter on top - a luxurious dessert - it comes from back in the day when people in villages did not have enough to eat - least to say, have butter on their bread.

- Djana, please stay with us, we really want you here. This guy meant nothing negative - he just did not know it is rude to refer to you in third case when you are in the room with us.

WOW. I love guys who aren't scared of a strong woman!

I walk to watch the sun setting down the mountains across the sea from the island.

Rest assured, the spirits have taken the amulet, as next morning we catch a minibus back to Irkutsk and I farewell the "Pearl of Siberia". A quick stop for coffee and *yazichok* - a layer pastry frosted with sugar. Off at bus station in Irkutsk. Run to train station. Let destiny run its course.

Line up for the ticket booth: train for Ulan-Ude at 8 p.m. and train for Ekaterinburg tomorrow at 4 p.m.

Great...I'm gonna stay here another day.

Quick dinner of shawarma, a kebab every Moscowit knows is deadly dangerous, as they can well be made from human meat, but since this is Siberia it might well be chicken as they proclaim it to be. Sherif and Amir buy two bottles of vodka: Gzelka and Stolichnaya, two jars of red and black caviar, a sack of pryaniki, we say goodbye//they leave.

I jump into my jogging shoes and run for an hour until the sun sets over the Irkutsk river promenade.

A gift store from Baikal. Mostly souvenirs of *beresta* - bark of birch with engraved designs and symbols from old rural traditions: jewelry boxes, keychains, magnets, bookmarks, even earrings.

Bookstore. Paulo Coelho. *11 Minutes*. *The Alchemist*.

Sounds too cliche....pick a book with the least beckoning name. *Zahir*.

I take my assigned bed. My neighbors are a strangely Philip-resembling man who really likes fishing - easily told from the magazines. He does not speak to me, except once asking me whether I need help moving my pillow. He is too high-strung as I feel a pattern setting on...it don't matter where he from...I will only be nice to him as his astral body yearns for my affection; neglect my emotional needs as he self-realizes and establishes himself in my eyes....sucks the energy out of me...leaves.

<<<<before that happens.

>>>>I give him no chance.

I stay to myself. Stop the astral dialogue.

My other two neighbors are an old woman with an even older mother. She moans and groans as she gets in, signs and makes noise in her flatbed, burps and farts. So old.

The train takes off as I open *Zahir*.

"I can tell so much about your personality from the way you love this woman."

This is what I want my book to sound like.

I love how...real this is. I love how...true this is. And how...

unreal it seems....it is fact...but seems like fiction.

A disguised story....of Paulo's wife's disappearance.

He searches for her and cannot find the answer as to what he'd done wrong for her to leave him.

He goes on to Kazakhstan to find her as that is where she had been seen last. He gives in to the obsession and longing to find her. To unite, be inside her body and mind. So....Brazilian. Dialogues with her...in his mind...in between times....in between realms....before and after he finds her.

In Arabic *"zahir"* means visible, manifest, evident. In Muslim countries, the word is used for beings or things which have the power to be unforgettable and whose image eventually drives people mad...

Visited many places, and drawn to places worst in their political, economic or social situation. *Want to play the saviour.* Karma. When I was 15 years old and first accessed a past life Dhyani told me that I don't listen to people enough. She said I need to be more responsive to what other people need. Pick access...into what other people are feeling. Not be so self-centered. What a way to teach a soul to care of other's needs = make it an empath. I involuntarily feel other people's feelings.

Buddhism teaches that the best way to learn is to incarnate as something one previously despised or ignored. What if the past life in China I uncovered with a boy from my early teenage of learning to consider somebody else's needs....and now suffering it being born an empath?

Could this be Truth.

Why would I even want to stop the time loop that began. *I lost my faith....just for a while? To complete the karma?* And then I regain it. What a mind-game. I used to ask Dhyani if she gets tired of so much mental work. She would tell me she does not...as that is not how she looks at it. She chose to look at it as enjoyment and a something she does day after day.

She used to tell me she does not judge as she cannot grow personally if she judges anyone. She told me once....that one day...I will have a website....and her name will be on it as my

first teacher. At the time I wish I had done a better job communicating that ....I need her guidance.
....and I need...the knowledge...she refused to give me.

They say knowledge cannot be given, it can only be taken.

Love transcends. Memories of love from past lifetimes have helped me heal. Back into the first year of my sexually active life I saw a GYN. As she inserted the spiculum I heard a loud sound in my ears....my vision became black. *I can go through any emotional pain....but not through this.....an erosion.* Memories from the shame of abuse. Past life>Genetic<Teenage. It occurs and goes. Like the bumps I had on my feet...when my depression hit peak. Then my face would break out in spots....which was even harder for me than anyone else as I was in the beauty therapy industry. Unable to cure myself....from something I study? Thus help others. But until you learn from the karma within an emotion causing the dis-ease, you can do any therapy in the world, but it will not go away. And so I had found, learnt...and healed.

There is a memory I have of the past....that I cannot heal to this day. During teenage I had bad stretch-marks. My mother gave me a blend of aromatic oils - to lessen the scarring. How do I get rid of them? Hairs on the chest. As a beauty therapist I should know that is due to the excess of male hormones in my body. As a nutritionist I should know I have to get beer out of my diet as it facilitates male hormones. As a holistic therapist I know it is suppressed anger directed inwards. As a regression healer I have a trench of memory....but it is too gruesome to write down. Until I let go of it...until...then.

The train makes a stop in Novosibirsk as I get off to walk and stretch. It is said this is the most beautiful station in all of Siberia.

Should I...or should I not go to Izhevsk........the decision must be made. what would it mean if I go there//what would it mean if I don't. If I want to speak to Chingiz I should go there, leave my bags at the station, catch a cab to the cemetery, bring flowers, talk, grieve, cry, leave town. Not even tell his parents I was there. But....I can't do it...I am scared. This will drive me crazy. I just wish there was a sign. A yes. A clear indication that I should go. Or no....I should not go.

I check my cell phone and get a message from Amina, asking where I am and how I am doing. I tell her I can't decide about Izhevsk. She tells me there is nothing to do there, come home as she misses me and can't wait to see me.

I decide I will go, otherwise it will drive me. I wont stay the night: arrive early morning....check the train timetable, leave that same night and go to Kazan to visit extended family. Thus....ending the journey via the Republic of Tatarstan - home to my entire family's family. Dad's family moved to the depressing town of Izhevsk in the Udmurt Republic due to a famine after a civil war back in the 1950s. Grandfather was a painter, mystic and a Pisces. Some 55 years and some 5 days are apart my birthdate and his birthdate.

Through the villages and woods of summer Siberia, laying on the top flatbed of the third class car, I remember the day I heard the news of his death. Mom was home and Ilfat, my uncle called. I held her tight. I remember how she dropped the phone. Just as she dropped the phone and burst in tears when we got the news from Chingiz's death....a year earlier. My father believed it was celestial...he believed he was taken for the better. By good beings. As I type this....my crown chakra opens.

Thank you.
For being there, for supporting me
You mean so much to me
It is all because of you.

It was that same year...clearly that same month....when I almost
did away. I was a teenager. I was sitting....on my window sill....in
my room. The pain was so incredibly bad.
I could not understand. I felt things that were different.
I felt things that were spiritual.
I could not tell. I tried to stop the thoughts. The voices. I locked
myself in the bathroom and let the water run.

*In my heart I feel I want to hug that girl if I ever see her again/ I
wish I could help all empathic, psychic, indigo children suffering
in search of love and understanding// I wish I could help them// I
wish this piece of work helps them//*

My train is following all the way into Minsk in Belarus. This ride
is costing me a little over two thousand rubles. Of course...this is
no branded train that foreigners take - the Baikal "9" or the
Rossiya "1". This is the cheapest and shittiest train, and this one
makes a thousand stops every day. During the stop, one cannot
use the bathroom, nor half an hour after the train leaves a so-
called *sanitation zone*.

No shower = no doubt.
Green-tea diet.

Ekaterinburg was named after Empress Ekaterina the Great and it is capital of the Ural Republic. Apparently not so long ago, scientists have uncovered an ancient city, which they called Arkaim. To gain publicity, it was named "Mandala City" in reference to its shape. The Ural mountains are rich in minerals, which carry heat, information and memory. The town is also known for the murder of the Romanoff's royal family last century and as the birth-city of Russian Federation's second President, Boris Yeltsyn. As I would learn later on, the name also has roots from the Russian patron Saint of mining.

I walk to *The Meeting Point* hostel, according to the directions the secretary gave me, and find a 1950s 5-storey apartment building. The floor-plan is exactly the same as the apartment my mother grew up in. There is no hall - you enter the living room through the kitchen and the bedroom through the living room.

Ekaterina, the owner, hands me a map of the city and runs off to a salsa class. Eric and Jeremy bounce through the door as I jump to hug them. I still need to make up my mind whether or not to go to Izhevsk. I check prices for the train online and lay in my bed restless, unable to sleep.

People like us - star seeds - are scattered all over the world - in major cities - with major patrons such as our fathers - and strong family ties - a religion, an ideology - and this is our purpose - to seek union with other aspects of ourselves - but never finding them. If we do....a glitch happens....*our meeting was a glitch.*

Which is precisely what happened precisely two years ago.

The vision of Chingiz's grave. If it is meant to be I will just go. As I sit next to the Church on the Blood - the site of the slaughter of the Romanoff's family...my heart pounding the decision that must be made.

I read another book by Paulo Coelho about a girl who thought she had experienced everything: love, sex, passion, pain, grief, frustration and felt she had nothing left to live for. She popped a bottle of pills, was taken to a hospital and had her stomach pumped. She survived, but she is told that she is going to die in 5 days as her heart is going to stop because of what she put her body through. She then learns to live everyday happier, making the best of her time, than ever before...[52]

The Church's golden domes atop whitewashed walls with a big sign in front "Only Christian Orthodox Can Enter," a woman consecrates herself and covers her head with a shawl.

I visit the Afghan War Memorial and walk back to the hostel as Eric and Jeremy are gone on the train to Moscow. Ekaterina and I talk in Russian. She has beautiful long curly hair, thus her nickname, Ekaterina Curly, she is only 26 and she is running her own business.

- It is amazing what you have going on here. You are so young, so smart. This is your parents' apartment?
- Grandparents'.
- How did you first think of this?
- When I traveled to the States, I was inspired! I just...did it!
- You're doing an amazing job! Did you go to salsa last night?
- Yes, I love to dance salsa.

---

[52] Veronica Decides to Die

- I ballroom-danced for five years...before I quit..for a stupid reason.
- What reason was that?
- They gave me a wrong partner.
- You call that a stupid reason!
- ...well...I mean...
- Dancing is all about getting to know each other! You are exchanging energy with your partner. It's a *big* reason!
- I know.
- Our university professor used to take us to dance classes.
- There was one older guy I went to dance tango at milongas with in Moscow. It was amazing...to dance with an older man...who can lead you.
- I know! Our professor used to tell us *men forgot how to lead...and women forgot how to follow!*
- What a line. Do you by any chance know Sofia?
- Sofia from Germany? I know her!
- I see that!
- She is such an amazing chick. She will only go in third class platskart *as the people are so friendly and the vodka is free!*
- She's crazy.
- She's done so many things, been to so many places. I see how you guys connected!
- By the way I saw your guest pics - I recognized a guy from there.
- Who?
- Philip...I met him in Beijing.
- Oh! Yes, he was here recently.
- Him and I got drunk and made out, then I wouldn't give it up and he couldn't get over that I got him hard and left him.

- He was very...to himself. Quiet...he didn't really care about girls when he was here.
- He asked me if I ever had a...broken heart.
- A broken WHAT?! Excuse me!
- Man, you're so good! And there was another kid...Mark.
- I love Mark! He is so cool, so tall and manly. Where did you meet him?
- Briefly in Irkutsk. He was cooking.
- I know! He was cooking here too. I took him to the opera. All girls were jealous. He is so big and manly. I felt like a little princess. I wonder if he had a girl...
- Oh, please. Nice clueless guys like him leave their girlfriends at home...in the search for something more. I don't envy English girls.
- You think he left someone?
- I know he did....I picked it up from him...he confirmed it.
- Really...wow I never would have thought.
- There's two things you need to know about English men. One: the Bond complex - desire a Russian woman at a near-collective unconscious level, and Two: they grew up in a monarchy with a prince and a princess, they want to be prince with a little princess.
- You're good.
- Bond wants to be a hot spy, live life of adventure and excitement...which they get little of in England.
- Damn.
- ...which I've been told by guys themselves.
- Wow. With your charm, I bet they tell you a lot.
- I can read them.
- Wow. I'll have to remember this.
- Test it: you'll see it is true. Besides, I've been through so much myself. It would be stupid of me not to know by now. I went out with an English guy after college: dull as

a bucket of sand. Then I had an important love with an American. Broke my heart.

- I haven't had anything like this.
- Men don't count for that shit. They want you when you don't want them.
- Wow. You've had so much experience.
- That's just how life goes.

A pillar...of light....behind her left shoulder.

- It's...7 p.m. What time is your train?
- 7.30 p.m.
- You're going to Kazan, right?

Uncle Ilfat picks me up. He is one of the top heart surgeons in Russia and he invented an adjustable back-up ring for annuloplasty of cardiac valves.

I haven't seen him since two years. He has gotten so old, his hair has gotten so gray.

- We can go to the studio-house and hang out there for the weekend.
- I wont be staying for long...I have to get going. I need to buy me a ticket.
- But I thought...maybe you can stay here...and relax...

...and soak up the pain and misery we are living in.

- I can't.

As we pass through the woods of my father's childhood I remember being here the year before traveling to exile = going to grandfather's grave just before Chingiz's wedding.

- Why did he die?
- I don't know. He was not telling us anything. Things were going good for him - he just got a promotion. One day I get a call from his work place telling me hasn't been in for a few days. So I go to his house and open the door and there he is...just laying there.

...pain taking over...

- ...can you not find out what the reason was...
- I did the postmortem examination. And there were no pills, no chemicals, no alcohol in his blood.

I burst out in tears.

- But how...and why...
- Ildar had told me Chingiz has been having heart murmurs - hums - he said his heart beats as normal but suddenly it stops for a few seconds and then goes on again.
- How...could he...

- ...we have always helped them you know and how could he keep something like this from me...??
- He never told...??

As the car pulls into the driveway I remember I forgot to buy flowers.

- Ildar says he didn't want us to worry. But I am a heart surgeon. And I couldn't help my own son???
- What about Elmira?
- She turned out to be a very selfish one. She never called us since he died. She hasn't asked if we had been okay. She only cared about herself. I mean, if Chingiz had been coming home and he knew there was somebody there who cared about him - not to mention - love him - it would have never happened.
- They were not living together?
- No, from what I know the first New Year they spent apart and the second New Years Elmira took off in his car. She didn't want to stay home. She wanted to be out there partying. She didn't take care of her husband or the house. She wasn't a homey girl. Did you know that Chingiz brought laundry for us to do?

I get out the car and walk to the grave. The old man bursts out in tears. It hurts to see him like this. I can't believe it. How much he loved his son. And they have been through so much together. And now he is gone. And nothing can bring him back.

You need to understand...we are having it very bad...I don't know if this pain will ever go away....

As I sit down in front of the gravestone seeing Chingiz's name with a Muslim Crescent and Star on top <>
I know he is protected by the Guards of Islam.

My stomach rumbles of hunger as I have not eaten since the day before. Uncle drives me home to eat fried chicken with potatoes. I put on a DVD of the wedding and picture myself there. As the memories come back to me of sitting in this very room....at the same time...as right now. Could I have changed anything, had I been *in* that video?

The story goes that less than a year before I chose exile I came to Izhevsk to attend my cousin's wedding. He had been going out with Elmira for two years. After they got married they moved to my grandfather's and grandmother's apartment. I had been there many times when I was a child - when my father would take me to visit his mother, Faruha Yamal, Faia, as we called her. My father says I look like her. His father was passionately in love with Faia when they were young - and they had two children. Faia was once coming out of the *banya* in the winter and having not covered her wet hair, she got meningitis, became disabled and grandfather started having women on the side. I remember meeting him...when my father took us to visit him in the hospital after a heart-attack.

When I got here for the wedding I did not like Elmira. I couldn't sleep in Chingiz's old room - I couldn't *fall* asleep in his bed. Something was *crawling* on the wall. I swore I am leaving this town as I cannot witness the wedding as it will kill him. She will kill him, smother him to death. I took off on a plane for Moscow.

As the video of their wedding comes to an end it sickens me how Elmira wipes her lips after Chingiz kisses her. She pulls away when her mother gives her a sip of traditional Tatar drink. How emotion-less and love-less the look in her eyes is. Then why *did* they get married?

I switch on "Chingiz-Khaan" and "Mongol" DVDs. A message will come through...like everything in this world is parallel and we can read and trace messages from one reality to another.

Ildar, Chingiz's younger brother, returns from his exam. He was studying to be a surgeon and then switched to psychology, psychiatry and paraphilias. He had come to visit Moscow and he stayed at my place two years ago...last time I had seen him. When I was sketching spirits watching me in unison. Exactly when...I had psyched everything I could tap into. Sitting on my balcony in my apartment in Moscow, listening to *Znayesh Li Ti* by Tatar songstress Maksim. Dying...dying...of *love*.
- We're coping. Dad is having it the worst.
- I know.
- You went to visit the grave?
- Yes.
- He dragged you?
- No. I asked him to take me there.

...as I wonder if this "calling" I felt was the calling of a suffering wounded soul for energy (love and compassion) that he knows he can get from me as I have all this energy to give someone in pain. I realize it.

I can stay here and try and be there for them....whereas in truth...it doesn't change anything. Chingiz is not coming back. The pain never goes.

I am tired but I cannot fall asleep.

Irina comes home and makes bliny, salad, tvorog with sweet milk, chocolate layer cake, milk tea with sugar and more fried chicken with potatoes and salad. I feel sick and bloated. She just does not understand when I say, no, thank you, I am full. I am going to be constipated until I leave here. Some places are just stuck in time. There is no release.

She tells me I should start tracing my family tree. Be *Thoth The Scribe* so-to-speak.

She takes me for a walk around town on to the Lizy Memorial: "lizy" means "skis". She makes a picture of me in every one of which I close my circuit - fold my hands and legs together. If my energy is closed, no-one can read me from a photograph.

The gardens around the Presidential House are nice and neat whereas the town itself is miserable - it has a monument and memorial to a dumpling on a fork and a memorial for Crocodile Gena - a Russian cartoon character from the 1970s similar to what a Micky Mouse is in America. As I gaze upon the lake, the smoke from the nearby industrial plants making Kalashnikov and other arms as per Venezuela's Chavez's order, covers what could have been a pretty scene.

Tears in Irina's eyes. She keeps it all to herself. She is suffering double...she had a third son...after Ildar...about twelve years ago, but he was stillborn. Ilfat did the postmortem examination.

My train leaves at 11:01 p.m. and as I try and sleep in my bottom flatbed of the second class train I can't get my uncle off my mind. I shouldn't have let him make tactile contact with me. My Rei-ki teacher taught me...if I can't get my mind off someone, it is the first sign of a subtle inner connection made. A sort of "attachment" made. It will drag you...

...I asked for pain.
It's just...where *I* feel comfortable.

I arrive to Kazan station at 5 in the morning. The writing on the buildings is in Tatar and Islamic "crescents" are everywhere. I walk to follow Spirit guide me to the Kul Sharif Mosque and catch a bus as I get off at the bus stop "Fuchika". Rakip calls on my cell and tells me to walk to their house East

....where the Sun is rising.

In Gemini right now.
....passing through my 4th house of ancestry.
Alsou busts me in. I get into the elevator to floor number 9. She has the door open for me. She also has a key for me, in case I want to go somewhere. We sit down to eat breakfast as she had prepared everything she possibly could - fried chicken with potatoes, cabbage and carrots for the hungry starved backpacker, pancakes full of grease and fried oil, sweet cakes, tvorog (milk tofu - sorry for not mentioning earlier) with sweet milk, grapes and apples, milk tea and black tea. Tatar moms are the best! I hungrily eat everything that can possibly fit inside me as Damir, the younger son, says he is going to be in Moscow after tomorrow - to meet with Rafael, his older brother - hang out for the weekend and watch a football game. I tell him he should call me to hang out together. I think...I should probably get on the same train if I want to make a connection with him. Otherwise he will feel too vain to call me. Then I think of my space. What my journey would mean if I...return to Moscow with him? Meet Rafael at the station. Meet father at the station. Would be fun!

Alsou and Damir leave for work as I shower in their state-of-the-art bathroom and fall asleep. Finally. I wake up late in the afternoon and run to the train station. I want to get a ticket on the same 12 train at 10:30 p.m. as Damir. That would mean staying here for one night. I don't know if it is what I want...so I decide to decide at the station. I will ask for a ticket for tonight - and then if they have no seats - I will go tomorrow night. But...I already told Alsou and Rakip that I am leaving tonight.

-   Train 12. One ticket for Moscow.
-   No seats.
-   Tomorrow?
-   No seats. There is an additional train to Moscow half an hour later.
-   For tomorrow?
-   And for today.

Great. Er?????

-   One for tonight.

I walk to Kul Sharif Mosque as I text my father with the details of my train. He tells me to visit the Kremlin and the Syumbike Dedication Tower which was proclaimed a Unesco World Heritage Site and houses government offices, cute parks and several religious buildings. According to legend, Ivan Grozny - the tsar behind the *Christianization* of Tatars, launched the siege of Kazan khanate after Princes Syumbike refused to marry him. To save her city, she had agreed to marry the tsar but only if he had built a tower higher than any other in Kazan within a week. He did and she jumped herself to death from one of the terraces.

Kazan is one of Russia's oldest cities dating back to 1005. In modern terms, Kazan is the city of the rich who had gotten their hands on the oil produce in the Republic of Tatarstan, which has autonomy and its own president. The flag of Tatarstan bears a green stripe - color of Islam, a red stripe - color of Russians and a thin white stripe between the two, representative of peace between the Tatar majority and Russian minority. An oil brand of the republic is named TatNeft. On to the National Museum as Alsou calls on my cell. Out onto the main drag of Baumana str.

Hop on subway of 5 stations and the announcements are in Russian AND in Tatar. Both my parents speak Tatar. My father was not accepted to primary school at first because he did not speak Russian and kids laughed at him. Twenty years later, he speaks five languages: Tatar, Russian, English, French and Arabic. He studied in Nizhny Novgorod, a major student town about 500 kilometers from Moscow. The Nizhny Novgorod State Linguistic University named after N. A. Dobrolyubov is currently full of foreign students.

I hop off and walk to Alsou's house. I smell fried chicken and potatoes. She is so sweet. I tell her about visiting Izhevsk and how miserable it had been. She gives no emotional response. She acts, but does not react. She is a lawyer in real estate registration. Who would have thought. She manages to do both things: be a loving, caring mother, homemaker and a business woman at the same time. Rakip used to be a Communist Party Official back in the Soviet Union and now works in development construction.

She explains that Damir and Rafael are not cousins to me...but *nephews*.

I am 24 and....an aunt to two guys my age!

Rakip arrives shortly after I finish my chicken with potatoes and gulp down four glasses of milk tea and two slices of chocolate cake.

- Djana. How wonderful to meet you. - as he holds my hands in respect and admiration.

He says I speak like Maria Sharapova. Maria's first language is American, Russian is her second. I see the golden implants in his mouth. Alsou gives me a big fat *chak-chak* to take home as a *gostinez* (a gift from home). Chak-chak is a national Tatar "cake" made of dough based on honey and eggs - extremely sweet. I tell Rakip that their kids should call me when they are in Moscow so we can hang out. I hop on the train and wave goodbye to my newly-found extended family.

As I lay back in my flatbed

Everything in the Universe is interconnected. The past, present and future exist at the same time. If you do something bad to someone, it comes back to you. I have raised five children all of whom were adopted. I told them, I will support you until you are 18 and then you're all on your own. One of my children was born disabled. I had taken care of him and he grew up healthy. 25 years later I told him I want him to find his biological mother. He said he didn't want to do it and to him, I was his mother, not the other.

I hear a woman in the neighboring compartment.

an uncomfortable night's sleep on the top flatbed of the train...
...I get up and she never stops.

Everything you do always comes back to you. You know if you lie or cheat on someone what a sin it is? everything returns to you, especially in the times we live in. I know so because I have to know. I must speak and preach the truths to everyone I know. These are pictures of my family - look. These are my children. All of them are adopted. I wasn't meant to make children of my own - but I raised other people's children as my own.

I brush my teeth and comb my hair as the train approaches Lubertsy - right after the ring road of Moscow ends - we are entering my birth city. Excitement is building up.

Home after so long!

The train brakes and slowly pulls into the station.

I line up for the exit.

A bang on the glass of the window catches my attention.

Daddy!

He waves a "thumbs up" at me.

I walk out the train.

I pictured this moment every day for the last twelve months.
  -    So where was the best place you had visited?

I love being home. I love being <u>here.</u>

The first experience of love - my mother.

As I walk towards her, she looks gorgeous. Her skin is plump and perfect.

She holds me in loving care. She sits me down to eat fried chicken with potatoes and salad as we open a bottle of wine.

I walk into my room with a sense of newness with my older self. My bed is just as I had left it - and my desk is full of gifts my mother had bought for me during the time I had been gone.

I get a text message from Eric telling me they are out celebrating Jeremy's birthday. I meet up with them to watch the fireworks at the Red Square adjacent to the Russia National Day. "The Kremlin sits high on a hill like the crown of sovereignty on the brow of an awesome ruler", wrote Russia's great poet Lermontov back in 1833. It is regarded as an inviolate nucleus of Moscow...which as I have found is sister cities with Amman, Athens, Mumbai, Bangkok, Beijing, Beirut, Cairo, Chicago, Cusco, Delhi, Dubai, Hanoi, HCMC, London, Seoul, Tel Aviv, Tehran, Tokyo, Tunis, Ulaan-Baatar...[53]

Iran and Saudi Arabia. Ancestors, I need to collide.

You must be kept.

For the significance of knowledge given.

The most karma is with the country of your birth.

Keep typing and I will speak to you

I go through boxes of storage of memories: journals, writing...the records. Must find where Spica speaks of *writing December 21, 2012. Do not find it.* I do find that *someone is moving my hand.* I find the predictions for the birth-dates of my children. Dad says Russia has signed visa-exemption agreements with at least five

---

[53] The concept of sister cities is to promote cultural and commercial ties.

countries in South America: Brazil, Argentina, Chile, Venezuela and Colombia...as I ponder why....just as I've traveled this far and gone through all that paperwork, they sign the agreement?

We pass by a stream in the woods and I tell him I am unsure just how accurate and Universal-blessed is the plan to go to the U.S. How am I going to make a living?
Things I enjoy doing. Being extravert, I get energy from communicating and exchanging. Travelers. People in transit. No commitments. Freedom. Open a hostel. It will be a 5-minute walk from Tretyakovsky Gallery, Kitay Gorod and a 15-minute walk to the Kremlin.
Shelves of travel guides, toast with peanut butter, whole-wheat bread, tea or coffee; option of eggs or *kasha* - porridge - at no additional charge. Friday nights of cooking *borsch* - beat-root soup. I will take people out to the Irish Pub two blocks away. Weekends I will take them to my father's country-house. Barbecues. Sleepover. Ride sleighs and skis. Ride past the fancy area of Rublevka full of *novyi Russkys*. Pick up from train station in a 4x4. I will have my own operating business.
I will forever stay unknown for my psychic and spiritual work.
The story of my lifetime to this day and I must make myself known. who, if not me?

Sabantuy, a Tatar National Holiday and "Feast of the Plough" after harvesting. Muslim *halal* foods and souvenirs, horse racing, sack-fighting sitting on a tree trunk, who's first to get a bucket of water to the finish line and catch a fish from a pond with your hands. Daddy buys me a metallic bowl with engraved scriptures from Al-Quran.
Back home I never had to change the light-bulbs in this room. It always shines...a channel of light through the center of my room in meditation and initiation exercises. *Unconscious art is a*

reflection of the subconscious mind and the all-knowing super-consciousness. The symbolism of the flower of life, the fractal and the spiral, time-looping, Eye of the beholder, the Circle, are all definitive patterns of psychic and channeled art. Color circles I used to train my sight to see the aura.

My jaw is beginning to swell up as I touch the wisdom tooth with my finger, it smells of rot. Inflammation process. Dad and I go to the country-house for the weekend to chillax and have a barbecue. I pick raspberries, plums and blackberries.

Monday morning. Diagnosis: pericoronitis - inflammation of the skin surrounding the wisdom tooth which has not erupted completely. Inflammation = due to top wisdom tooth pressing on gum around wisdom tooth on bottom jaw. If extract the top third molar - it will stop bumping on the jawline of the bottom = inflammation will go away. I tell the doctor I had a mild surgery about a year ago...as he says if I want we can cut the skin around the tooth again and see what happens. I am scared and tell him I will come to visit on Thursday. I can't do it today...as the moon is waxing into a full moon Tuesday. There must be no surgeries or any kind of interventions into the body, as inflammation can occur stronger and healing would take longer.

I change into boots, jeans and go to STA Travel to buy my pre-booked ticket to MIA. In the office a girl tells me my ticket cannot be issued...as the last segment on my flight cannot be confirmed because American Airlines is closing the flight from Chicago to Moscow come September. She tells me she can put me on a Delta flight with a stop-over in Atlanta or Aeroflot to New York and then I can buy a ticket to Miami from Newark airport that way it is cheaper.

I leave the office, call my mother as she tells me to go see Shumilova, another doctor nearby my house. Last January she told me there was nothing there but hypersensitivity and calcified debris that had formed underneath the retainer I still wear from the orthodontia I had done when I was 12.

My father tells me to call one of his clients who owns a clinic in the center of Moscow. I describe my sensations and the doc, Prikus, tells me to get a gargle and an anti-inflammatory gel and come see one of his doctors tomorrow afternoon.

Tuesday morning I see Shumilova and she ignores my inflamed bottom left wisdom tooth and makes a photograph of the top left. She looks at it with a surgeon. They agree that it is full of caries...which sits in between the third molar and the second molar - and to get to it they would need to remove the third molar. I say I can't have surgery today. The surgeon puts me in for extraction on Thursday afternoon.

My mother advises that I stick with the first doctor I saw and have the top extracted. I can't decide who to believe or listen to. How am I supposed to intuitively make a decision what tooth to extract if different doctors tell me different things?????????????

I catch a subway to the center of Moscow for my appointment at Prikus's clinic, two blocks from the Kremlin. The surgeon, Andrey, comes in, I open my mouth and he starts filling a syringe.

- What are we...doing?
- Mild surgery on your last left bottom molar.
- But I'm...not...ready....what is my diagnosis?
- Pericoronitis - inflammation of the skin around the impacted tooth.
- I can't...do it today....can you explain to me....
- If you do nothing it will continue to hurt.

- I can't...do it today...
- Then don't do it.

He walks away as I am left sitting in the chair. The nurse tells me if I just gargle it and watch the hygiene, the inflammation will go away. I walk out the examination room to Andrey smoking outside the clinic hallway.

- Can you just...take a look at this...photo here...
- There was no point taking this photograph. You have classic pericoronitis. The top tooth might be pressing onto the bottom jaw but that is secondary.

He shuts the door in my face to continue smoking.

I sit in the waiting room. The receptionist asks me if I am okay.

I am silent.

She dials the doctor and hands the phone over.

- I don't understand what he is saying...he wont tell me the complete picture. I am leaving in two weeks and I wont be back in a while.
- Where are you going?
- The U.S.
- Dental surgery over there will be like buying a car.
- I know...that's why I need to have it over with here, now.
- Okay give the phone to Andrey.

I hear Andrey tell Prikus that I need to have all four wisdom teeth extracted. There isn't enough space in my mouth to have all these teeth.

The receptionist hands me the phone and Prikus tells me that it will continue to hurt and inflame, we can't extract now as it is too inflamed already - we need to open the *hood* (dental operculum), the inflammation subsides and the tooth can be extracted worry-free after a week. The healing period will be about a month - before we can do anymore extractions as the body needs to re-adjust and re-coop from the intervention. I should be healed before my flight in 2 weeks but just in case...it's a good idea to change my departure date if I can afford to do so. But nobody...no doctor will agree to do a surgery like this a week before an international flight.

Aggravated and confused, I walk into the subway. I can't decide but if I continue to do nothing I will just go with one of the doctors I saw before as they are close to where I live and have surgery on the top wisdom tooth. This will not solve the issue. If my father had recommended me this doctor then his Higher Self had known the time it would take me to heal and be ready to travel again. I trust my father's higher self and what it is telling me. I stop halfway and walk back to the clinic.

- I'm not going to operate you.
- Why not???
- I have other patients to see and I am going to the other clinic right now.

He walks off to smoke. I sit down and weep. Just as I have made up my mind about what I am doing, he refuses to work with me.

- Please come in.

The nurse gives me a sanitation robe and the doctor wipes the gums in my mouth with a sanitation gel and gives me a shot of two cubes of ultracaine. As I see him move a surgical knife in my mouth, in one simple move, it is over. He puts in a cotton ball to cover the bleeding as I sit outside the examination room and catch the doctor before he goes to smoke.

- What is next? Should I come next week for an extraction?
- For what?
- My...wisdom tooth...
- What's the point? You need all of them extracted.
- Well...I am leaving...so I don't have the time for this right now.
- Where are you going?
- America.

\-   So do it there.

He shuts the door in my face and continues to smoke.

I ask the receptionist to book me in for Tuesday next week.

I return home and my mother gives me mashed potatoes with broccoli and fried chicken strips mashed into a paste.

She da best.

I gulp it down.

Amina cannot decide what university to enroll in as she had been accepted into two for her Master's in Art Management.

Shiver and chills run up and down my spine as I am shaking, too sensitive to run a shower, the water would just hurt my skin. The nerves would start running all over the place. I lay in my bed and cover myself with four blankets. Amina comes in, sticks a thermometer into my armpit. Fall asleep.

Wake up, sweating. Archangel Michael's gigantic feather wings wrapped around me in a loving and protective embrace.

I am ready to be with you again.

I wake up from a place I drifted to for a few seconds...to the sound of my sister going through the first aid kit. I pop one, two antihistamine pills and fall back asleep to Manjushri Mantras.

Om Ah-Ra-Pa-Ja-Na-Dhih

...feeling absolutely fucked up with a fever of 38C. Dad calls the doctor. He says to get antibiotics, anti-allergy pills and a gargle. Amina runs to buy my pills as I lie half-awaken and my father starts a panic.

Run around in hysteria that life hurts so much. Somehow it all makes sense and I understand why I am in so much pain.

I have so much love, energy and positive vibrations that everyone wants to just feed off me.

Nobody wants to give me *something*, everyone wants just to *take*.

Moreover it is my innate nature to want to sacrifice myself for the needs and happiness of other people. And who are the people I find!? The crappiest of the crappiest. I just manage to pick the shittiest people to take care of - make sure I don't get tied down. Make sure that they use me up - and leave me. And then I remain this way, forever.

And I am happy!
I am comfortable like this!
I am sick of it!
I need help. I need a shrink.

I see my father. My poor father. The man who had given me life - sitting in my kitchen looking lost, confused, puzzled.
a strand of hair falls out. 8 years ago...in the summer after my first year of living alone abroad - hiding in the bathroom and letting the water run...

I am sick of having gone all this way and *still* feeling I intimidate people who are lower than me. I take such pity on them that I lower myself. A fucking martyr!

I never tell anyone about my spiritual work. About what I have learnt from the *other side*.
No-one can be better than bringing themselves down and keeping themselves secret.

I burn out of talking this way.

Amina brings me a book of spiritual meaning underlying diseases. She quietly points out a line for me to read: wisdom teeth and gum problems are manifestation of longstanding indecisiveness, inability to become stable and back-up decisions.

My affirmation must be *I am a decisive person, I walk to the end and support myself with love*.

completely out of energy. my stomach so thin it touches my spine.
too fucked up to stand up.

Daddy says fever is a good thing as the body naturally increases the temperature of environment so that all the bacteria die off. Strong immunity...as I survived a dangerous virus back in Iraq when I was 4. Shit all day, went to hospital, slept all night, woke up healthy, was kicked out of hospital. This reminds us of our eternal bond.
...doze off having popped three pills of amoxicillin and clavunolic acid. The swelling on the tooth is not going. I call the doctor and ask him to extract the tooth. He says he wont do it as you never extract a tooth from inflamed tissue.

Then why do you wait for it to inflame? And how do people have them removed until they even find out about the need to have them removed - *unless* they inflame?!!!!!!!!

Something is just not right around here.
I hate having to be here alone and having to do everything on my own. I am so fucking tired of setting myself up for challenge, loneliness and pain. Like in Thailand after a fucking motorbike

accident in a hospital getting stitches fucking breaking down of pain and crying out for the Angel's help and for the ability to just hold your hand ONCE!

Boots. Mini-skirt. Black leather jacket. Silver hoops. Attitude.
- Okay so the puss has come out, it will be healing, can't do anything now, it is inflamed and needs to heal naturally.
- But when can you extract?
- When it heals naturally. Her reaction is very severe to the mild surgery we did.
- What should we do?
- Wait until it heals.
- How long will it be?
- One week.
- ...and in the meantime?
- Continue taking your antibiotics and painkillers.

We leave the clinic as I hold on to my daddy....*I will always be alone. I hate this about myself. I am so comfortable in my loneliness. The man I want in my life is just...not there. He does not exist. If he did, I would find him. And all I need to do is* want to find him. *That's the secret conspiracy of the entire life that I call* mine. *I just don't want to find a man to be happy with. I constantly need challenge, people who hurt me and help me grow. I just don't...want to.............I am so....so sick.....of coping with my own self all the time. I am so angry with my self for creating this. I am so sick...of my body letting me down when I need it. Giving up on me. Just as I had a plan and knew what I was doing, everything just changes. My body changes my plans.*

Daddy reads a prayer while holding his hand on my jaw. He rubs Prophet's (May Peace be with him) Oil into my cheek. I shred tomatoes, chop lettuce, slice chicken strips, wash peanuts and dice cucumbers and carrots. Yes I am making kung pao chicken.

I look at myself in the mirror.

- Daddy, the pain is gone!

He kisses my forehead.

My mother says she will be going to the hospital for a week to have some analyses done and see what is up with her. She had been feeling down, low on energy. We sit down to eat. Amina eats a very little bit - she says the Chinese food I make is too spicy for her. I mentally prepare myself and my facebook status is *so scared of the upcoming surgery*. I post an album of emotion-provoking images of the Rei-ki symbol, the Heart Entwined, the Sankofa symbol, the Family of Light, the Heart Chakra, Dolphins and South Floridian paintings. I will not be accessing facebook until this surgery is done with. Recollect and spare my energy.

I wear a grey dress from Nepal and 5-inch stilettos.

I'm not religious...but I feel so good...
...this makes me wanna pray...that you always be here...[54]

Get Into the Groove and *Express Yourself.*

I rather have it over with, right now.
August is just such a hard month ahead.

- Why are you here?
- Extraction.
- I am not going to do any surgery with you until you come back and stay here for good.
- She is not going anywhere. - says my dad.
- She's not?

Andrey looks into my mouth.

---

[54] Nothing Fails by Madonna.

- It's healed. It's ready to be taken out. But you know what? I don't care how much you pay me - if you're gonna act like that and misbehave I wont operate you! I don't care how much you pay me !
- Act like what??
- Doc, she was in a lot of pain! - says Dad.

Andrey cleans the gums as I watch Iguazu Falls on the screen for relaxation.

- You promise to behave?
- Yes.

He gives me a shot of ultracaine and sits back at his computer. His main job is prosthetic implants. He must know teeth and their structure well since he makes fake ones. He said that the orthodontist who did my braces did a shit job - as instead of trying to make the teeth fit into the little space they have - he should have expanded the space - that way the teeth would have the space to settle in. This was before the wisdom teeth erupted though. Both my top ones are fully erupted with no problem - it is the bottom ones that are bothering me.

- Can you feel it? - asks Andrey as he sticks an extraction tool into my mouth.

Interesting. My jaw is numb, I know he is doing something, but it causes no nervous response. I hear the screeching sound of the tool, as he pulls in and out and tries to shake the tooth up.

- Oumph - as he sweats - this is hard. It doesn't want to come out.

Please...just go....

- Hold on a minute, - he says to the nurse. - I need to rest. My arms are tired. Just make sure she stays in her chair. Or she will run away out of here with a half-extracted tooth.

I giggle. He shakes it off and comes back to my business.

Pop!

-   Wash it and put it into a bag. - he says to the nurse.

He makes a stitch and a knot on the softness underneath what used to be the tooth's bed, puts an ammonia-smelling medicine inside and a cotton ball to cover the bleeding.

-   No food, no water, no swallowing or rinsing until the cotton ball falls off. Understand?
-   Yes.
-   A blood clot should form and healing of tissue shall begin.

A zip-loc bag with a label: D.F. 14/7/09

I walk outside and into the car as dad rushes to take me home past Sadovoye Koltso.

-   Yours are very good! Apparently there are different types of impacted teeth - sometimes they can even be inside the gum and you need to cut inside the gum to take the tooth out!

As I lay in bed I await for the swelling to begin. I was told that you can swell up bad and get fever...bleed...all the nasty things. I feel nothing. No swelling whatsoever. It is so mild that it is strange to me. I finish my course of antibiotics and painkillers. My life is no longer about me. I find salvation in helping others. Animals and nature will never be as ungrateful as people. I want to join greenpeace or go to Ecuador and teach children English for free, if they give me a place to sleep and food to eat. I would be so much happier. It is no longer about me. A week later I visit the dentist for a check-up as he removes the stitch and tells me it is healing well and puts some more ammonia-smelling stuff on top of the hole.

Amina is putting together photos of my grandfather's art for a brochure. Dad is looking for a house in Tatarstan nearby grandpa's birth village to open a museum.

- I remember when you text me when I was on the train...I was asking the Universe to help me decide...and then I fell asleep and you text me that same moment.
- I knew you were in Siberia. The dolphins and Angels painting fell down.
- ...
- I took it as a sign.
- !!
- I saw you have *The (Secret) Doctrine*?
- Yes. Why?
- He had one too.
- Sacred art enters the realm of the sacred when it transcends personal and cultural expressions and mirrors the deeper levels of our minds. In this realm, art has the power to illuminate dimensions of consciousness inaccessible to our physical senses; it can awaken our most subtle perceptions, and show us the true nature of our being.
- It's true. Art in the higher understanding was never considered as means of personal self-expression. It always served as means of focusing the spirit. A work of art shows the Godly archetype and is the bridge between the ending and the endless, by which the dedicated one makes a journey into another reality of being.
- I mean it is very high frequency. It is both imaginative and transcendental. It's about love, truth and protection. Spirit art is created through the intuitive wisdom of the unconscious.

Amina and I visit mom in the hospital and bring her a care-package. Her hospital is clean, her roommates are funny and she looks promising. I am lying. The hospital is miserable, her roommates are old farts, she looks pale. Diagnosis: leukocytic meliosys. Chills down my spine. The disorder is not curable, but controllable. The origins are...unknown. She is still waiting for the results of her other tests to come in. I break out in tears of how much it hurts not to have her home.

We sit outside in the courtyard as I am frying in my knee-high Nine West boots and mini-skirt in the summer heat. Mom says I look hot. She asks me when am I going to the States. I tell her I can't decide. She says she wants me to be there - not staying here. Amina is deciding between the two universities: weighing the pros and the cons.

Tremendous pain in my left upper jaw. It must be all the talking the doctors have been doing that is making me almost create the decay in the upper left jaw. The pain drives me crazy, I call dad and he tells me to call the doctor to arrange to see him. I really....must...help my mother. I search for color healing and gemstone healing - what I think is best that would work for her condition. I pack up one of my Angel-channeled paintings - red and orange to stimulate the red blood cells and the second chakra of life force - and the spiral which heals all illness and brings us to the source of health and well-being. Amber energy cures blood disease. Ill with despair and need to heal her. If my significant others are healthy, I am happy. I want my mother to heal. I will do anything for her to heal. Jade.

The pain in my upper left jaw subsides and I fall asleep. In the morning it drives me crazy again as I call Andrey he says he cannot see me as he is booked for the day. He tells me to call the other hospital in Taganka to arrange for tomorrow. I call dad. The pain drives me nuts as I cry and can't decide what to do. I call Shumilova and arrange for extraction with a surgeon in one hour. Dad calls me back and says he had spoken with Prikus and he said that no extraction must be done now - as a hole underneath a hole is very bad and can cause problems eating and your mouth mechanically opening and closing. The bottom hole needs about a month to heal first before we can extract. He says he spoke with mom as well and she had said that the surgeon at Shumilova's place is not a good surgeon - and we better just let the first doctor finish my treatment. Dad had arranged for me to see Andrey. I cry on his shoulder as he says that everything will be okay; the reason for all this is coming back from traveling and the changes: my body is re-cooperating. It always happens when you come back home: your body lets go. It knows you are safe, sound, and home.

Andrey looks in my mouth and says the pain is due to the decay that had formed in between the third molar and the second molar. To eliminate it, we need to extract the third molar and treat the second molar. Unless the pain is absolutely unbearable, we cannot extract now. It is highly *not* recommended as it can cause more problems.

- What do you want to do?
- Wait.

Amina leaves for the weekend to St. Petersburg.

I start uploading the video of my bungy jump in Thailand.

James: hi

James: its been a while

me: hi

how are you?

James: do you want the real answer :)

me: of course

James: been tough. Though on paper it prob. seems pretty good. if you know what I mean

me: is this really you?

James: yes

I mean I presume

who you think it is

James

from Nepal
me: :) its you
i know what you mean i've been pretty tough too but on paper it looks pretty good
James: :)
where are you?
me: home, in Moscow
i thought you'd never speak to me again
James: no
in all honesty
I got your e-mail long ago
not sure how to respond
and I was going through a depressive episode
when I returned home from Asia
last June
and it lasted a long time
till maybe Feb this year
its still hard but I am better and functioning more than before
me: i always wanted to know how you are doing
James: and I always think that I am a bad person for not getting back to you
to be honest I don't know where the last 6 months have gone
like a tornado
been so tunnel visioned
def. not living in the moment
me: i know what you mean
James: but changing that in every way I can
I mean trying to ;)
me: are you taking medication?
James: yes and no
ha
for sleeping
toying with anxiety stuff

but don't want to take it

me: don't they give medicine marijuana in the states?

James: no

me: they should :P

James: I mean in some states

maybe only California

me: it's so good to speak to you again

honestly i've been praying to have a chance to speak to you

life is full of miracles isn't it

James: I believe so. Just don't see them enough

or open myself to them enough

but yes

it is

full of them

me: still hard on yourself? :)

James: for sure

yeah. y u know me so well?

me: do you see a shrink?

James: :)

me: i always wanted to know how you deal with pain

i felt you were the only one i ever let know about mine

i'm sorry maybe i shouldn't bring it up

James: sorry djana. just saying goodbye to someone

no it's totally fine to bring it up

I don't care

not hard for me talk about

me: okay i'm glad

did you say you returned june last year

James: yes

when did you return?

me: june this year

guess what happened first day of my trip

James: when did you leave?

me: uhm well june 2008 i left, and returned this june

James: ok

so first day??

hmmm

me: i have so many paintings you should see them

bummer, wisdom tooth pops, out of the blue

first day in lima, and i wasn't exactly ready for surgery en-route the inca trail

James: ouch.

me: so i was sure it would never bother me again and had a bit gum cut around the tooth

so to make the story short, it just popped earlier this month and it changed a lot of my plans

James: you see a dentist?

me: but glad i had surgery last week

James: oh

good

and they give you good pain medication :)???

me: yeah it's changing the chemistry in my body it's not good

did you have wisdom teeth?

James: still do

no problems

knock on wood

me: knock knock!

who's there?

:P

James: lol

dork :)

so 1 year away

how was it?

me: challenging, stressful, fun, amazing, tiring...addictive!!

you would know

James: all sounds great

that's what it should be
when its a year
one week. all fun
one year = everything
still life
me: it was a journey
James: :)
and you said you came to hoboken too ??????????????
me: yes by the PATH :P
James: haha. I ride it most days
amazing that you know of it
me: wouldn't if i didnt know you :)
James: :)
when were you here?
me: april '08
was visiting friends in brooklyn, and around nyc
James: right. I thought I was still away
I was in Dharamsala or Rishikesh
me: did you see the Dalai Lama speak?
James: yes
me: omg
James: 2x
me: your journey was amazing you know that
James: it was
but I just got so depressed and tired
me: did you put your blogs into a book yet?
James: and lost for the 2nd half
me: of the trip?
James: no. my blogs stopped
when things shifted in my head
they were great when I met you
and the whole journey was amazing
but I def. got in my head again and quite down

spent last 6 months in India

many meditation retreats

me: i've been depressed and tired too after the 8th month

but couldn't settle down to stay anywhere to do a mind-calming course

James: ah. I think it's normal

me: how did you know it was time to go home?

James: djana. sorry. I am here. my best friends mother went to hospital and he is calling me now.

me: no prob, take your time

James: the mind calming didn't do me well

I went home

b/c June had many events that were important to be home for and I was sooooooooooooo tired

physically and mentally

and I lost 25 pounds

me: awww

James: which I still haven't gained back

me: mom must have been shocked

James: well i gained 10 back

I didn't know it

she said get on a scale

and I said no

me: :)

James: like I didn't think I lost any weight

I couldn't believe it

but yeah

so

I had a wedding

my fathers 60th b-day

my brothers b-day

lots of things

I was going to go to Ladakh

but felt I would not be so receptive to it
being in the state of mind I was in
so figured best to come home and believe that I will get back
there when the time is right :)
me: :)
James: how did you know when to come home?
me: i flew into kuala lumpur and wanted to get to moscow all
overland
and estimated it would be 3 months
lol
little did i know
took a little more
James: wow. thats an awesome trip!!!!
me: 5 months in total to see as much as i could without getting
distracted by the thought of homesickness
James: so it sounds
me: you would love mongolia
James: amazing
ooooohhh
I want to go!!!!
me: you should
take the transsiberian train
James: no money!
yes
I want to take that train!!!
stop getting me excited
me: it's a filthy, old train, no food, just dried fish, goes for 5 days
in cold desert
you said stop getting you excited :P
James: sounds like my kind of train
me: it's a luxury first-class train with caviar and champagne
bubbling from the tap
:P lol

James: eh. doesn't sound so good.

me: are you offline?

James: just invisible

usually do that to get work done

me: it's 4 p.m. on a friday afternoon a little overcast in new york city. what is James doing online?

James: sun is out now :)

in jersey city

me: what do you do?

James: what is it like in moscow?

I am going back to school for social work in the fall

september

me: july is the hottest month

James: ooh

me: really? thats wonderful

James: I guess :)

me: heal yourself by helping others

James: yeah

me: i knew you find yourself in some form of healing

James: I know. THis doesn't feel like the exact path

me: i studied sociology in college but left it cus of really bad attention deficiency

bummer

James: but feel it can lead me there

oh

me: don't you take the PATH everyday?

James: yeah. I am ADD too

me: ;)

i know it's so difficult

James: and worried about it

to be honest

me: my mind goes out the window

James: me too

me: when i start reading something i don't connect with which happens to be most stuff

James: I know!!!

haha

me: :)

James: what about you

what are you doing?

me: getting myself together from the surgery

James: oh

me: writing my book

James: of travels?

me: off and on

the trip to nepal, tibet, buddhist course

James: oh

wow

me: you're in it :P

James: :)

perhaps I should do the same

me: i'm putting together a website of my art..

James: excellent

me: i discovered there are other people out there who paint similar patterns

James: ooh

me: you should definitely put together memoirs of Dharamsala and other places and courses

your whole journey

James: I don't know where to begin :)

me: you kept a journal?

James: yes.

periods of time did not get recorded when I was a bit down and those are parts probably some of the juicy

me: i'm so sorry to hear you felt that way

James: don't be sorry

it's ok
just signs of things to change
me: ok
:)
James: easier said than done
but it's true
me: i haven't met many people who were depressed like us
during traveling
James: I felt that way too
I mean so many people are depressed
me: yeah
James: but it seemed that while traveling
there weren't so many
but who knows
I mean do you think all the people you met knew you were
depressed
me: many leave to have a good time and don't have time to be
depressed don't you think
hardly anyone actually
James: I don't know
some may be escaping
and underneath are sad
never really know
though you read me like an open book
but I think you have special insight and powers
personally
me: :)
you opened them...again
:)
you don't believe me do you
James: didn't say that
I believe you
no reason not too

me: i found out how it was working btw
and no nobody knew i was depressed
most thought i was friendly and giving and enjoyed taking while
they could...
till i was exhausted and needed to get my energy together
meaning detach from the vampires
but honestly
this is getting really deep and emotional
but listen
James: take your time. 'you don't have to say anything
if you don't want
me: i knew if i ever speak to you again
i would tell you that i never meant
to intrude into your destiny
but i couldn't help feeling a purpose within our meeting
and i had to tell you everything i knew
whatever would happen next
my mom says i always make a mess and then run away
you said i leave abruptly
but another human being telling me i have a gift instead of
proclaiming hysterical ad hypersensitive
is a whole different story
phew
i write about this a lot in my book
now that i have time on my hands i'm editing it and
James: you are def. gifted
I am going to go back as soon as I have time to read many of the
things you wrote to me
They were powerful
and seemed on target and wasn't sure what to do with it all
I didn't mind you telling me things
cuz I need to be told things
ultimately we have to find freedom on our own.

but I know I need help along the way
you were flighty when we would meet
me: of course
James: I didn't know what to make of you
but I knew that you were hurting
and that you were also special
me: James
what is flight?
bummer. flighty
James: maybe wrong word
me: flaky?
James: hey. stop focusing on negative
!!!
during that time period you were very emotional
me: empaths are yeah
James: and so you were there talking to me but you would leave quickly to
no def. not flaky
that is the wrong description
I think it was a lot for you
me: i felt so many subtle energies connecting both of us i wasn't ready for it
James: so you just left sometimes
yeah
it was just for your comfort
not bad
me: yeah i wanted to run away from you
James: I didn't see it as negative
just hard
I saw you hurting and thats how you dealt sometimes
me: how can you know this?
James: you did sometimes!!!
and yes. I focus on neg too

unfortunately

me: that's why you say i do hey

James: well I complimented you just before but you asked about the part that sounded negative

me: it sounded confusing i'm sorry english is not my first language..

:P

cus i always want to work on myself

and focusing on bad things within helps me see what i need to work on

i can't help it...i'm hard on myself

but i wouldn't have it any other way

i felt it was a lot for you

when i was like this

cus i know you are like that

we never have it easy

i'm sorry..

that was a lot to take

i just want to make the world better

help people become aware

save turtles in costa rica

conserve the amazon rainforest

James: djana: i just want to make the world better

help people become aware

that is all I want to do too!!!

that's it

that's all

me: i know

i saw it in yours eyes

and you told me

in the monastery

you have the sweetness in your soul

that i've never seen in anyone else
the purity
and you came from the blue
James: why do you say blue?
me: it's a metaphor like
   "out of the blue"
James: oh
got that
me: cus your eyes are blue
and
pure souls have a signature color = blue
James: just curious b/c it is a signif. color in my life
I don't know if I should 'waste' two years in social work school
me: you're trying to balance out the energy of your root chakra
by soaking up the blue color
James: or practice in a monastery or some shaman camp
or something else
you know what I mean
?
me: monastery and camp!
right now

this minute
well...maybe tomo :)
James: ::)
I think school will be good as it is helping people that REALLY
need it
the most
poverty
violence
substance abuse
ADD
ha

but

It's consciousness and energy and universal love, the cosmos etc.
holistic
things
me: yes
James: that really get me going
me: yes!!!!!
me too
James: it'
this decision has been plaguing me all summer
actually don't know
if I should go to NYU or Columbia
I got into the best schools in the country
me: yess!!! wow
congratulations
James: and have the best internship
and don't even know if I want it
I'm fucken nuts
me: i know how you feel, i had to make that choice many times
i always chose holistic
simply bcus when i pushed myself into traditional school i
couldnt handle it

James, listen to your heart
when you left and i stayed in the monastery i did what you told
me
i listened to my heart, for the first time, i really did
how did i know i was listening to my heart?
cus it kept jumping out of my throat
giving me a rush
an energy so high
nothing was more powerful
and i gave in to it

and explained myself to the monks, and went to tibet
and got an experience of my lifetime
i would not change it for 12 months of courses in the monastery
James: I can't access my heart hun
me: of course you can
James: I rarely can do it
I hear too many voices
I mean like other people - not fake ones
haha
me: oh
:)
James: not schizo
just society
I am super self-conscious
me: i know i feel the same
but what matters more than what WE want?
James: this is hard
nothing
me: who's that speaking, your father?
James: a little bit
but I have distanced myself from that a lot
everyone knows I might be going to Columbia
or somewhere
and they finally see me as "on the right track"
b/c of course I was the weird one

haha
me: who they?
James: everyone I know
listen if I knew exactly what I wanted to do I would
I am very unclear
and the WORST decision maker in the world
social work school seemed like a good option

thought about it for years now
so I applied
and invested much energy and time into it
more than any normal person
and got the fruits of the time I put in
but don't even know if I want it
ahhhhhhhhh
enough about me
thanks for listening
me: if not school, what is the other option?
James: no idea
nepal :)
me: would you go back and help in orphanages, elderly homes
teach kids english
eat chapati
isn't that why you left in 2007 cus the system wasn't working for you?
look i've been a free spirit and on a spiritual journey ever since i first dropped out
and if thats who you are - a free spirit
that's where you need to be
your soul needs are so much more important now
if your soul feels more comfortable in nepal, india, go there
and if your soul feels comfortable in nyc - in school - that society has told you is the right track
then do that
its simple
James: :).

yes. so it sounds simple
but my heart is not sure
and for sure I need money
to go anywhere

I have kinda run out
of course I can just work anywhere and save
for a year
me: you can work teaching
James: you mean abroad?
me: nothing more rewarding than working with and teaching
kids
yeah
James: I know
love those kids man
me: for real
i have a friend he lives in brooklyn
he took a 40hr tefl course online
and leaving to china for a year to work and save up
James: I did that too!!
me: really
so you have taught
James: yeah. before I left for india
just in case
me: wonderful
use it
you can even go to korea or japan
or russia
lol
James: I want to hang with the Dalai Lama :)
lol
i was to St. Petersburg for a few days
once
me: isnt he travelling all the time?
James: yeah
he is

me: i remember you told me, you came from helsinki i think?

James: yeah
good memory
me: ;)
consider teaching
they pay for your expenses too
i wanna do it once this is over and done with
the surgery i mean..
school is a great thing...but for me, personally, if you want my opinion
James: but what next. I just have no fall back. I think this degree is imp. bc I am than accredited to help people
and in many capacities
me: yeah
James: I mean it goes along with what I want
just not exactly
its not spiritual enough in nature
for me
that's the prob
me: i know, i know
James: but it's real life
real people
real needs
me: you can be a yoga instructor
James: yes. I could be
it's so good to talk to people that are outside the box of thinking
that things are one way
me: oh! my favourite saying
James: meaning you right now
me: :)
i was trying to get into the greenpeace work
i love nature and animals
after kids of cours
James: awww

we should find a number of people that think like this and start our own org.

me: YAY

James: Hey if I graduate from Columbia I can get a loan anywhere
most likely
:)

me: for a business you mean?

James: yeah
to start one
an ngo
or non-profit
but maybe with the right connections and right marketing wouldn't need it
from bank

me: right

James: this is more my dream

me: it's what i always wanted to do

James: in the future
:)

me: i think the theosophical society is something close to what we are talking about
they have headquarters in nyc
and india
chennai i think
how would we make money from it?
membership? lectures and education workshops..
combine columbia with some workshops maybe - then you are doing both things
for your mind (school)
and for your soul (workshops, lectures..fun stuff
spiritual

i'm uploading a video its taking ages
James, are you there?

James: Yes!!love what you are saying. I am with you. taking phone call. sorry.
I am off and reading
me: :) you're at work arent you?
James: no
ha
me: home?
James: yes. it's evening and many people calling and making plans. Just trying to organize it all but want to speak to you and do some practice before I leave
me: practice?
James: like self-practice
like for the soul
though I never get to it
most important thing
but I avoid it
very weird
me: is that an audio course?
fall back in meditation and ask your higher self to guide you to your true soul's desire
James: um I have some audios
but just exercises
to feel a higher self
I took a course that made me cry over the summer
it was one weekend
me: i remember your palm said
your purpose will be fulfilled abroad, away from your country of birth
if that links to your profession or daily job, i'm not sure
more to life?

how was it?

sounds powerful

you're famous, your picture is on their website :)

James, i'm gonna have to go soon its past 1

you write very well, keep doing it

i think you're taking a phonecall?

James: hey

how did you know

More to Life

?

me: it's international

James: but how did you know I took it?

did I say that

me: lol sorry no you didn't tell me

your picture is on their website

James: wait. did you just find my picture

I am so confused!!!

did you know I took that workshop before we started talking

me: nope

James: how did you know???

djana

!!

me: ok ok

i think i was surfing and surfed into their website there was a
weekend course and i think your picture was there

i didn't really read what it was though

James: yeah. i wrote something that they put on their blog

but crazy that of all the courses in the world you surfed into that
one and found the little blog they put up of me

me: you write beautifully

what is it that made you cry?

James: ha. I just googled myself

it was a process they did
but basically
I never get what I wish to get out of these courses
to much expectation
me: me neither
James: but this one process
the last one of the course
did something
and all it was was to accept myself as I am
and they use a mirror
called the mirror process
and you stare at yourself
for like 10 minutes
and you have someone guide you
and you tell yourself what you need to tell yourself
and stare at yourself
and I told my self that I am enough
over and over
James: and everything else doesn't matter much
this is embarrassing :)
all the worrying is for nothing.
And than you move on and stare straight into another persons
eyes and 'let go' and let them accept you for who you are. and
after about five minutes of staring at the other person I let go
again and he saw that in me and I saw that he accepted me for
me and nothing else.

I didn't have to be anything else.

You are gone.

??

you are very sweet and therapeutic and I like having this

conversation with you.

Happy to reconnect

Hope you feel the same

feel free to tell me anything

I will listen if you like :)

I wrote a bunch but not sure that you received it

me: got it just reading now

sorry was disconnected

James: brb

me: i don't geddit! you look at the person and accept them..and then they accept you?

oh! just got your other messages

i'm happy to reconnect as well

one thing i want to tell you

relax, unwind and ask the Universe to guide you..

i have to go cus i'm sweeping off my feet its 2 in the morning thank you for starting this conversation

i will wait until you wish me goodnight otherwise this will feel

like a dream tomo morning

James: goodnight djana :)

sweetest dreams